I0731157

NOTORIOUS

Poisonous Passions
Book One

Mae Thorn

ARE YOU SIGNED UP FOR DRAGONBLADE'S BLOG?

You'll get the latest news and information on exclusive giveaways, exclusive excerpts, coming releases, sales, free books, cover reveals and more.

Check out our complete list of authors, too!

No spam, no junk. That's a promise!

Sign Up Here

www.dragonbladepublishing.com

Dearest Reader;

Thank you for your support of a small press. At Dragonblade Publishing, we strive to bring you the highest quality Historical Romance from some of the best authors in the business. Without your support, there is no 'us', so we sincerely hope you adore these stories and find some new favorite authors along the way.

Happy Reading!

CEO, Dragonblade Publishing

CHAPTER ONE

New York City
Spring 1778

FOOTSTEPS SCUFFED AGAINST the cobbled street behind Foxglove. She swayed forward as her feet froze and her body advanced. Her shallow breaths ticked by and rose above her in puffs against the fading light.

A shiver brushed over her skin but not from the chill air. If someone followed, it would be her final rescue. She didn't hazard to look behind her but bounded forward as fast as her heeled boots would take her.

Foxglove darted through the door of a burned-out building and scrambled out the skeletal back wall.

A crash ricocheted off the alleyway buildings.

A gasp caught in her throat, and her legs consumed the distance, heedless of her skirts' limitations. She wove through the building next door and, once again, across the alleyway. There she stopped and forced a deep breath past her stays.

Whoever trailed her must be on patrol. He made enough noise to shake the crumbling neighborhood to dust. The British had reinforced their numbers. She had counted on the foxglove poison in their rum to clear the way. What she hadn't counted on was a soldier who didn't partake, an unexpected newcomer.

The faint drip off the roof was the only sound. Outside the side entrance, the street stood vacant. Neither a shadow nor a wind stirred.

Her shoulders loosened, and she continued up the street at a normal pace. A few streets down, the Wilsons waited for her. The patrols were active tonight, and pouring the poison into their drink had never been more of a challenge. Her friend, Felix, knew to continue to the ship without her if she didn't arrive before dusk, assuming Felix followed instructions this time.

A trio of singing soldiers rounded the corner, their voices in sync with their alcohol.

Foxglove forced her quaking lips into a smile and instilled the practiced sway into her walk.

One of the men whistled, and another punched him in the gut.

The whistler grunted. "What did you do that for?"

"Be respectful to the lady."

The other two men snickered, and the third man slapped the whistler on the back.

"Bill, that's no lady. She's a whore."

Bill pushed the other men aside. "No, she's a lady."

Foxglove rolled her emerald eyes and gave the men the bulk of the road.

"Listen here, she's a whore." The second man caught her arm. "Aren't you?"

"I'm off for the night." Her face hardened, and she tugged at his grip, her wig jostling over her pale hair. Her knife and the remaining poison were in easy reach in her skirt's pocket, but she couldn't bring them all down. On second thought, they didn't look too particular about their drink.

Her lips widened on an easy grin, and just as she meant to offer them some trouser-dropping, delicious rum, another voice sounded behind her.

"Get ahold of yourselves, men." The newcomer's words were all bark with a bite at the end. "Don't you set out tomorrow?"

Foxglove snapped her mouth closed against her yelp. A web-like fear clung to her chest and sharpened into a buzz. It took all her self-preservation to keep her eyes forward as the British officer's boots shuffled closer.

The trio froze, but their drunkenness seemed to melt onto the cobblestones.

The second man saluted the officer. "Captain, sir, we had business to take care of with the rebels."

"Business with the taverns and whores, no doubt." The captain stood in the corner of her vision. She could reach out and touch him, or he could run her through with his blade. "No matter. Be watchful. Word is Foxglove is out tonight."

A laugh bubbled in Foxglove's throat, and a tear rolled down her cheek. She pinched her arm to ward off her laughter. Any one of these men could bring her down. This was death she courted and not an awkward suitor at the Riverton ball.

Bill's face scrunched up. "Now you've upset the lady."

The first man rounded on him. "For the last time, she's not a—"

"Take yourselves back to camp." The captain's tone was low, but it reverberated like a shout. "All women are ladies."

Foxglove's heart beat a tattoo. Who was this man? She pictured a rotund, red-nosed officer with a well-kept wig, but as the men hurried off without a backward glance, the man who matched the voice came into view.

Her lips gaped open. This captain must be new; she wouldn't have forgotten his dominating presence. Not since the British had captured New York when Washington had fled. Not since her first steps on the earth. Not ever.

He towered over her, and the shadows only enhanced his dark features and serious disposition. A smirk peeked out into the dying light. She didn't know whether to draw her knife or leap into his arms.

"That goes for you as well, ma'am. The streets are dangerous at this hour."

Her pulse fluttered at his concern. "How do you know those men weren't working with Foxglove? Or"—her hand caught her lower lip—"maybe they are Foxglove?"

His smirk deepened, and he waved a hand in the direction the men had left. "If they had anything to do with Foxglove, then they're off the streets, at least, as you should be."

"A girl's got to make a living." She cocked her head. "I have it now. You're Foxglove."

The captain made a strangled sound and shook his head. "On with you."

She clicked her tongue. "I'm already on my way." Not home, not yet.

He threw his hands up and pivoted on his heel, leaving her admiring his firm backside accented in his breeches.

She counted the minutes as they slipped by. A tightness remained where the danger had resided. Instead of easing, it flooded restlessness into her limbs and gave her a craving for danger.

When she was convinced the city's husk had swallowed the captain, she broke into a sprint. Her skirts tugged at her legs, and she hiked them to her knees.

Her body pulsed and fueled her steps in a burst of energy.

Twenty yards.

Twenty-eight.

Thirty-five.

The moon cast doubt over her path. She wasn't just late; she may be doomed. A second too long and the Wilsons could be captured before they set foot on her father's ship. If they waited on her, they would miss the tide.

She threw herself through the appointed doorway, and the door clicked behind her.

Empty.

She squeezed her eyes shut and allowed herself a long breath. The suspected rebel group must have moved on. She had never missed a rescue.

Her lids slid open. A frowning face was drawn in sloppy lines on the back of the door in what looked like plum jelly, as if she needed a reminder that Felix was still a child and not a responsible associate.

She heaved through the back door. A fallen oak guarded the entrance, but it was a direct route to the docks and worth the time gained.

The neighborhood was draped in darkness. Now even the moon had hidden behind the clouds. Hands out in front of her, she pressed her way through the streets. Her muscles hardened, and her legs twitched to run, but she was no use to anyone if she fell on her face.

She gained the warehouses, and every darkened building she passed seemed to tighten the grip on her throat. The ship should be gone, and yet, up ahead, lights floated where the boat docked. The dock gave off sufficient light, and she rushed over the wooden planks.

Had they lost all reason?

Felix balanced on a wooden pole and waved.

"Why haven't they left? How will they leave?" she asked.

He hopped down, and a wide grin emphasized his teeth in the dark. "We had a problem with patrols."

Panic slammed its weight into her chest. "The Wilsons?"

"Gone." He frowned and examined her blanched face. "Aboard."

Foxglove slapped her chest in relief.

A deeper voice came from behind Felix. "Everything is ready now, Foxy." The Wyvern bowed. "Have you come to sail away with me?"

"As much as I appreciate the offer, I'm needed here." A blush ran up her neck in the presence of the ship captain. He worked for her father, who was unaware of the man's sympathies.

In another life, she would've run off with the notorious blackguard, but she only needed to make sure things ran smoothly under Felix, since she was late to escort the Wilsons.

She didn't need more complications in her life, which meant no men. Her mind flittered to the mysterious captain who searched for Foxglove. Men were trouble.

"I don't know what you did to explain away the patrol, but thank you."

He nodded. "Anything for the prettiest rebel in town. I explained nothing. I let my good brandy do the talking."

"Funny, that's my favorite method as well."

He saluted her and climbed aboard the *Mary*. As the ship vanished into uncertain waters, she couldn't help thinking he was the safe one.

CHAPTER TWO

B RITISH OFFICERS GATHERED in bright red against the feminine pastels of the crowded ballroom. Hundreds of candles created false daylight over the hum and murmur of excited conversation. Theirs was a gathering more dangerous than the streets.

Delia Wolcott was prepared.

A shift in the crowd brought Helen Perry's long, angular face into view on the far side of the room. Her pale-yellow gown revealed her out of mourning for her fiancé, Arthur, Delia's second-oldest brother.

Seeing Helen brought back fond memories of Arthur's smiling face and quick humor, but the memories shifted all too fast to those of Helen's broken sobs amid blood-soaked clothes. For a moment, the room was awash with spilled blood as the officers milled about the crowd in their uniforms.

Delia brushed her fingertips against her lavender dress to call herself back to her task. It had been too long since they'd met, and Delia had questions about that night only her friend could answer.

A too-loud whisper stopped her progress across the room. "Did you hear the Wilsons escaped? The traitors dodged arrest just last evening. It was that loathsome Foxglove again." The shrill voice rose above the din of conversation. Those within earshot craned their necks at the name *Foxglove*.

Delia caught her breath and moved closer, her way momentarily blocked. She hardened her features into the mask to which she had become accustomed. It would do her no good if everyone got a glimpse of the traitor beneath.

Mrs. Sarah Willoughby's face crumpled into a frown. "Where is the justice? Foxglove has robbed it from us. It can't stand for long. Mark my words: Foxglove will fall to the king's justice. Already the patrols have been tripled. No man will exit the city without suspicion."

But what about a woman? The British would never capture Foxglove so long as they searched for a man. Women were above suspicion, and Delia remained free as Foxglove to rescue rebels from the city. She moved on. Mrs. Willoughby was a foolish gossip. This wasn't news.

"We are fortunate to have Lord Carrington to lead the investigation," Mrs. Willoughby said.

As if sensing the exchange, the man turned and flashed his dark eyes on Delia. His pupils were enlarged, leaving an inky pool she could sink into. A shiver tickled over her, and she forced herself to look away. Still, she couldn't help but notice Lord Carrington's commanding presence advancing toward them with an athletic stride. She mentally kicked herself. He was *the* captain. The man following her from last night, who was beyond off-limits. Her pounding heart refused to listen.

She caught Mrs. Willoughby's gaze. The other woman took the hint with open enthusiasm and snatched Delia's arm. Not for the first time, she wondered why Mrs. Willoughby was still invited to these events.

"Captain, may I present Miss Delia Wolcott?"

Lord Carrington gave a short bow of his head, and his blue-black hair waved with the movement.

Delia's traitorous gaze searched his bottle-brown eyes, and she inhaled a quick breath. The natural tilt of his brows suggested a mischievousness she could only guess at. She sensed the bold interest in his eyes even as his visage remained silent. Her every fiber stood at attention under his examination.

She steeled herself and dropped into a graceful curtsy, but she failed to hide her contemptuous frown as she rose. Carrington arched a brow, and amusement sparked in his gaze but with the same expression of stony seriousness.

"Sir, how do you suppose the Wilsons escaped?" An oblivious Mrs. Willoughby interrupted the introductions as she stepped between them.

He cleared his throat, and Delia peered around Mrs. Willoughby's pencil-thin form as he took a noticeable step back.

"That, Mrs. Willoughby, is still under investigation. However, as before, Foxglove left his mark. This time, in the form of three dead guards."

Delia grew numb, and her mind raced over the fatal error. She needed to adjust her measurements again. The plant was a difficult and unpredictable ingredient to factor. Drinking too much would make the man purge the poison, a violent sickness not always fatal. Ironically, drinking too little was beneficial to the heart and she might as well join the redcoats herself.

If the man consumed enough of the foxglove plant and did not expel the poison in time, he would die. It was a fate Delia wanted to avoid, and as much as she tried, she could not reason away the deaths. Some of those men were colonists themselves, but the people fleeing the city often had nowhere else to turn.

"I apologize, Miss Wolcott, for this unseemly topic." The captain's concerned tone brought her back to the present. He watched her with downcast eyes. "Let me make it up to you with punch for you and Mrs. Willoughby." Carrington summoned a nearby footman who carried drinks and handed a cool glass to Delia. Her gloved hand grazed against his, imprinting her with the heat of his touch.

For a brief second, Delia wondered at the contents of her drink. Imagine, the man who led the investigation against her fetched her wine punch. She suppressed the urge to smile. Now was not the time for humor.

The icy liquid steadied her, but she wanted to escape this stifling room. She needed this captain's information about Foxglove. Her conversation with Helen would have to wait a little longer.

"It's an ugly mess." He sighed and gave her a faint smile. The first real smile she had seen from him. The small movement warmed her from the inside out, and she had to remind herself who stood before her. "Are you well? Is there anything else I can get you?"

Patrol schedules, troop movements, a detailed map, and maybe a nice long bath with you.

"I'm fine." Her cheeks blazed. "I'd like to get some air. Would you care to accompany me, Captain?" At least outside, the press of bodies wouldn't choke her.

The captain answered with a warm smile.

Music started up to signal the first dance as they exited, but her awareness focused on the arm of the man she held. His touch burned through her glove.

An uneasy flutter brushed her stomach, but there was no helping it. She didn't know this man, and her mother would not be pleased; she was denied her thorough investigation of the officer.

Delia adjusted her skirts and reassured herself when her fingertips caught the top of her knife nestled against her right leg.

Already a few other groups roamed the garden's stone-covered pathways, taking advantage of the privacy from the low light of the torches and the moon's dull presence.

"Miss Wolcott, I've become acquainted with Mr. Andrew Wolcott and his son, Mr. Jeffrey Wolcott, this past week." Carrington's statement trailed off into a question.

Curious, she allowed her gaze to wander to him, but he stared ahead.

"Indeed." She nodded. "My father and older brother. My father took ill this evening, but Jeffrey is here." To her surprise, she realized Jeffrey was a little older than the captain. He would be closer to Arthur's age or how old Arthur would have been.

"That's unfortunate. I hoped the warmer weather would see him at the party. Although, I wouldn't mind discussing a few things with your brother." He paused as he watched her expression. "What is it you wanted to talk about? I don't believe you brought me out here for polite small talk."

A flush crawled up her neck. Had she been that transparent? She grasped for a topic that would excuse her actions. Discussing Foxglove would only give her away further. She already risked his recognizing her. This was why she didn't usually do the spying.

"I can't desire an innocent turn around the garden?"

His mouth tugged up as though he read the lie on her face. "Miss Wolcott, I find it unlikely you would lose your opportunity at dance partners to stroll with a stranger in the cold."

"You were just remarking on the warmth but now it's cold?" She grinned at him to hide her struggle to maintain calm.

The garden became a prison under his assessing stare.

"Oh, it's pleasant enough for some activities. Although, I don't believe a stroll can make up for the cold." His tone was light and offhand, his face the epitome of solemn decorum, but his meaning was plain to her.

She bit back her shock at his veiled comment. Was he teasing her or propositioning her? She should have known he would create meaning out of their walk. This man was dangerous and far too attractive for his own good. If she wanted any useful information out of him, she would have to be more careful.

"I think a walk can be quite invigorating. What else would you do in a garden?" Her tone was even, but her quaking lips betrayed her. The warmth of his eyes lit with humor. She rose to their banter as each of them underestimated the other.

"I could show you if you'd like, though I'm afraid your frock would suffer for it."

She concealed her titter behind her hand. "I'm quite fond of this dress. Pray, what did you have in mind?"

"You know, gardening, playing cricket or golf, and riding. That sort of thing." Oh, he was teasing her. A hint of regret tugged at her senses.

"Riding? What a novel idea." She burst into a wide smile as he gave a nervous laugh at her boldness. "I'm afraid the grounds aren't large enough for such an occupation."

Just then, two bulky forms came into view, and she attempted to hold back her frustration as she recognized her brother, Jeffrey, along with his best friend, Mr. Richard Bradshaw. Her two overbearing shadows would make it impossible to steer the conversation into the right answers. Not to mention, they robbed her of much-needed entertainment.

Jeffrey greeted them and folded his towering frame in a mocking bow.

Mr. Bradshaw lingered above her hand, a suggestive smile spread over his features. Both men were taller than Carrington, yet among the three of them, Carrington owned more of the space around him.

"Lord Carrington, I see you've met my troublesome sister." Jeffrey gave her a crooked smile, and his chocolate-brown eyes lit with mirth. "Tell me, did my dear Delia trap you into some maidenly schemes? Surely she has bewitched you as she has half of New York."

She held back the embarrassment kindled by his words. Instead, she studied the man on her arm, wondering at the weight of her brother's comments.

Lord Carrington glanced back toward her, his ears tinged red. He cleared his throat but stayed silent. His face mirrored her thoughts, though his features were touched with guilt. Jeffrey also caught his expression and looked from him to her. He would scare away her quarry. Again.

"She's my most beloved, you know." Jeffrey's tone dropped. His bared teeth looked not unlike the way she pictured Cerberus, the three-headed dog that guarded much worse things than himself. It was an apt description, since there was no escape from the situation.

Mr. Bradshaw stepped forward and extended his arm to Delia. She stared at it in distaste. As protective as Jeffrey was, he was blind to Mr. Bradshaw's attentions to her. He saw him as more of a brother figure than a threat.

Delia sighed and took Mr. Bradshaw's arm. There was no use arguing the point. She flashed Carrington a regretful half smile and allowed Mr. Bradshaw to lead her away.

The captain's absence left an emptiness behind. What was wrong with her? The man was her enemy, a threat to her freedom and life.

Jeffrey followed them with Lord Carrington. Jeffrey spoke to him but in a brighter tone, not seeming to notice the change in mood. Carrington eventually took to him as everyone did. The conversation sounded amicable enough.

Mr. Bradshaw's curious stare took in her behavior.

She scowled back at him. "Was that really necessary?" Mr. Bradshaw had always believed he was correct in all things. He was not unlike Jeffrey in that regard, but the men's opinions aligned so closely it didn't usually interfere with their friendship. She fought the urge to strangle him.

He gave her a small smile. "If anything, you should be thanking us. You of all people wouldn't want to get involved with Lord Carrington."

She paused midstride as she considered his words. Did he know? Only two people were aware of her identity as Foxglove, and they were trustworthy, loyal to a fault. Had she slipped somehow? No, that couldn't be right.

"What do you mean?" She kept her tone even and continued forward.

"Really? Lord Carrington is an earl's heir, a British officer. You know how they are."

She stiffened. Well, that didn't matter as long as he was willing to talk. She came from a family in trade, and Carrington would consider her beneath him. She had no illusions about a relationship. He was a glimpse into the investigation, one that could lead to her discovery and subsequent hanging.

Wait...what?

"Do you think he's better than me?" She bristled and drew back, lightening her touch on Mr. Bradshaw's arm, though her nails ached to carve gashes along his arm.

She had no intention of marrying an Englishman, leaving everyone and everything she knew. That didn't mean she couldn't have an innocent flirtation. It would give her an excuse to get close to the captain. He would open new avenues of information to rescue more rebels and avenge Arthur's murder.

Mr. Bradshaw, like her family, still saw himself as a British subject. "That's not it. Remember what happened to Anna Barrow? She has never recovered her reputation from being compromised. And if I recall, your father and Jeffrey went to great pains after your incident with that one fellow."

"Anna Barrow is a fool. It was obvious he wasn't after marriage. As for my idiotic suitor, that cad had it coming. Besides, he marched out. No real harm done." He really must think her stupid. She would avoid Carrington compromising her; besides, he didn't seem like the type to take advantage of a woman. Although, it was hard to tell these days.

"Delia, you pushed him off a balcony. Remarkably, he didn't see the knife you were holding. It was a good thing Jeffrey and I were nearby."

As they always were. She could barely breathe without an escort, but she had gone unnoticed at the party when the man had cornered her with his straying hands. Now, he was terrified of heights, though he had left for battle with only a few cuts and scrapes, having landed in some handy but prickly bushes. Hopefully, one of the rebels would make coyote food out of him.

She had loved that knife, but Jeffrey had taken it to "protect her." Honestly, it was lucky she had left her other knives at home.

"Of course you're right." She nodded to him, and her gaze lowered as she withdrew from the lecture. "We should return inside. Mama will think me neglectful if I don't dance with at least half a dozen different partners."

She turned down the next path and forced him back toward the house. Her brother and Carrington were not far behind.

Mr. Bradshaw's muffled words brought back her attention.

"Excuse me, what were you saying?" she asked.

"Let me have the next dance, or better yet, the next three."

"Three? You know Mama wouldn't approve of your taking all my dances. Sadly, I've already lost some of them to this walk." Her mother would probably be delighted and happily scandalized to see him pay her so much attention.

It was a matter of debate between them whether or not Mr. Bradshaw was serious about her. Already some of her former suitors had given her up to the big man. The fewer partners she had to dance with, the less information came her way.

He laughed and grabbed her hand in answer, not letting go until they reached the other dancers. He was gentlemanly enough and not a bad dancer, but the way his eyes lingered over her suggested a familiarity she did not wish to explore. Their conversation was innocent but sparse. He seemed preoccupied with keeping her close, an unwelcome notion that caused her to flee the floor as soon as their first dance ended.

During their dance, she had scanned the crowd for any sign of Helen, but she wasn't where Delia had last seen her. They couldn't have wandered the gardens for more than a half hour. Finally, Delia resolved to ask her mother if she had seen her friend.

Mrs. Elizabeth Wolcott was seated to the side, watching the dancing couples with Delia's younger sister, Lynette. Her mother was a colorless woman. Her white hair, so similar to Delia's, was lined in gray, and with her pale-slate eyes, she appeared washed away. Her turquoise gown only distracted from her lack of color enough to render her a ghost.

In contrast, Lynette had the coal-dark hair of their father and the same dark-brown eyes they shared with Jeffrey. At eighteen, she was a miniature female version of their father in pale blue.

Delia's mother didn't bother to meet her eyes. "My dear, why aren't you dancing? This isn't a good beginning to the evening."

"I don't see Lynette dancing." Delia snapped out the words before she could stop herself.

Her mother gave her a sour look. "Lynette isn't twenty."

"I'm sorry, Mama." She cast her emerald eyes down but not from deference. She did not want to get into this again. She had plenty of time to get married and had no intention of doing so anytime soon. Too many activities consumed her time that a husband and children would complicate. People to transport, officers to sabotage, and patrols to kill. She flinched at that last thought.

"I do intend to dance more, but I wanted to speak to Helen first. I haven't spoken to her since before." Delia avoided mentioning the loss of her brother.

"Then I'm sorry to have to tell you Helen went up to rest. I doubt she'll come down again tonight. Really, I don't know what the Perrys were thinking, holding a ball while their daughter was still recovering. You might as well plan to postpone your reunion. I think we may be able to call on her tomorrow if you like." Her mother dismissed her and turned back toward the dancers.

Like Mrs. Wolcott, the Perrys thought Helen was three and twenty and unwed. Yet Helen had lost the love of her life a short year ago. She couldn't entertain suitors while in mourning.

Leave it to her mother to bring her bad news while also inserting herself to further the impact of it. She couldn't have the conversation she wanted with her mother and sister present.

Unlike them, she still needed closure, which meant she must know what happened the night her brother and father carried Arthur's bloodied body home amid Helen's choked sobs. What had really happened and not the fairy-tale story everyone told her.

Exasperated with this whole mess of a ball, she wished she had decided to stay home. She briefly considered sneaking upstairs to talk to Helen but abandoned the idea. Maybe she was ill.

She was startled to find a lieutenant asking for a dance. A welcome proposal that could prove fortuitous. With the right amount of pressure, he could be a font of information for Foxglove. She accepted with a bright smile and a short nod.

For a man out of shape, Lieutenant Chambers was a competent dancer, a nice change from Mr. Bradshaw's unwanted attention. She spotted Carrington frowning in his direction, and she glared back at him. Why didn't he like Mr. Chambers? The man was jovial and good-natured, at least to her.

He studied her features. "I'm surprised you agreed to dance with me."

She tilted her head toward him. "Oh?"

"I'm sorry about your brother."

Her eyes widened. "You knew Arthur?"

He gave her a grim smile. "For a time. We didn't exactly move in the same circles, but I knew his work. I can't say I approved of it."

Delia frowned. Her mind raced to untangle his words. Arthur had done business all over the city with her father and brother. She supposed profiting from war could be considered wrong to some, but it wasn't a reason for Arthur to be killed.

He continued, "Still, I feel responsible."

"Nonsense." She hadn't any proof it had been murder. Unless he had he sought her out in order to appease his guilt? He was a British officer, after all. Although it was unlikely he was involved, his words prickled at her mind. She was missing something.

"Now with Foxglove"—the creases at the corners of his eyes seemed to deepen—"at least we have something."

Her head spun at the change of topic. "What is it? How will you catch Foxglove if no one has ever seen him?" She studied him with what she hoped was wide-eyed wonder and innocence.

Mr. Chambers puffed out his chest. She guessed he didn't get much credit for his work. "That's just the thing. The captain has an eyewitness account this time. We're sure to catch him now."

Delia almost missed her step in their dance.

"How wonderful." She swallowed back her panic and steadied her voice. "Do tell me, what does this awful man look like?" Her grin shook as she feigned excitement. "I would like to avoid one of his nature."

"Unfortunately, the captain has kept that information to himself. Don't worry, Miss Wolcott. The traitor only seems to attack those who get in his way while smuggling other traitors. You and your family are perfectly safe." He bowed, their dance finished.

Her brows scrunched together. She was hardly reassured. What witness? There hadn't been anyone around when she'd tampered with the soldiers' drink unless the three drunks or the captain had seen more than she thought. Had Carrington followed her last night?

Maybe her past successes had made her careless. She needed to retrace her steps and talk to Carrington, though she doubted he would be forthcoming. If he didn't trust his men with the information, it was unlikely he would tell her, a stranger, and a woman at that.

All too soon they returned to her mother, and Mrs. Wolcott smiled at the pair. Lynette was nowhere in sight.

"Would it be all right if I called on you, Mrs. Wolcott? Miss Wolcott?" Mr. Chambers's face shone with hope.

Her mother's smile widened. "Of course. Tomorrow afternoon we're free." After Mr. Chambers had retreated, she added, "Delia, I don't understand how you aren't married. So many eligible gentlemen."

Men who were loyal to the king. The only men worth considering had fled New York and were likely dead in a field.

"Also, I've invited Lord Carrington to luncheon tomorrow. Your father spoke highly of him, and I think in this troubled time, he would be a good connection to have."

"But, Mama, you said we would visit Helen tomorrow."

Delia's nails bit into her palms through her gloves.

"Don't be ridiculous. We can't ignore this opportunity." Her mother's voice grew stern. "Now, stop looking so glum. You're scaring away potential suitors."

Her frown deepened. How about she scare them away with her blade? She giggled to herself and resigned to get through the rest of the evening without killing anyone.

After all, that was Foxglove's job, not Delia Wolcott's.

CHAPTER THREE

L ATER THAT NIGHT, Delia was in her room overlooking the back garden. A room her mother had decorated in accents of purple and green to match Delia's usual wardrobe choices and her preference for nature's company.

She dismissed her maid and worked on the numerous pins placed in her near-white wispy hair to hold it up high. She supposed her mother was right about a connection with the captain but for different reasons than she would think. With the combination of Mr. Chambers and Carrington, she was bound to get tidbits of information to piece together from their investigation into Foxglove and their knowledge of Arthur. It didn't hurt Carrington was a tempting enigma.

As for Helen, Delia would be lucky to call on her anytime soon. Her mother was always controlling her life and making plans for her without telling her. No, she would have to run into Helen somewhere. Right now, it was more critical she found out about this witness and what he or she knew before it was too late for Delia to fix her mistake.

A faint knock sounded on her door.

She sighed and opened it to Felix, who bolted inside. She shut it behind him with a faint click. "What happened?" Already she calculated how fast she could change and be out of the house.

He noticed her tension. Not much got past his quick mind.

He was small from his underfed childhood, but it helped him scramble into places to overhear talk. He did much of the legwork to make up for the information she failed to gather at social functions. A battle on two fronts.

"Isn't urgent. Nobody to save or poison." His stance was relaxed, his mask as a carefree boy. "There's another family, the Davises on Pine Street. The father was questioned. He's not much of a liar. The officers saw past him."

"What did he have to lie about?" She settled back onto the plush green chair near her covered window.

He followed her lead and took up a place on the chest at the foot of her bed. "His son is a soldier on the rebels' side." He crossed his legs and continued at her raised brow, "He gave hints that he knew what happened to Arthur."

"I thought there were no witnesses."

"I don't know. All I have is what I overheard. Does it matter?" He fidgeted with the knife at his belt.

"Maybe, maybe not. It could open other leads." She let out a long breath. "All right, we're going to have to come up with a plan and soon. The rebels aren't giving us enough information as it is. Unfortunately, we also have to figure out a new way to get people through. I'm afraid I heard tonight there was a witness from our last rescue."

Delia nibbled her lip, her eyebrows drawing together.

Felix cocked his head and studied her expression. "What are you thinking? You have your scheming face on." A wide smile spread over his face.

"Do I? Hmm."

He leaned forward and uncrossed his legs. "You do have a plan."

"Just a little bit. We would need more people if we're going to get information from Davis. Say, his account for an escape from New York. Get at least two people but also someone good at woodworking. Can you handle finding people? Men well trained for driving and service. We must be able to trust them completely. Better yet, have damning information on them."

"Why, Miss Wolcott, such language." His voice transformed into an infuriatingly accurate impression of her mother.

She hurtled a throw pillow at him, which he deflected off his shielding arm. "Well, can you?"

He got to his feet. "Of course, my dear." He turned back at the door and saluted her. "There's one more thing. The kitchen's in a whirl with the visit from the captain. Be careful. I've heard stories about him around town. Each one contradicts the other. At the worst, he's a butcher and a womanizer. They say he abandoned his wife to die. They say he kills prisoners for fun. The British soldiers call him a hero, but many of them fear him."

She waved her hand, dismissing his concern.

He disappeared into the hall and headed to their kitchen for his nightly lessons with Cook.

She finished undressing for bed, and her mind lingered over the events of the ball anew. Where would her conversation with Carrington have led if they hadn't encountered her brother? A smile tugged at her lips, and her fingers worked over the front fastenings of her stays. Carrington's knowing eyes watched her in her memories.

She shook away the thought and donned a long nightgown for the chilly night. She nestled under the thick quilts of her four-poster bed and tried to forget the thoughts invading her peace.

Peace wouldn't have her.

Delia didn't like her plan. Creating a false bottom to conceal passengers in a carriage occupied by a British officer was crazy, if not suicidal. Carrington was the only person she knew who could leave New York without being questioned. Or so she hoped.

She rolled to her back and stared at the ceiling. She barely knew the man, but the challenge excited her. A man sent to lead the investigation was likely observant enough that deceiving him would be difficult. He had shown as much during their conversation tonight. What if what Felix had said was true? Would she be in danger, aside from the chance of discovery?

She decided the risk wasn't too high, even if he was a danger. She needed answers, and the Davises needed rescue.

The captain's future was at stake. Her father and her brother were respected members of the city, but more importantly, they were rich and would believe her if Carrington did anything. Or at least, this was what she told herself.

At the back of her mind, attention from Carrington was thrilling, like playing with an open flame. She ached to read the danger hinted at in his dark eyes and flushed with pleasure to flirt with the noose, but her tangle with the handsome captain would have to wait until tomorrow.

The next morning, Delia rose before dawn, an unreasonable hour for her station but a necessary one for her inclinations. She dressed for the morning in a woolen brown dress, several seasons old, and prepared to practice her knife work in the back of the shed, unseen and unheard.

The air had a frosty bite to it as she made her way over the frozen ground, her breath preceding her. The old carriage in the shed that had been replaced months ago was crucial to her plans, but the carriage was nowhere in sight. It was clear from the gathered dust the carriage had been gone for some time, but she hadn't noticed nor had anyone mentioned it to her.

Foxglove's plans were not just obliterated, but the carriage left a gaping hole in her memories. The last time she had spoken to Arthur, they'd been riding in that carriage.

When the crunch of footsteps came from behind, she rubbed at her face as if she could erase the disappointment and loss from her features. Felix approached. His eyes were downcast and his pace reluctant.

A frown creased her brow. "Do you know what happened to the old carriage?"

He shook his head. "But it doesn't matter. None of it matters." He met her eyes. "The Davis family is gone. There's no one to rescue."

She covered her mouth and stumbled to a bench set along the

path to the shed. Felix dropped down next to her.

"How?" Delia's voice came out a whisper.

"They must have found out where their information leaked. They went around my interception point. Foxglove forced them to take preventive measures. I had no warning they would act, but the arrest happened a few hours ago. There was nothing we could do."

"We'll have to find new avenues of information. Maybe the arresting officers learned more about Arthur in your absence. We'll have to track them down." She clenched the polished antler handle of her knife, which she'd brought out for practice. Arthur's knife.

She stabbed the bench between them, taking out her frustration at their failure. Felix jumped. His reaction checked her volatile outburst, though she left the knife like a struck flag in the wood.

"There's something else." He hesitated. "The soldiers arresting the Davis family didn't just take them to jail." His voice shook as he spoke. "They took the father, John, out into the street and held him down. He could still see into the house, the same way I could. The soldiers stripped his wife, Mary, and his maiden daughter, Rebecca... There was so much screaming. I wanted to look away, but I couldn't."

Delia went numb, cold, and yet dampness crawled along her cheeks.

"I saw them afterward, Mary and Rebecca. After John was taken away. The soldiers didn't kill them, but they weren't alive. They just lay there, silent, and nobody dared move to help them. I was about to find some way in through the back. Mary, though, she slit Rebecca's throat and stabbed herself in the gut. It was so fast. So much blood." His eyes were vacant, lost in that last act of despair and defiance.

Cold air stirred around Delia as though the women's ghosts passed over her. She shivered and folded her arms against her body. She hadn't known the family, but she had heard their story before. Rape was not uncommon in the occupied city. A murder and suicide were not unheard of. Yet she couldn't help but feel responsible. If she and Felix had acted last night, none of this would have happened. How they would have pulled it off didn't matter but only that they would have tried. She owed Arthur that much even if the rescue would have yielded no answers as to his death.

Felix tugged at her arm, bringing her back to the yard. He reminded her she was still alive and had to deal with the business of the living. She squeezed his hand and got up to dress as the loyalist daughter she was supposed to be. A costume that would mask her intentions as Foxglove.

AFTER SHE HAD changed to a contrary, sunny yellow dress, she discovered what had become of the carriage. Her father had sold it as a favor to an officer who intended to repair it for his wife's arrival from London. The information left a sick twist in her gut. It was an insult to her memory of Arthur. They didn't even need the money.

She busied herself in the sunlit drawing room with the hemming and repair work her mother had brought in, for the soldiers. A small, round table sat between the red damask chairs she and her mother perched on, and light threatened to blind her as she worked. She had the urge to fling down her work and escape to her plants.

"Delia, you've been fiddling with that seam for too long. If you aren't going to do anything helpful, then you might as well stop." Her mother sniffed. "Besides, you missed the news from your father."

Delia glanced up at her in disinterest, fussing with the stitch she had placed.

Her mother continued in an even tone, "He was told he must

take in one of the officers, since there's an overcrowding of soldiers and we have a spare room."

Delia narrowed her eyes at her mother. The spare room was Arthur's.

"Don't look at me that way, dear. At least we were given a choice of officers. They could have simply thrown us into the street. We'll be able to house a man of the best of character. Your father has insisted on this, since he has two unwed daughters in the house. Some of the things the soldiers do, well, let's just say you won't have to witness them." Mrs. Wolcott's face contorted in disgust.

How would she continue her efforts if she had to work under an officer's nose? Then again, it may be useful to know where Foxglove could strike next. She returned to her sewing.

"If all goes well at luncheon, we will ask Lord Carrington to reside here."

Delia stabbed her finger with the needle. Hard. She brought the wound to her lips and looked back at her mother, who was contentedly replacing buttons on a coat.

Her pulse drummed in her ears at the prospect of having the deliciously troublesome captain in such close quarters. "Is there no one else?"

Her mother ignored her stare. "It's your father's decision. He has already met Lord Carrington and simply wants my agreement."

Which meant her father had already decided and wanted to keep the peace with his wife. The illusion of giving them a choice. Her mother realized this but liked to pretend there was equality to the union.

They wouldn't ask Delia. Lynette had escaped off to a dress shop with their mother's maid and would probably love an officer in the house. This luncheon must be to appease Delia. Maybe they did pay attention to her moods after all. That was not reassuring.

She supposed she always had her poison handy.

A small smile brushed her lips. No, foxglove was a painful way to die, and she would rather avoid using it. Foxglove was also present in many of the gardens in their neighborhood, which made it convenient for her.

Unfortunately, it was too difficult to predict. She had to take into consideration the individual ingesting the poison as well as the conditions in which the plant grew. She had gotten careless last time, a fact she no longer regretted after the events of this morning. The men who'd survived had likely spent a good deal of time with vomiting and diarrhea, wishing they were dead. It was an excellent distraction to hide escapees from the city.

Deep in her thoughts, she hadn't heard the footsteps approach. The door to the drawing room creaked, and she looked up as the butler, Mr. Henshaw, announced Lord Carrington. Delia rose with her mother.

They curtsied as he approached, and he bowed to each of them in turn. He was out of uniform, and it suited him. His clothes matched the inky black of his hair and the coldness of his smile and eyes. Yet she sensed the wicked spark behind his calm exterior, and her pulse quickened to meet it. This man could be sleeping a wall away from her soon.

"I believe our refreshments will be ready shortly." Mrs. Wolcott gave him a pleasant smile. "We're missing a couple of members of our little party. Jeffrey and Mr. Bradshaw are expected to join us. Also, Captain, your Lieutenant Chambers is invited to come after luncheon if you wish to stay."

"Wonderful." Carrington sounded anything but sincere. He handed off his hat and coat to the butler and seated himself in the upholstered red chair across from Mrs. Wolcott.

Delia took the chair next to her mother.

"I think I'll stay," Carrington said. "In all honesty, I find Mr. Chambers a questionable character and I'd like to form a more solid opinion of him."

Delia's eyes flashed to him in surprise at his plain statement. "Then you're new to working with Mr. Chambers?"

His dark eyes searched hers. She had the sense he could read her mind and every traitorous detail lay naked to his piercing stare.

"We're all new to each other. We were transferred from different places with the sole purpose of catching Foxglove. Unfortunately, I didn't have a say in who was included, and Chambers has uncertain loyalties, which is why he was assigned to the case."

A British officer with New York sympathies? It seemed not all Englishmen were bad—just the one in her home. That must be how Chambers had been involved with Arthur. They shared similar views of the war.

"Ah, let us move to the dining room." Mrs. Wolcott gestured toward the butler in the doorway.

A cloud pushed across the sun when they moved to another set of large windows. The long chestnut dining table rested on a carpet of light blue and cream, which matched the curtains to precision. Her mother held her chin high as she showed the guest into her favorite room. The place where matchmaking often began.

At last, Jeffrey and Mr. Bradshaw arrived. While Mr. Bradshaw apologized repeatedly, Jeffrey grinned and gave Carrington and his mother elaborate bows.

Mrs. Wolcott frowned at Jeffrey. "Awful boy. Can't you ever be on time? And you denied us Mr. Bradshaw's company in your tardiness. I do apologize, Lord Carrington. What must you think of us?" She took the seat at the head of the table.

"There's no need for apologies. We're all here now." Carrington grinned at Jeffrey as if sharing a private joke.

Delia took the seat on her mother's left, and Jeffrey sat across from her. Mr. Bradshaw moved to take the place next to her, but Carrington got there first. Mr. Bradshaw was forced to sit next to Jeffrey, away from Delia.

Mr. Bradshaw eyed Carrington with disdain, and she tightened her fists in her lap. Who was he to think she belonged to him? She had never given him any hope or led him on. His behavior was intolerable and his attentions growing bolder.

Their food comprised dainty sandwiches and small pastries. Delia had to pace herself to avoid looking gluttonous. The food would only tide her over for a full meal at dinner, the afternoon meal that was always too late for her schedule. Her mother had also found tea for their snack, and Delia sipped it in content oblivion. If this was going to be a regular occurrence, then she would gladly welcome Carrington.

Her eyes were half-closed, her hand against the steaming cup and a lemon tart resting on her plate. Her mother was saying something.

"Then you'll stay? We thought you the perfect choice when Mr. Wolcott met you, and we would like to get you out of those dreadfully crowded sleeping arrangements."

Delia flooded back to herself. She stared at her mother, who favored Carrington with a proud smile. She had hoped he would refuse. He could always visit for tea, and they would probably run out if he was in residence. She frowned at the lemon tart as if it was to blame for distracting her.

Her life was at stake here. What if he found her dried fox-glove hidden behind her other herbs? Arthur's bedroom was next to her own. He would hear much of what went on in her room, and she would have to pass his door when she left, an intolerable circumstance. It didn't help he was tempting enough without the added proximity.

She caught him studying her from the edge of her vision. Her cheeks warmed, and she averted her gaze. How would she get through the war like this?

Mr. Bradshaw drew her attention. "Miss Wolcott, would you like to take a walk? You look like you could use some fresh air." He sounded genuinely concerned, but also, this was an opportunity to reclaim her from Carrington.

She offered him a small smile. They had once shared a strong friendship through Jeffrey, but now his possessive behavior suffocated her. She could see no way around his suggestion. Her mother would lecture her for weeks if she refused Mr. Bradshaw.

"Very well, but only if Lord Carrington and Jeffrey agree." She stood, and her mother patted her hand in approval.

Mr. Bradshaw rose and glared at Carrington, willing him to refuse. Carrington smirked at him and took her arm as a manner of acceptance. They led the way to the barren garden. How very like and unlike it was from the time at the ball. They had turned the situation upside down and with her mother's approval. She grinned conspiratorially at Carrington, and the answering spark in his eyes sent her stomach fluttering.

When they outdistanced Mr. Bradshaw and her brother on the cobbled path, Carrington spoke, "Forgive me, but it seemed you were trying to avoid Mr. Bradshaw."

She bit her lip. "Why do you say that?"

"You appear to resent his attention. I'm surprised no one has noticed or commented on it, most especially him." He scanned her features, and his warm gaze soothed her uneasiness.

"You're right, sir. I tire of him, and I've told him so, but he doesn't want to believe me. I think he's too vain to accept I would refuse his advances."

"Then let's have fun with him. I noticed his improper advances to you at the ball, and I think your lack of interest in another partner only reinforces his thinking." His smile was mischievous and conniving, and it embraced her like a lost friend. Or a lover.

She returned his grin. "How do you suggest we do that?"

He leaned his head closer to hers as if to whisper a secret. His breath tickled the tiny hairs across her neck, and she shivered but didn't move away. "By making him believe what he will."

"You're mad." She giggled. She leaned forward and whispered back, "He's bigger than you and has a bad temper. You better hope my brother approves of you now." She watched him through her lashes. The space between them hummed.

"You're a natural. One can only hope for a reaction. That's

the best part." He winked, and her smile brightened. "Now tell me what objections you have to my taking the extra room."

Her face fell, expressionless, and her heart sank at the change of topic. "I have no objections."

His face grew solemn. "Nobody would believe that."

"It was my brother's room." The words escaped her of their own accord.

"Aw." He looked away. "I'm sorry about him. I heard what happened but didn't make the connection until today."

"What did you hear?" She straightened, coming alert at his words. From what she knew, Carrington hadn't been in New York when her brother had died. She hadn't imagined he would be a source of information concerning Arthur's death as well as for Foxglove's enemies.

He cleared his throat. "There are two stories. I haven't found out which is true."

"Tell me."

"Have they said nothing?" His gaze moved from side to side as though he would see her family there. "This isn't a proper conversation."

"Neither is making Mr. Bradshaw jealous. I don't care. Nobody tells me anything. All I got was a story about a riding accident." She lowered her eyes.

He sighed and leaned toward her again. "I haven't heard that one, which leads me to believe they lied to you, but you didn't hear that from me."

She raised her brows.

"One story claims a robbery by soldiers while your brother was defending Miss Perry. The other story claims assassination by some unknown party. I believe it was no robbery but it was meant to look like one after the fact. From the report I read, Miss Perry fainted and was unable to identify the murderer. It could have been anyone." He shook his head. "Is this what you wanted to hear?"

"Yes, it brings me some consolation to know I was right." She tapped her lip with a finger. "It was the soldiers."

He halted their walk and glared at her. "I know there are robberies, murders, and such crimes committed by my country-men, but you mustn't make rash judgments."

She stepped aside. "And what if I do?"

He didn't have the chance to answer. Mr. Bradshaw caught up to them like a furious bull. Jeffrey was close behind, and a worried frown creased his features.

"Is he insulting you, Miss Wolcott?" Mr. Bradshaw stationed himself in front of Carrington. His false concern pained her ears.

"I'm perfectly fine, Mr. Bradshaw."

"You look upset. I'd hate to see you used badly." Mr. Brad-shaw grabbed at her arm, but she pulled away from him and Carrington.

"I'm quite well. Leave me alone." The lie shook in her voice as her mounting discomfort sizzled around her. Why must he always touch her?

His jaw dropped as he stayed his hand.

Her mind muddied at the news from Carrington and the possessive presence of Mr. Bradshaw. She fled before she said something she would regret. Her feet tripped over the uneven ground as she skidded back toward the house. She rested at the partially frozen pond, clutching her middle with her arm.

Mr. Bradshaw's rustling footsteps followed her and then a brush of air as he tentatively reached for her shoulders from behind.

"Please, leave me be."

He clutched her shoulders and turned her about to face him.

She snapped, and she pushed him off. Her teeth clenched, and her breath came out in a hiss.

His eyes widened. "What are you doing?"

Jeffrey and Lord Carrington halted as they came on the scene.

"Mr. Bradshaw, I think it would be wise if you left now." Carrington's level voice held a stern warning. The most sensible thing she'd heard all day.

Mr. Bradshaw turned on Carrington, his fists raised. "You." His voice came out a growl. "This is your doing."

"Richard, stop." Her once-familiar use of his given name startled him enough for Carrington to throw him off.

"You will pay for this, Carrington." Mr. Bradshaw spat out his words like venom and pointed at the captain's chest. He turned on his heel, not wasting time as he retreated out the yard's gate without looking back. They watched him go, silent and still.

Her body shook, the anger escaping through her tremors. She fell to her knees. She sensed someone crouch in front of her and looked up to see Jeffrey.

Her throat clenched tight. "Why did you bring him here?"

His gaze jumped away. "I knew he was interested in you, but I didn't know he would get this bad."

She stilled her tremors with a gulp of air, rose to her feet, and brushed out her skirts.

A flicker of concern shone in Lord Carrington's eyes through his usual solemn mask. She gave him a weak smile to reassure him. Encouraged, he offered his arm, and she tentatively took it to steady herself.

"You should rest your nerves. Mr. Wolcott and I will make your excuses." His calm manner and steady presence comforted her as they continued to the house. Jeffrey, on her other side, was quick to agree.

They walked in silence, and Delia found the trip far too short to wrap her head around everything that had gone wrong. Leaning into Lord Carrington eased her overwrought mind but kindled new questions in her heated breast.

Chapter Four

After a sleepless night, her thoughts continued to tug at her conscience the next day. Her future as Foxglove was like a dead weight pressed on her heart. Her days of dressing up and roaming the streets were at an end, but she refused to believe her role as Foxglove could not be salvaged.

She would start by questioning the officers who had hurt the Davis family. They had to know something about what happened to Arthur. If only someone knew where the men resided. It was risky, but she would have to find them through balls and parties. Unfortunately, gathering answers meant witnesses, and witnesses talked.

The deep, crushing sensation she'd experienced for the last year surfaced. She wasn't a killer. Not intentionally, but crimes committed by British soldiers were rarely investigated. Robbery and rape were common occurrences. At least she could rid the city of soldiers preying on civilians.

Nothing was as it had been when Arthur was there with his carefree smile and boyish laughter. This was war, though, and Washington had left the city. Those who remained would have to defend themselves. Those who could not fight, like Arthur and the Davis family, had Delia and Felix to fight for them. It was a promise and one she would see through no matter the consequences.

Lynette entered the room, stirring Delia's attention. Her sister dropped onto the foot of the bed. She set down a familiar box carved with leafy vines and stars. The air was heavy between them. They sat in silence for a moment until Lynette spoke.

"Dee, is it true?" Her hands held a tight grip on the box.

"About what?" Delia gave Lynette a crooked smile. Her sister could mean any number of things at this point.

"About what happened with Mr. Bradshaw." Her sister's voice was low, as if she was sharing a secret.

"Probably. It depends on what you heard."

"One of the maids was talking to Cook. She was spinning a story of how you've led Mr. Bradshaw on, and that although you're as good as engaged to him, you...uh... How do I put this nicely?" She gave Delia a pained look.

Delia's brows drew together. "Just use the words she did. It's not like Mother is here."

"She said you were whoring yourself to Lord Carrington." Lynette's voice came out in a rush, and she averted her gaze.

Delia paled, and her heart twisted in her chest. How could anyone reach those conclusions? Did everyone think she was attached to Mr. Bradshaw? She barely knew Carrington.

"Of course, that's not true. You know more than anyone I've no intention of marrying Mr. Bradshaw or anyone soon. I can't believe the servants have such a low opinion of me." She hardened her jaw. "I suppose in Mr. Bradshaw's point of view that's what happened, but it's a bit exaggerated. Did Mr. Bradshaw say anything to the servants before he left?"

If a story like this spread, her plans for a desirable marriage would be on a permanent delay. She could survive as a spinster, but she had always thought she wouldn't mind marrying and having a family of her own after the war.

"That's another thing. I know Mr. Bradshaw said nothing because I passed him when he went directly out of the yard." Lynette frowned. "There's something I haven't told you but only because it kept slipping my mind. That same maid is in love with

Mr. Bradshaw. I see her pay unnecessary attention to him."

She blinked at Lynette, seeing her with fresh eyes. "This all happened while you were present?" Maybe her sister should be the spy.

"Nobody notices me. I'm the sweet, invisible girl, but what they don't understand is I'm quiet, not deaf." She said the last part with that same passionate tone Lynette used for all her strong declarations. Delia had had no idea her sister felt that way, and she told her as much, earning a smile for her understanding.

Delia rubbed at her forehead. "Hopefully, this ridiculous story hasn't spread too far."

"I doubt it has. Cook looked at her like she'd grown another head, and I think most of the household won't believe it either. In any case, Jeffrey wants to turn out the gossipy maid, but I think that will make things worse. He's planning to talk with Mr. Bradshaw and is worried Lord Carrington will retaliate."

Lynette brought out a deck of cards from the box. "I thought these would help you." They had preferred to use playing cards since they were young, their old nanny having taught them how to read them. Lynette excelled at reading, and they often used the cards to make decisions.

Her sister shuffled the cards and fanned across the bed. Delia focused her mind to think of a question, but so much entered her thoughts she decided to choose whatever card called to her. Her finger caught the edge of one, and she handed it to her sister.

Lynette brought it to her face and gave a sharp inhale.

"What is it, Netty?" Delia reached to take the card back, but her sister clutched it tight and shook her head. She turned the card to face Delia.

The ace of spades.

Surely this meant transformation and not death in her circumstances, although death was also a transformation.

"Do you know what it means? Does it answer your question?"

"I think so." She had no idea in the least.

Lynette furrowed her brows in concern. They had drawn the same card shortly before Arthur had died, but the question had been some frivolous one that neither of them remembered.

"This is silly. It doesn't mean anything." Delia's hands shook as she stacked the cards. It was just a game, after all. Fortune-telling only gave answers when reflecting on the past, and any possible meaning would be useless to them. In her haste to gather the cards, one of them slipped off the bed, to the floor. The two of hearts.

She blushed, and Lynette's face split into a wide grin.

"Dee, what have you been doing?" She tut-tutted when Delia remained silent. "Do be careful." Lynette's face fell, serious. "I don't know what will come of all this." She gestured to the cards. "We can consider ourselves warned now." Yes, but warned of what?

Delia lost her appetite for fortune-telling. The prospect of marriage seemed to shadow her like a drunken soldier in an alley. If only she could tell her sister the truth, but Foxglove was a part of her Lynette couldn't share. Delia couldn't take the chance her actions would hurt anyone but herself.

"Dee, Lord Carrington is handsome and titled. You could do worse." Lynette smiled at her brightly and left before she could reply.

If Delia was honest with herself, she didn't know what she was doing. She was drawn to Lord Carrington, but what kind of relationship was founded on the threat of the scaffold? Yet his rare smile kept invading her thoughts when she least expected it.

She didn't know Carrington or even his full name or title, thanks to their interrupted introduction. He often seemed cold and distant but with a mischievous streak that had probably landed her in this mess with Mr. Bradshaw in the first place.

As much as she wished to unravel the clothes—er, layers—of the captain, he was her enemy. No good would come from a dalliance with him. Besides, men like him didn't marry into new American money like her, and she had no interest in being anyone's mistress.

Quieting her thoughts was a futile task, and she finally gave up that night. She threw on a simple dress and left her pale hair loose to stream down her back. The hour was late, and she reached the kitchens undisturbed, where the fire was always in full force. Felix, or one of the other boys, would be on duty to tend the fire, but they were nowhere in sight. Sounds echoed off the far walls as she shuffled inside.

Delia set her candle down and located her valerian root with her jars of dried plants in the back of the larder, undisturbed. She kept her dried foxglove hidden behind her harmless plants, well sealed and unlabeled. Nobody touched her jars, but the possibility never left the back of her mind.

The water boiled, and she steeped the tea. The smell made her heavy-headed, and she wondered a moment if she should skip it and go back to bed. She drained the water and combined it with cooking wine.

She allowed the wine mixture to cool. At last, she swallowed the drink, and it slammed into her like a heated ram. She took a long breath and continued to sip the liquid, flinching at the taste. When she finished, she was light-headed and drowsy, but she started off to her room.

She stopped at the stairs when voices emitted from her father's office and traveled through the hall. Their words became clear as she eased closer to the door, behind which could only be her father, her brother, and Lord Carrington.

"It's a horrible thing, but what can we do? They've operated in the city from the beginning and spoken for us all when they've no right to do so. A band of ruffians. Our family has lost enough to them." Jeffrey paused. "We don't know if they're connected to Foxglove, but it's possible."

"I don't believe they are. Foxglove seems to have different motives, and they're certainly not quiet about their crimes," Lord Carrington said.

Jeffrey raised his voice. "For Foxglove's sake, he better not be or I'll kill him myself."

Delia covered her mouth over a gasp. She had held out hope her family would sympathize with her. Who were they talking about? The soldiers? The gangs? She had no idea. Foxglove was not working with any group of people. Nobody she thought of made any sense.

"However misguided Foxglove is, he has saved the lives of people who faced certain death in those prisons." Her father's declaration caused her to weave, and she caught her balance in a crouch.

"Father, how can you say that? He's a murderer."

"I make no secret of my concern for the well-beings of the prisoners. Most of them die without any kind of trial. Make no mistake, I don't support the Foxglove killings, but I think his heart is in the right place." Her father's voice dropped, and Delia strained to hear. She slid closer to the door and prayed to whatever god that nobody would spot her there.

"Regardless of whether his actions are just, I've been ordered to find him." Lord Carrington's voice was steady. "I would prefer to keep him alive but have been given the option to stop him by any means necessary. My commander and the king want results soon, and I think my leads are solid enough to give them what they want."

Silence fell beyond the door.

Her cloudy mind couldn't grasp the conversation anymore. The king knew about her? No wonder men were assembled to capture her. Foxglove was a royal embarrassment. Yet, as much trouble as she was in, she would hate herself more if she quit.

"I think I'll retire for the night, if you'll excuse me?" Lord Carrington said.

She staggered upright and hurried up the stairs, bumping into the stair rail as she went. Her feet flew over the steps and swung her to the hall to her room. She ended up sprawled outside of her room while the sounds of footsteps continued. Laughter broke the stillness around her.

Carrington stood behind her, in front of his door, his stance proud and captivating. He cocked his head and watched her with a keen intelligence in his gaze and a wide smile.

She frowned back at him. "You might as well help me up."

He closed the distance between them, and merriment sparked in the darkness of his eyes as he stared down at her disheveled state. His smile sent a rush through her body and warmth to her cheeks. She shook her head to steady her thoughts and fought the urge to trip him for laughing at her.

"Learn anything interesting?" He offered her his bare hand. She hesitated and eyed his ready palm. The world spun around her, and she didn't think crawling away would help her dignity.

She grasped his hand. A jolt shot up her arm and settled in her chest, awakening a hollowness she hadn't known existed.

Without much assistance from her, he brought her to her feet and steadied her by her shoulders. The hollow sensation spread from her chest, up to her neck, and down deep between her legs. She met his gaze, and her eyes wandered to his lips. A grin tilted up his mouth as he noticed her attention.

"You're drunk." A deep laugh rocked over him. She scowled at him and held out her arms to her room as if she could wish herself away. He moved his arm under her shoulders and guided her along. She hated herself for needing his assistance, and yet she wouldn't refuse the chance to be near him.

"What gave me away?" Her body barely reacted to her attempt at movement. She rested her head against his chest, cocooned in the scents of leather and brandy.

"You made some noise. Maybe a gasp? I thought it was a servant." He paused at the threshold to her room. "Can you make it?"

She snorted. "Of course."

When he released her, she staggered to her knees. She whimpered at the loss of his solid presence. No doubt he thought she had hurt herself.

He chuckled above her and lifted her to her feet. She let out a long breath and collapsed against his chest. A moment passed as his heart hammered into her ear and her pulse galloped after his.

He cleared his throat and led her to sit at the edge of her bed. His hands remained long enough to keep her steady, and then he spun away from her and strode for the door.

A smile lingered over her lips. "I've always been a terrible spy."

He stopped midstride and peered back at her. His expression was a mask to her alcohol-riddled brain. "You spy often?"

"Don't be ridiculous. I prefer gardening." She giggled and fell back onto the bed.

"Of course." His smile filled his voice. "Sleep it off."

CHAPTER FIVE

DELIA'S EYES FLUTTERED open as she struggled against her sealed lashes. Her heart drummed in her skull, and her tongue stuck to the roof of her mouth with a sour taste. A dry groan escaped her throat as she tried to roll over, and she yelped at the pinch in her back.

She had added far too much wine to the tea. An idiotic, careless, and overindulgent thing to do, but she liked it. It had been a relief to forget things for a while. Now every thought was blurry, and she didn't trust what she remembered.

Had Carrington been in her room, or had that been a dream? At least he was honorable and had left her alone in her drunken state. What a mess she must have looked, and he had seen it all. She wanted to bury herself under her bed. What had possessed her to listen at her father's office door? She could have reached her bed before the drink had taken full effect.

She grasped her head and rang for a maid. Her embarrassing state last night would do nothing for her innocence or Carrington's good opinion.

After some time, a servant appeared, one she didn't know well. Maybe Gladys? Where was her maid, Hope? She requested fresh water and clean linen. Seeming not to hear her, the maid went to the curtains and threw them open.

Delia gasped at the jolt of pain as sunlight struck her face.

"Shut them." She hid her face under the crook of her elbow. The maid ignored her plea.

Gladys smirked. "Or what? You'll tell your mother? Imagine what she would say if she knew what you do at night."

Delia's mouth dropped open. "I don't know what you're talking about."

"Oh, but don't you? Late nights with Mr. Bradshaw? You don't deserve him."

A moment ticked by as Delia digested her words. "You wouldn't." A dalliance wouldn't get her hanged, but her mother would push her down the aisle faster than she could blink.

Gladys had a smug look.

Sweat dripped down Delia's spine. "What do you want?"

The maid paced the room, and a wide grin grew over her features. "First, I want you to stop your visits to Mr. Bradshaw."

She chewed her bottom lip. "Done." No more late nights? She could handle that. Anything she needed to do she could do at parties. Or at least, she hoped so. It was a risk she had planned to take.

"And I want a raise."

Delia shook her head. "I don't have any control over that."

Gladys pursed her lips. "How about your allowance?"

She snorted. "Might as well make an appointment with my mother."

"All right." The maid fanned away her suggestion. "Four months of your allowance."

"Three?" Delia slid her feet off the bed and stood. She rummaged through her jewelry box and found the piece she was looking for, a yellow topaz bracelet set in plated gold. She displayed it in her palm. "This is worth at least that much." It was a piece she never wore. She thought the yellow made her skin look sallow.

Gladys's eyes brightened, but she straightened her face into indifference. "I don't know."

"I'll throw in a pair of matching earrings."

The maid couldn't hold back her squeal as she took the bracelet from Delia without another word. Gladys's dark eyes seemed to spark as she stared at the jewels. The girl had probably never owned anything so expensive. Delia neglected to mention there was a necklace too.

"Do we have a deal, then?" Delia held her breath.

Gladys grew serious. "You have to leave Mr. Bradshaw *alone*."

"He's all yours." She tried out a frown, but tears would have been preferred. It was too bad she couldn't cry on command like her friend Abigail.

The maid clutched her new valuables to her chest and headed for the door. Delia would have to get her own water. When Gladys was gone, Delia let out a long, steadying breath.

She stopped herself from screaming in frustration but only because it would hurt her head worse. Not because she didn't want to alarm anyone. Who was to say whether Gladys would keep her word? Then again, who would believe she had given the jewelry freely? Besides, Gladys wanted Mr. Bradshaw for herself, and if she told her mother, Delia would end up attached to Mr. Bradshaw forever.

Pushing the subject out of her mind, she threw herself into getting dressed.

She studied herself in the mirror and tidied wispy strands of escaped hair. Her red-rimmed eyes presented a haggard appearance. The pain echoing through her skull rendered her attempts useless. At least her looks supported her story of being sick.

Facing Carrington made her uneasy, but she saw no way around it. He was boarding with them now, and she couldn't hide in her room forever. She made her way to breakfast, where food was laid out. Thankfully, Jeffrey was the only one seated at the table. Even though the long table was mostly vacant, her brother occupied the space like an oversize bear.

Jeffrey gestured to a chair beside him, out of the pale sunlight, and she hesitated to take it. He would lecture her; she was sure of it. He cleared his throat, and she planted herself in the chair.

"Where do I start?" He tapped his fingers against the glass, holding his steaming coffee.

"By telling me what a talented and beautiful sister I am?" She eyed her plate of bacon, scones, and jam with reluctance and poured herself some coffee, adding too much sugar.

He frowned at her. "Well, you are, but I'm serious. How do you make so much trouble for yourself? First with Richard, then the maid. Now I hear you were drunk in the hallway."

She nearly choked on her coffee. "How do you know about that?"

"Lord Carrington talked to me before he left this morning. You just missed him." He was calm now, shoveling egg into his mouth. The runny egg slathered over his plate turned her stomach and forced her to look away.

She itched to track down Carrington and land him on his pompous ass. He had no business discussing her when she wasn't there to defend herself and to her brother of all people. Jeffrey didn't need any more reason to try to control her. She choked down the thought with a sip of coffee. Later.

"You're going to have to talk to Richard." He held up a hand when she began to protest. "I'd like to avoid getting caught between you two. I haven't said anything to Father, but he will know soon if Richard gets the idea to court you formally."

She reined in her voice just below a yell. "He'll never listen to me." If Gladys got word of it, she would have worse problems.

"You'll have to try. I still consider him a friend, but he's blind when it comes to you. He nearly bit my head off when I tried to talk about what happened."

"Fine." She attempted to cut the conversation short. Mr. Bradshaw could wait, and she would have to navigate around Gladys somehow. Right now she had more pressing concerns.

Jeffrey had other plans. "Were you really going to hurt him, Dee?"

Her gaze dropped to her plate. "I don't know. I just wanted

him to leave me alone." She let out a breath and comforted herself with some of her scone.

"Why didn't you say something to me? I would have kept him away if that was what you wanted." He placed his palm on the hand she rested on the table.

"I didn't think you would believe me. He's been such a good friend to us." She stared at their hands as she nibbled her lower lip.

"Why wouldn't I? You're my favorite. I will believe everything you tell me if something happens again." He patted her hand and went back to his coffee.

She raised a crooked brow. "I thought you said Lynette was your favorite?"

"Her too." He smiled into a sip of his coffee. "Now, I assume your drunkenness was from one of those potions of yours?"

"My potions, as you call them, work. I may have added too much wine or valerian or both."

"Either way, Carrington had a good laugh."

"Did he now? I so wish to provide entertainment for our guest." Her words hissed through her clenched teeth.

Their conversation and her further humiliation were interrupted by the entrance of their mother and then Lynette.

"It's a good thing you're well this morning, Delia. We still have plans today. Your dress for tomorrow's dinner at the Rivertons is ready." Her mother scowled, looking her up and down. "Goodness, have your maid straighten you up before we go."

Delia sighed inwardly and left to follow her mother's wishes. Her mother was another spoke in the wheel governing her life, but nobody controlled Foxglove. Yet she needed all the help she could get to prepare for Foxglove's new direction at the dinner. An interrogation would go smoother if she dazzled the eye.

The Rivertons' dinner wasn't much of an event, but her mother insisted she had new dresses when there was even a remote chance she may meet a suitor. Her mother's actions were wasteful and futile, considering she didn't give them much of a chance. This time her mother had picked her dress, and it was unlike anything she had worn before.

Her mother wasn't messing around anymore.

The fabric was indescribable. It was either pale peach or pink, depending on how the light hit it. The neckline was cut low, lower than she liked. Not to mention the dress was formed to fit her upper body in such a way to accent her breasts.

Her mother was trying to serve her at dinner. She was ruthless; Delia would give her that. Lynette's dress was what she would have preferred: a teal gown with a modest but flattering cut.

By the time they made it back from their errands, it was suppertime. Delia let out an exhausted breath as she entered her room to fix her appearance again. Through the faint lighting, she made out a form on her chair. She jumped before she recognized Felix and hurriedly closed the door behind her.

His wild grin split his face from ear to ear.

"What is it, you scamp?" She moved to tidy her hair.

"You've become too fearful. I have something for you." He handed her several sheets of paper filled with his quick, precise handwriting. They consisted of a long list of names in neat rows, with information on each.

She frowned down at the paper. "I'm not too fearful. You try being a woman in this city. What is this list?"

"It's a soldier roll call of sorts, or several. Names, companies, ranks, and duties." He nodded at her wide-eyed stare.

"But how did you get this?"

"It was on Carrington's desk." His mouth curled into a smug smile. "The original was, anyway. I spent most of the day copying the lists. It turns out he isn't just investigating our side but every side. That and I think he's trying to predict the next target."

"I can't believe you went into his room." A nervous flutter unsettled her stomach. She wished she had thought of it. "What if he had come back?" And what if he had found her there instead of

Felix? The flutter transferred to her chest, a pattering like hummingbird wings.

He quaked with laughter. "I'm a servant. Are you daft? You're probably the only one in the family who has noticed me at all."

She tapped the pages with her finger. "Still, how will this help us?"

"You know, Miss Dee, if you keep this up, I'm going to strike out on my own. Maybe pour all the foxgloves in the water supply. It would make things interesting."

"That wouldn't work. You'd probably just induce vomiting with such a high dosage, not to mention poison innocent citizens. Be serious." She pinched the bridge of her nose. He was joking, right?

All mirth left his face. "Nobody is innocent here." His cold tone sent an icy shock down her spine. It made her glad he was on her side. "We can use this list to match up crimes to duties and the like. Here." He pointed to a spot on the list. "These men are the ones who arrested Mr. Johnathon Davis."

"You're sure?"

He gave a quick nod.

"Well, I guess I better get to work on my extract tonight. The officers seem to be at every event this year. They're like parasites. I'll try to question these men." She scrawled a copy of the four soldiers' names: Frederick Baker, Benjamin Forrest, Peter Norris, and Nigel Weston. She handed the list back to Felix.

She mulled over the names, committing them to memory. "We weren't trying to kill them before, and I'm going to use something different this time." She chewed her lower lip. No witnesses, she reminded herself.

"Then how will they know it's Foxglove? I think giving them a healthy dose of fear may get them to think twice about their actions." Felix had a valid point, but she would be more at risk if the men survived. As much as she wanted answers for Arthur and the Davis family, she wouldn't be much help to anyone hanging from a noose. She told him as much, and he grudgingly agreed.

After he left, she finished freshening for supper and made her way down the stairs. Being the last to arrive, she stole a glance at Carrington through the candlelight. He leaned toward her father and brother in deep conversation and didn't seem to notice her admiring look. A footman poured her some wine, and she turned her attention to the food. The light meal consisted of a roast chicken alongside cold meats and cheese with bread and fruit.

At last, her mother took notice of her appearance at the table. "Delia, you are becoming as late as Jeffrey. Don't make a habit of it."

Before Delia could answer, Jeffrey said, "I was on time."

She resisted the urge to stick her tongue out at him and settled for kicking him under the table, causing him to choke on his food.

He coughed and then turned to Carrington. "Our Delia is such a lady she can be fashionably late to even our humble family supper."

She gave an airy wave of her hand. "One must take great care of one's appearance, or one may find himself at thirty and still a bachelor."

He gaped at her in mock horror, hand placed on his chest. "Dear little sister"—his tone was flat—"bachelorhood is better than spinsterhood."

She considered putting nettle in his bed, but then their mother interrupted their banter. "Speaking of spinsterhood, Lieutenant Chambers is also invited to the Rivertons' dinner."

Up until now, Carrington had been engrossed in conversation with Delia's father, but he looked up at the mention of Mr. Chambers. Her cheeks colored as he witnessed her mother's thinly veiled criticism.

Mrs. Wolcott continued in her flat tone, "He made a point of letting us know, since you missed his visit."

Delia looked down at her plate, sensing Carrington's continued gaze on her. Her mother would play all eligible men against one another in a bid to get her married as soon as possible. She suspected her mother had long given up on Jeffrey giving her grandchildren, and with Arthur gone, it was now Delia's turn. Marriage was the last thing on Delia's mind, and a husband would just be in the way.

"How fortunate." Delia's voice came out just above a whisper. As enjoyable as her conversation with Mr. Chambers had been, she couldn't risk showing her sympathies. She had long since ruled him out as a murderer. He'd been on Arthur's side, after all, but that didn't mean an association with him would be safe.

After the meal, she pretended to read as she waited out the others so she could prepare the tincture for her next encounter with the officers. It would be a weaker consistency, but she didn't have weeks to wait. The poison should be strong enough for a quick death. Since the movement of soldiers proved unpredictable and frequent, she didn't want to take the chance her targets would leave the city or turn her in.

When her family went to bed and the servants were dismissed, she carried the brandy from the library to the kitchens. She located the water hemlock she had gathered last summer. At the time, she had mistaken it for Queen Anne's lace. It was an error that would have gotten her killed if she hadn't discovered the hemlock's true identity in time. The plants were similar, but one was beneficial and the other was almost certainly fatal. Delia had decided to keep it for further study, far removed from her other dried plants. She was grateful now for her curious nature.

She donned work gloves before she carefully washed the dried plant and minced it. Then she placed the pieces into a dark-blue jar, which she filled with the brandy, and shook the contents. It would last her for some time and would get more powerful as the days went by. It was in the soldiers' best interest to appear later, since it would be a quicker death. Before she left tomorrow for dinner, she would pour some into a smaller bottle.

At last, her bed called to her.

Distracted with her plans, she collided with Gladys. The

chamber pot in the maid's hands streamed its contents over Delia. She froze, speechless as she stood there staring at her gown. Piss ran down the fabric, ruining her shoes and drenching the marble tiles. Blood boiling beneath her skin, she gawked at the spotless maid.

This was no accident. The maid had no reason for collecting chamber pots at this time or carrying them near the kitchen. A roar filled Delia's ears, and her hands shook at her sides. Why did this girl think she was beyond reproach or dismissal? Delia's mother or father had to see reason after this incident.

"What is the meaning of this, Gladys?" She kept her voice quiet but cold.

Gladys curtsied to her. "I'm so sorry, Miss Wolcott, but you must watch where you're going."

Delia's fists clenched and unclenched. She couldn't let this unsettle her, not when her life was at stake. "Yes, I believe you're right." She took a deep breath. "I was just thinking of Mr. Bradshaw, and my mind got carried away. He hated this dress anyway. So really, you've done me a kind favor."

The maid gaped at her. Maybe Delia had gone too far.

"Now, I don't have time for your childish nonsense, so let me pass." Her voice was surprisingly steady. She had already given up her jewelry. What would be next? She made to move past her.

Instead, Gladys stepped forward to push her back toward the kitchen, but Delia had other plans and ducked away, sending Gladys sprawling on the stone floor.

"Much obliged," Delia called behind her as she left the girl on the floor and hurried to her room. With brisk movements, she shut her door and wedged a chair under the handle. This couldn't continue. She needed Gladys and Mr. Bradshaw out of her life.

For now, she would make sure her maid knew to keep Gladys away. A door lock would be ideal, but until then, she would keep the chair in place. She grasped Arthur's knife that she usually carried and placed it under her pillow before throwing her soiled dress into a heap on the floor.

CHAPTER SIX

O N THE DAY of the Riverton dinner, Hope helped arrange Delia's unruly hair high above her head and accented her coiffure with pearl drop clips. They struggled to adjust her dress correctly, and now her air and all her comfort were restricted.

When her hair was completed, Hope left Delia to stare at her reflection. She didn't feel like herself at all, and she certainly didn't look like herself. Another mask for a different type of crime.

A half hour later, she rode with Lynette and their mother to the Rivertons', through the cobbled streets as sunlight struggled against the clouds. Once they caught up to Jeffrey, Carrington, and Mr. Wolcott, Mrs. Wolcott took her husband's arm and led the way.

Delia wove her arm through Lynette's, and they exchanged a smile.

Jeffrey gawked at the sight of Delia's dress and took her other arm. "What are you wearing?"

She self-consciously snatched her arm back from him and placed her fan in front of the ample view her dress provided. "Mother's idea of a fish hook."

He shook his head as though to erase the image of her. "You mean a bear trap."

She lifted her gaze to find Carrington staring at her, face

white. Her pulse drummed in her ears as she caught his widened eyes and smiled. His lips curved up, and he tripped on his feet. He righted himself and quickly moved ahead of them to join the dinner party.

She raised a brow at Carrington's straightened back. "What's wrong with His Lordship?"

"Damned if I know. Am I going to have to trail you all night to beat off the bears?"

She considered but remembered the task at hand. "No, but thank you. Besides, I think this is my punishment for not making an effort at the last ball." Jeffrey kissed her forehead and left them, doubtless to join up with his friends.

The Rivertons' dining room was smaller than the Wolcotts' but made up for it with ample windows and bright white-and-yellow trappings. Delia had to make do with the men seated next to her during dinner.

One of them happened to be Mr. Chambers, while the other was an aging bachelor. Mr. Mayhew wore a curled wig and neat, well-tailored clothes. Mr. Chambers looked as he had at the ball in his officer's uniform and a curled wig not dissimilar to Mr. Mayhew's.

Mr. Mayhew eyed her chest until the food arrived, but at least he was silent for the most part, having dispensed with the usual courtesies about the weather and food. Mr. Chambers, however, completely ignored her attire and proceeded to discuss whatever came to mind.

Then he chattered on about another soldier he was friends with who was moved out of the city. She let him talk, relieved to be at ease to scan the table. Delia didn't let on that she knew about his loyalties. He was still in his British red, after all.

It occurred to her that his friend, Mr. Ritter, was no ordinary friend, which only meant a marriage to him would lack the type of love she desired. Maybe her mother would take a hint and look elsewhere.

She barely noticed the three courses served, except for the

cake, which she couldn't help but moan over. This led to a few stares from men, while the women looked the other way.

Lord Carrington caught her gaze. The world fell silent, and she forgot about the cake as her mouth dried around it. She swallowed and dropped her attention to her plate. If she wasn't careful, he would enchant her with those devastating eyes that saw everything.

Although the dinner party was small, officers were there with whom she was unfamiliar. Mr. Chambers pointed them out for her, but none of the names were on her list. She lowered her guard and relaxed, relieved to put off the task for another day.

"I have to apologize for my countrymen. We are usually more polite when it comes to attractive women," Mr. Chambers said.

She studied him. "You can't help what they do. Besides, I prefer the men of New York."

"Aw. In that, we have something in common."

Delia's cheeks colored, but her heart warmed that he confided in her. "Indeed? It's a shame they can't be more like Arthur."

Mr. Chambers tensed and cleared his throat. "That would be unfortunate."

Her eyes widened, and she rubbed her fingers under the table. "What do you mean, sir?"

"A man's loyalties are everything. When one doesn't have a clear side, there can be only chaos. Picking no side is picking the wrong side."

Her tongue seemed to freeze in her mouth. Hadn't she jumped from one loyalty to another? By all accounts, she had once been an English subject, but how did this relate to Arthur? Out of necessity, he spoke in half meanings, and the more she conversed with Mr. Chambers, the more uncertain she became.

Yet Mr. Chambers had her rethinking her own loyalties. If he sympathized with New York, there could be other men in the British army with similar sentiments. Mr. Ritter was probably one of them. Could Lord Carrington be as well? Better not to take chances.

When dinner concluded, the women moved to the drawing room. It was an expansive space occupied by upholstered deep-green chairs with gold accents and a couple small round tables supplied with tea. Candlelight made up for the room being on the dark side of the house.

Delia was seated alone with her dear friend, Abigail Riverton, the daughter of Theodore and Constance Riverton, the hosts of the dinner party. Younger than Delia by a few months, her friend was dressed to subtly impress, with her jet-black hair set off by the deep plum of her curve-emphasizing dress.

"I see your mother is at it again." Abigail eyed Delia's cleavage. "It seems to be working or at least drawing stares. I think some of the women want to kill you. I know I do."

Delia smirked and refused to show her shame by covering up again. "This wouldn't have happened if you had agreed to run away with me, Abs."

Abigail laughed, her golden-brown eyes lit up in her round, smiling face. "I don't think they have marzipan on the Nile."

"You've had too much anyway."

Abigail sniffed and snuck another off the plate in front of Delia. "Who was that officer you were talking to during dinner?"

"Lieutenant Chambers? We had a wonderful conversation."

"Yes, people noticed. Some of the men had the saddest looks. It was like your officer had killed their favorite hunting dogs."

"He isn't my officer, just a nice man." If only she could explain to Abigail about Mr. Chambers's decent nature without raising more suspicion. Lord Carrington already watched him.

"Dee, I never thought I would see the day you called a British officer a nice man. I've heard you have the captain staying at your house." Abigail shivered. "He makes me uncomfortable. I had the pleasure of sitting next to him at dinner. Does he always look so sour?"

"Most of the time, though I have seen him smile and laugh. It's terrifying." Delia held back a grin.

"I believe you. He seemed to be in a mood that must be his usual winning character. Although, it was directed at your officer. The captain must have a fancy for you. I would love to hear the conversations the men are having right now. Do you think they've decided to sacrifice Mr. Chambers?" Abigail tilted her head to the side with a faraway look and took a sip of her tea.

Heat blossomed over Delia's cheeks, and she glanced toward the doors. "You're exaggerating, truly."

"Oh, we will see. I plan to take full advantage of the entertainment your mother has created."

They were summoned to join the men in the Rivertons' ballroom. The decorations bordered on gaudy in the family's favorite room. Candles illuminated the yellow paint and golden scrollwork, but the large window curtains were open to take advantage of the remaining daylight. Yellow roses sat along the walls, giving off a pleasant smell that would soon be overshadowed with the presence of people.

Upon entering the room, Jeffrey hurried to meet Delia. He led them off to the side, where they wouldn't be overheard.

"I would rather you didn't dance with these men, little sister. If it weren't for some of them being officers and Lord Carrington restraining me, I would've gotten into a couple of fights already." He held on to her arm, ever her devoted guard.

"I told you, Dee. Isn't this exciting?" Abigail whispered.

Jeffrey ignored Abigail. "I'm going to take the first dance with you. Also, I've convinced Lord Carrington to dance with you, and plan to ask the Riverton brothers."

"You convinced him? I don't want to dance with someone who doesn't want to dance with me or has some misplaced need to protect me." Frustration balled up in her throat, and she pulled Abigail away from Delia's meddling brother. She would never know if Carrington would have asked her himself. The mere thought of being close to him filled her with an anxious giddiness that left her mind senseless.

She didn't make it far before almost colliding with a pair of officers. They were introduced as Mr. Gardener and Mr. Mason. The taller one with a crooked wig, Mr. Gardener, asked her to dance. With a haughty glance in Jeffery's direction, she accepted and let him lead her to the floor. He wasn't exactly the dashing captain, but he would serve to irritate her brother.

For much of the dance, his hands strayed but artfully enough that it seemed like an accident. Instead of stomping off, she inhaled a deep breath to steady her nerves and took advantage of the unwanted attention.

"You're a good dancer, Mr. Gardener, but I dare say Mr. Baker is a bit more talented than you." She mentioned one of the names on her list at random.

"Mr. Baker? You mean Freddy? I can show you a better time than Freddy can." His breath traveled between them, a mixture of onions and copper. She forced herself not to flinch.

"Oh, it's hard to say. I would have to dance with you both on the same night." She gazed at him through her lashes. "Are you sure we're talking about the same Mr. Baker?"

"I know no other, and I know all the officers in New York." She doubted that but figured all the awful ones must gravitate to one another.

"Where can we find Mr. Baker?" She glanced at the other dancers as if he was in the room.

"You don't need Freddy." He guided her forward, none too gently.

"I'll have to judge that for myself." She knew it was terrible, and she would probably regret it, but she trailed a gloved finger along his hand suggestively.

"All right, but you'll have to remember my skills tonight. Freddy is going to be at the Marsdens' ball on Saturday." He rubbed his palm over her skin.

She clenched her teeth, suppressing the urge to flee. "How do you know this? As far as I know, you want to keep me to yourself."

"Freddy talks too much. He'll probably talk about his dancing with you. It doesn't matter if he has you Saturday. I'm being sent out tomorrow."

Of course, they were no longer talking about dancing, and Delia couldn't decide if she had meant it that way initially. The conversation made her stomach churn, but at least she had discovered the whereabouts of one of the men to question, and if he was anything like Mr. Gardener, she would have no trouble killing him.

They fell silent and moved through the last of the dance. When she went to leave him, he held her fast and tugged her off the floor.

Delia's stomach leaped into her throat, and her attention went to the comforting weight of her knife. Thinking fast, she asked Mr. Gardener to get them some drinks.

He handed her a glass and forced her to a shaded part of the room near a door. Unsure what to do, she sat, shaking, as he left her there with the drinks, to find a more private place. If she ran off now, he would warn Mr. Baker away or, worse, be a witness against her after she killed Mr. Baker, revealing her as Foxglove. All her work rested on this one man.

Mr. Gardener would have to die.

When nobody was looking, she poured the contents of the poison bottle into Mr. Gardener's glass before putting the bottle away just in time, or so she thought.

He stared down at the glasses. "What's that you have?"

"I don't want to be in the family way." She gulped down her drink. "Let's finish our wine so we don't have to carry these glasses." He obliged her and quickly drained his drink. Impatient man.

She dropped her glass, which made a loud crash as it shattered. As she'd intended, heads turned toward them. She pushed Mr. Gardener aside and hurried into the light, tears in her eyes. Jeffrey, Carrington, and Mr. Chambers rushed to her side. Once Jeffrey and Carrington saw she was unhurt, they left her to Mr. Chambers, who led her to Abigail, Delia's mother, and Lynette.

Another crash and scuffling resounded behind her. The other men gathered around Mr. Gardener, except for her father, who sat with Mr. Mayhew. A man shouted, and the group moved away. Carrington and Jeffrey came into view, dragging Mr. Gardener. Blood dripped from his scalp, into his eye, and his nose looked broken.

Mr. Gardener groaned.

Jeffrey's lips pulled back in disgust. "You're barely hurt."

Mr. Gardener shut his eyes as he wobbled against Jeffrey and Carrington. "I'm going to be sick."

Before they had a chance to release him, he vomited on Carrington, which would have been amusing in other circumstances. The men flung him off and moved a safe distance away as he continued to vomit. He clutched his stomach and went into convulsions.

A woman screamed, pointing not at Mr. Gardener but one of the rose vases. Among the yellow roses sat a deep-purple, almost red, foxglove.

CHAPTER SEVEN

*W*HAT HAVE *I done?*

The next morning, she lounged in the library, staring into the fireplace, her hand stroking her mother's scraggly gray terrier, Pierre. She awaited Lord Carrington's interrogation as she dreaded her fate. This time, seeing the captain could carry a death sentence.

After the convulsions had started, her parents and Lynette had pushed her into the carriage. Later that night, Jeffrey had returned home, tired and jumpy. He'd told them Mr. Gardener had lasted another half hour before his convulsions had stopped with his heart. Jeffrey wouldn't give any more details except it was an unpleasant way to die and they didn't think the poison was foxglove. Carrington had stayed behind to investigate.

She looked up, disturbed from her thoughts. Abigail sat beside her, but she didn't remember her entering.

Abigail watched her with upturned brows. "Dee, please don't fret. You're safe, and no matter what anyone else says, I don't believe Foxglove kills women, so you were never in any danger."

Delia exploded into a fit of giggles, and Abigail blinked back at her. She wiped a joyful tear from her eye and smiled at Abigail. "I think you're right, Abs. Foxglove doesn't kill women."

"I know it's wrong to speak ill of the dead, but Dee, Mr. Gardener was a sick man. Now he's gone, and the gossip is dirtier than ever. I think Foxglove spared you and the rest of New York from the misery of his presence."

Delia sobered. "Are you glad he's dead?"

"Goodness, yes. I've heard some of the women calling Foxglove a hero in private."

Stunned, Delia fell silent. The papers and soldiers had erupted anew at calling for her head. But a hero? She was relieved the man could no longer hurt anyone else, but she wished there was another way. Where was the justice for Arthur? For the civilians? Too many innocents had already been victims of the war.

Her father and brother profited a great deal from this war, as did other businessmen. They were devoted servants to the Crown. It wasn't for the women to involve themselves in politics. She was expected to follow her father's lead, and by all accounts, she was a devoted Tory. If she could not share her real opinions in public, then she would in secret. She would fight as Foxglove.

Abigail held Delia's hand protectively as they sat in silence. She squeezed her fingers when the door to the library suddenly opened.

Carrington entered looking uncharacteristically disheveled, his hair mussed and clothing wrinkled in a careless but seductive fashion. His tired eyes told of long, sleepless hours, yet she couldn't help but think he had rolled out of bed, and once her mind settled on the picture of him in bed, it wouldn't disappear.

He gave a quick bow and looked them over before addressing Delia. "I'm afraid I have to speak to you about what you witnessed last night."

"Whatever for?" Abigail answered for her.

"Miss Wolcott was the last one to talk to Mr. Gardener besides myself and Mr. Wolcott." He paused and met Delia's gaze. "I can come back later if you need more time."

Abigail shot him a piercing glare. "As you can see, Dee's still recovering, so how about you come back never."

"It's all right. I'll speak to him." Delia gestured for him to take the seat across from them.

He hesitated before lowering himself to the edge of the chair and leaning toward them. "Miss Wolcott, did Mr. Gardener seem at all unwell to you before you left his company?"

"Unwell as in mentally or unwell as in physically?" Was anyone well in this city?

"Either one." He shook his head.

"Yes, and both."

"How was he unwell mentally?" He smoothed his face into a mask of stern patience, but she sensed his annoyance, like an itch under her stays. His frustrated impatience was almost as attractive as his smile. What other emotions lurked underneath his solemn manner?

"He was male and British." She shrugged, not quite an apology.

He scrunched up his forehead. "All right. How was he unwell physically?"

She gave him an impish smile. "It's improper for me to say."

Abigail choked on a laugh behind her hand. Carrington leveled a stony frown at Abigail and waved her to the door. Her friend dashed out of the room, and laughter erupted in the hall.

Despite himself, Carrington's face softened into a rare grin.

The corner of her mouth crept up, and her gaze traced the contours of his smile. Her breath caught as he moistened his lower lip. "I shouldn't be alone with you." She didn't care much for propriety, but she didn't trust herself to be with him without an escort.

She regretted her words when he got up and called outside the library. A footman came and stood inside the door, out of earshot but in view. Carrington fell back into his chair and rubbed at his face.

Concern tugged at her conscience. She ached to smooth away his troubles, to knead the tension out of his firm shoulders. "You look tired. You should rest."

He cleared his throat. "That's of no concern to you, Miss Wolcott. What concerns you is what happened last night between you and Mr. Gardener."

"Happened? Nothing happened. He was a cad. I got away when I could." Her voice shook at the memory.

"Did you notice him acting strangely?" He held up a hand to elaborate with a slight tilt to his lips. "That is, behavior unfitting of a regular cad."

She crossed her arms. "He was sweating when we danced, and he kept complaining of the heat and his stomach." The lie left a sour bite on her tongue.

He cocked his head. "Is that why you went to get drinks?"

"Yes." Sure, why not? A dozen other innocent reasons could have prompted them to get drinks.

"We found a broken glass nearby. Do you know how that happened?"

"Yes, I dropped it." She should have thrown it at Mr. Gardener. Nobody would have blamed her.

"Did anyone approach you and Mr. Gardener after the dance?"

"No, not that I recall." The man could have been poisoned before their dance. Let Carrington think that.

He leaned forward as she slouched back. His eyes held devilish intent, and for a heartbeat, and she forgot what they discussed. "You're sure Mr. Gardener was sick when you danced with him?"

"Yes, I'm sure." She drew out her words, and her eyes fixed on his. "The man was probably sick from birth. Can I go now?"

He threw up his hands. "You need to take this seriously. A man is dead."

"Yes, I know." She released a breath. "I'll never have his filthy hands near me again."

Carrington stopped at that, his gaze assessing her. She thought she glimpsed concern etched in the corners of his eyes, but he stifled her notion when he spoke. "Do you hate all my countrymen or just British soldiers in general?"

"What does that have to do with Mr. Gardener?"

"Nothing really, I'm just curious. You dislike me, and as far as

I know, I've given you no reason to hate me." He got up, strode over to the fireplace, and leaned on the mantel.

She winced. "I don't hate you." This interrogation didn't gain him any points with her, but she couldn't help her body's reaction to him. Those intelligent eyes and that mischievous smile left her aching to touch him, explore his depths.

She quickly added, "I like Mr. Chambers, and he's both British and a soldier."

He peered back at her, his expression thoughtful. "What do you know about Mr. Chambers?"

"I know enough." She met his eyes, and he nodded.

"You'll know he's looking for a wife, then, or at least a wife in name. A woman to keep his secrets. He would be wise to keep his ideas to himself." His voice was steady as he gauged her reaction.

Her mouth grew dry. "I thought as much." She dismissed the subject as though it was of little importance. "Do you have any more relevant questions? I'm weary of this interrogation."

He drew himself up and moved back to his vacated chair. "Why do you carry a knife?"

She stilled. "I didn't used to. It makes me feel stronger, more in control." She hadn't meant to tell him the truth, but she was unprepared to lie. She hadn't realized he was aware of her knife.

"Since Arthur?"

A solid knot lodged in her throat. She nodded, eyes tightly shut.

Her eyes snapped open as his chair groaned. He headed toward the door.

"You're not going to reprimand me? Tell me not to carry a weapon? Chide me for putting myself in harm's way?"

He glanced back. "No, I can't see what it will hurt unless you stab someone like Mr. Bradshaw. If I did tell you, would you listen?"

"Well, no, I would carry it anyway." Her smile revealed her teeth. "I hadn't planned to stab Mr. Bradshaw, but I haven't ruled it out."

He smiled faintly. "Do let me know if you plan to stab him?"

She blinked. "Why? So you can have my family confine me?"

"No, I'd like to watch." The humor in his voice sent a rush through her. Where had this man been during the interrogation? Just when she thought she could get him out from under her skin, he enthralled her with this side of him.

Before she could reply, he let himself out of the library, and the footman followed. She couldn't understand him. One minute he was stern criticism, the next he was indulgent charm. For a fleeting moment, she wondered what it would be like if she weren't Foxglove. If there was no war and they had met under different circumstances. Already the library was hollow without him.

To make matters worse, Jeffrey came in shortly. He took the space formerly occupied by Carrington and studied her harried appearance.

"You have a fine way of causing trouble. Maybe we should send you to a nunnery or lock you in your room. Of course, you would probably escape." He had no idea. She wanted to laugh, having already been out her window and with no intention of repeating the ordeal.

"We'll be keeping an eye on you more." Really, more? How? Dodging him at parties was already an ordeal for Foxglove. Was he going to put her on a leash? "Lord Carrington and I thought we would have to kill Mr. Gardener. At least, I thought he would've killed Mr. Gardener, but Foxglove did it for him." He lowered his head, not quite hiding his smile.

"You mean Father?"

"No, Carrington. He was giving Mr. Gardener a sound beating until a couple of us held his arms. I couldn't get a punch in."

Her heart pitter-pattered through her pulse. She would have liked to have seen that, but a retelling from Carrington would have sufficed. Had the stern captain defended her honor?

His face brightened. "By the way, you've been receiving flowers."

"Flowers?" Her eyes widened in surprise.

"Flowers to help with your distress." He laughed at her expression. "Let me think. You have a bouquet of roses sent from Mr. Chambers. Richard brought over a bouquet arrangement. Also, I'm not supposed to tell you, but you also received a vase of foxgloves with no card. Mother threw those out."

Her heart stumbled in its disappointment. She hadn't missed the absence of Carrington's name. Not that he had any reason to bring her flowers, and he appeared under a great deal of stress from the investigation.

"Foxgloves?" Her mind labored over the possibilities. "Who would send me foxgloves? Do you know who received them?"

He gazed off in thought. "I believe it was Felix. Yes, I'm sure it was him. Why?"

She chuckled and shook her head. "Never mind, I'll talk to Felix about it later. What color were the foxgloves?"

"Purple, I think. Aren't they always?"

"Of course not. Don't you ever visit our garden?"

"Yes but not to see the flowers." He gave her a wide grin.

She narrowed her eyes at him. She was reminded of her conversation with Carrington. "I don't want to know what you're doing around my innocent plants."

His smile straightened. "Let's keep it that way. Also, for the sake of our mother and father, please stop being alone with men. Foxglove and I can't always save you."

She figured he was probably right, and she wouldn't always be able to poison them. She left the room when Mr. Bradshaw entered, not wanting to stir up any more trouble.

Her mind filled with thoughts of Arthur. She smiled at the memories, for once not letting the death of her brother eclipse her mood. Her mind was still absent as she turned down the hall that led to the stairs. She halted as she came across Gladys, who walked toward her, holding a mop and bucket.

What more did the girl want?

Gladys took a step forward and set down the bucket. The

maid closed the distance between them, wielding the mop. Delia backed up and fell against a solid male chest, and hands went to her shoulders.

"Don't you have work to do, Gladys?" Carrington's voice rumbled through her back as he spoke. The girl stopped, wide-eyed. She gave a quick nod and took her bucket and mop around the long way to the kitchen.

This had to stop. How was she supposed to avoid the maid and Mr. Bradshaw?

Delia let out a long breath. Carrington's chest nestled against her back like he sought to shelter her. An expectant air rose between them like a hum asking to be answered. She wanted to melt into him and allow him to pull her out of herself, to make her forget the misery of Arthur's death, and to escape the war and her suffocating family. In another world, maybe, but they were in the hall and he was out to capture her.

She straightened and turned toward him. "Thank you for getting rid of her."

"That wasn't getting rid of her, but I soon will. Why is she bothering you?"

She didn't know what to make of the concern in his voice or his willingness to help her. Maybe he saw her as some damsel in distress.

"She isn't just bothering me." Her voice caught in her throat. "I think she wants to kill me. She thinks I have somehow wronged Mr. Bradshaw, and she's jealous of his attention."

He arched a brow at her. "Really?"

"Yes, really."

"I believe you. I'd imagine Mr. Bradshaw's visit didn't make her any better. Let me get rid of her." He stepped toward the kitchen, but she grabbed his arm to stop him.

A sharp pang slammed into her chest. "Please don't. I can't be responsible for forcing her out on the street." Plus, Delia had no doubt Gladys would open her mouth if she was let go.

He scanned her features. "Then I will find a situation for her."

His gaze fell on her hand on his arm, but he didn't shake her off. They stood dangerously close, and the earthy scent of his shaving soap lingered over him. His brown eyes darkened as he looked down at her mouth, and she bit her lip nervously.

Her breath caught as he leaned forward.

Footsteps and laughter echoed down the hall, coming toward them. They stepped away just as Jeffrey and Mr. Bradshaw came around the corner. Mr. Bradshaw frowned at them but said nothing. Jeffrey's attention jumped between them as if he'd entered a lion's den.

She pivoted on her heel and led the way to dinner, but her thoughts were engraved with the deep-brown eyes of the off-limits captain and the kiss that would never be.

CHAPTER EIGHT

T HE NEXT MORNING, she made her way to the greenhouse. The atmosphere cushioned her in an earthy scent and musty air as Pierre trailed behind her. Upon entering, she noticed her foxgloves were sloppily cut. She didn't usually harvest from the greenhouse in case the garden didn't thrive. If Felix insisted on leaving foxgloves with their victims, he would either have to find more for her greenhouse or clip someone else's for the task.

She worked steadily on her plants. Although it seemed only a short time had passed, her lower back ached when a footman came in. Pierre had curled up on a patch of dirt, and his head perked up at the entrance of the footman, Sanders.

"Excuse me, Miss Wolcott. You have a visitor." Sanders's stern face appeared sincerely apologetic.

She knit her brows. "Who is it, Mr. Sanders?" Her attention moved back to the orchid in front of her.

"Miss Perry, ma'am."

Her brows rose as she looked to the greenhouse door as if Helen waited there. "Well, send her in here." She gazed down at herself and wiped her hands on a semiclean portion of her skirt.

When Sanders returned with Helen, Pierre rushed at her skirts, a mass of wiggling fur and saliva. Helen smiled at the little beast and patted his head.

"I missed you too," she told him. Satisfied, the dog resumed his place on the dirt, his head resting on his paws.

"Hello, Helen."

Helen offered her a weak smile. "I didn't know if you would receive me." Helen's mournful blue eyes were accented with dark circles.

"Whyever not?"

"You haven't visited me since I returned from the country. I thought maybe you blamed me for what happened."

Delia rushed to embrace Helen, and her arms found a slimmer version of her friend. "I could never. I apologize for not seeing you sooner. I've been neglectful recently." She drew back from Helen and eyed the orchid. "You see, even my plants are suffering."

Helen laughed, the sound like a clear bell. Warmth swelled through Delia. "That's a good sign, Dee. It means you're living your life."

A weight like a small stone caught in Delia's throat. "I wanted to talk to you about that night. We never really had the chance. I heard you were unconscious through the worst of it though. A small blessing."

Helen's gaze shifted. She was taller than Delia, but right now she seemed almost childlike. "That's just it, Dee. I wasn't unconscious."

"Then how did you…"

"Arthur told me to faint. He thought they would be less likely to harm me, and he was right. I don't know why, but they left me alone. So I kept as still as I could. I was afraid to breathe."

Delia wanted to spare Helen the retelling, but she sensed her friend needed to talk as much as she did. "I can't even imagine. What happened?" At last she had the opportunity to find some answers.

"I only heard some of it. I turned away. While I lay in the dirt, Arthur stood over me, pretending to check on me as the men got closer. He said he loved me." Helen's expression turned vacant. "They called Arthur a traitor, but then Arthur argued that they were the traitors and he wanted nothing to do with them. They beat him then. Three men against him." Helen was shaking now, her arms crossed protectively over her body. "I was terrified. I wanted to help him, but he made me promise to stay down. When they finally left, I crawled over to him." Helen's glassy eyes met hers. "There was so much blood, Dee. His face, I could barely recognize him."

Delia's eyes fogged over, and tears escaped over her cheeks.

"They told me later my screams were what brought help. My throat still hurt days after." Arthur had been alive but unconscious when they'd brought him home with Helen. His death had been drawn out to agonizing hours. "Mostly I remember the blood and the look in his eyes when he closed them for the last time. It haunts me."

Helen reached out to her, and Delia lost control, sobbing into her friend's chest. Helen held her tightly and allowed her to lose herself in her tears. "I'm sorry. I shouldn't have told you that. It was selfish, but I needed to tell someone."

Delia peeked up at her friend. "I needed to know. Who were those men?"

"I don't know. I could only see their figures as they walked toward us. You know my vision isn't the best, but Arthur must have recognized them when he told me to faint. I think only one of them spoke, and the voice wasn't familiar."

"Do you think Arthur was acting strange? Maybe he mentioned something about them before." She released Helen with a step back and rubbed at her wet cheeks.

"If he did, I don't remember. Before we noticed them, he was going to tell me something, but he didn't get the chance. I just thought it was about the wedding before, but now..." Helen shook her head and shrugged. "...I'm not so sure. It seemed important to him, but everything he said was important to me."

Delia didn't remember much of the days leading up to her brother's death. She had been busy preparing for what now seemed like trivial social events. Arthur had just returned from a reunion with some of his Yale classmates, and she had only seen him at breakfast that day. It seemed a lifetime ago.

Pierre, pawing her leg, brought her back to herself. She invited Helen to come in and have refreshments with her, but Helen declined.

"I wanted to make amends with you and see if you were coming to the Marsdens' ball. Mother has me on what Joseph has dubbed an 'apology tour' for my exit from our ball. I have more calls today." Joseph was Helen's younger brother and worst critic. "I heard about what happened and insisted on visiting you today."

"You have nothing to amend." She squeezed Helen's arm as she escorted her through the house to the front door. "To my mother's delight, I'm planning to attend. I think our mothers must be competing against each other for who can be most overbearing. You should have seen the horrible dress she made me wear to dinner that night. I think it was the true misfortune of the evening."

This earned a deep laugh from Helen, who Delia suspected hadn't done much laughing recently.

Her mother found her in her bedroom a few hours before dinner, a bundle of raw energy. "Your father informs me I can't make any more dress purchases anytime soon."

Delia inwardly celebrated and pressed her lips tight together to avoid smiling.

Her mother seemed to take her reaction as disappointment. "I told him it was out of the question, but he insisted things are too uncertain and he wants to recover from some disaster. My unwed daughters not wearing new gowns is the true disaster."

Her mirth fled. "What happened?"

"How would I know? Something about a ship and supplies taken by rebels. It's nothing for us to concern ourselves with. We will make do." Her back straightened like a marching soldier's.

This must have something to do with the dress she had worn to the Riverton dinner, and she silently thanked her father for his intervention. "Maybe it's for the best. Other families are doing without. It's a bit of a fashion statement in itself."

"I suppose." Her mother huffed and turned to leave. "Delia, do take a bath. Your face and hands are caked in dirt."

She sighed and rang for Hope. Not long after, the tub was fetched and buckets of heated water lapped over her skin. She faced away from the door and sunk her head under the water. Her eyes were closed against the world, cocooning herself in the comforting void. When she emerged, a cold draft drifted into the room, and paws rested on the edge of the tub.

"Pierre, what are you doing here? If you wanted to take a bath with me, then you shouldn't have run out." Pierre shivered against the tub and whined up at her. "What has gotten into you?"

Footsteps sounded too close in the hall. She peered back over her shoulder at the wide-open door. "Wonderful, you opened the door."

"No, I didn't." The voice echoed from the hall.

She gasped and searched for anything to cover herself. She hoped whoever was in the hall couldn't see over her head.

"Miss Wolcott, you seem to have a problem." Lord Carrington's voice became recognizable.

"Are you joking?" Hers raised an octave. "Of course I have a problem. Would you kindly shut the door?"

"Not the door. The view isn't a problem." He chuckled under his breath. "You should come out and see for yourself."

"Can you at least close the door first?" she said through her teeth.

"No, I... It would be better if I didn't come in there to try to shut it." Clearly, His Lordship had lost the ability to pull a door closed.

"Fine, turn around." She stood quickly, not waiting for him to obey. She smiled to herself as his footsteps stumbled down the hall. Served him right for ruining her bath.

She wrapped a robe around her, not bothering to dry, and

marched to the door. Carrington returned, his face blazing red. His gaze was dead focused on the door. A knife was jabbed into the floor, forcing the door ajar.

She inhaled a sharp breath. A foxglove was pinned to the floor.

Gladys. Delia told Carrington of her suspicions.

"I don't think so. I convinced your father to have Gladys moved to a new situation. She started at the Marsdens' house this morning. They were in a hurry for help to prepare for the ball."

The oppressive weight of dread lifted from her, and a mixture of happy gratitude and guilt took its place. She couldn't be indebted to him. It meant obligation and proximity. Already they shared a house. He was too close. She needed to create space now, or he would soon learn her secrets. Or even worse, she could fall for him.

He was trying and failing not to look at her wet hair and bare feet. The tips of his ears were tinged pink, and his pupils had consumed his eyes in darkness.

"Thank you. That was fast." A thin smile creased her lips as she watched his distracted state. "I hope you enjoyed the show."

He averted his gaze and gestured with his hand. "Your door was open, and I heard the dog whining. I thought I would see why." His gaze wandered back to her and glided over her body. Her smile widened, and his face returned to scarlet.

She bent to the knife and pulled it free. "Next time, why don't you knock?" She winked and clicked the door shut on his stunned expression.

A giddy sensation bubbled in her chest, but at its depth was leaden guilt. He had acted like a gentleman in an impossible situation. She had the wild notion of seizing him by his waistcoat, dragging him into her room, and kissing him until he forgot his name.

He probably believed the knife was a threat from Foxglove, and meant only to do his job. Either someone was trying to scare her or someone knew the truth about her identity. Neither was an agreeable choice.

The carving knife in her hand was from their kitchens. It had her father's monogram of "AW" engraved in the handle. She set the knife down and picked up the ruined foxglove she had left on the floor, the door having brushed over it. It was a cream shade she didn't grow.

Nausea settled heavily on her stomach. Someone wished her ill. He or she had opened her bedroom door in one of her most private times and threatened her. Of course, they could have easily killed her in her bath. They must want something. To scare her? To warn her? Or was it some sick practical joke?

This ordeal, mixed with the conversation with Helen, had left her exhausted, but it was still early, and she had to survive dinner. She rang for Hope, and they dressed her in a gown of burnt orange. It suited her aspirations for dinner, an attempt to be cheerful and grounded.

Tonight she was one of the first to arrive. Her mother and Lynette were seated in the drawing room, and they were chattering about the Marsdens' ball tomorrow. The occasion had already slipped her mind. She took a seat near them.

The rest of the family and their guests entered the room in pairs. Jeffrey came in with their father, and Lord Carrington with Mr. Bradshaw. She wasn't surprised to see Mr. Bradshaw, since he often dined with them, but the fact that he and Carrington were in amicable conversation was beyond her.

At last dinner was announced, and Mr. Bradshaw escorted her into the dining room. She sent a regretful look to Carrington as she sat next to Mr. Bradshaw. Lynette took the other chair next to her.

Mr. Bradshaw turned to her once the soup was served. "I'm concerned about your safety. I heard about Foxglove's threat. I will not have you harmed." His tone suggested she was one of his prized horses.

Of course Carrington couldn't keep his mouth shut long enough for her to explain things to her family. Mr. Bradshaw was the last person she would have wanted to know. She glowered across the table at Carrington, who caught her eye and quickly turned away. Coward.

Mr. Bradshaw dropped to a whisper. "He can't protect you. He's already shown he can't catch Foxglove, let alone keep those around him safe." He paused until he caught her eyes. "But I can."

"Thank you for your concern. The captain provides more than enough protection in our home." She settled back into her chair, waiting for the inevitable. "How do you suggest you can help?"

"That's what I would like to discuss with you if you allow it." He smiled, a look he must have thought reassuring. Oh no. Did he never give up?

She gave him a hard stare. "I'm not prepared to have that conversation with you. Nor will I for some time, if ever."

His face fell. "How do you expect to be safe? You need my help, and it's a sensible solution. I know your parents would approve."

She grew pale. "You've spoken to them?"

"No, not yet, but they encourage my visiting you."

"Don't. Please."

He squeezed her hand under the table and lowered his voice to match hers. "Dear Delia, that's all you had to say. I will wait."

She pulled her hand back. Aside from her clipped replies, she avoided Mr. Bradshaw for the rest of the meal. Finally, when dinner concluded, Jeffrey and Carrington joined up with Mr. Bradshaw. As she exited the room, Jeffrey whispered to Mr. Bradshaw, who shouted as the door shut behind her. She paused outside the door, but it had grown quiet.

Her father was the first to join the women in the drawing room. He beckoned to Delia, and she sat with him in chairs flanking a table, away from her mother and sister.

"I don't know how you do it, my dear, but you always manage to stir up trouble." He shook his head. "I'm putting a lock on your door, as you requested. I never thought my daughter would need protection in my own house." He paused and studied her. "Tell me, my little Helen of Troy, what do you intend to do about them?"

She gave him a quick smile. "Who, sir?"

He raised a bushy eyebrow. "Who? The men beating down our door. I thought Foxglove was enough trouble."

"You exaggerate. Nobody is beating down the door for me." Her mind shifted to Lord Carrington outside her bedroom door, but he hadn't even knocked. The only time she would have the pleasure of seeing the dashing captain break down her door would be if he came to arrest her.

He scanned her face and grunted. "Keep it that way. Now be off. I want to catch up on my reading."

She nodded and left him to find her own reading in the library. When she entered the hall, loud arguing came from the dining room. Learning her lesson from the last time she had eavesdropped, she ignored them and turned away. That was, until she heard her name.

She clenched her fists and stormed over to the dining room. They had no business discussing her. Jeffrey was the only one in that room who had the right, and it wasn't him she heard. She paused outside the door at Carrington's voice.

"No, I have no interest in her."

His rejection knocked the breath from her. She shook herself. What did she care? The man would turn her in to his commander faster than she could blink. She didn't need his prying eyes in her life anyway. His prying, beautiful, searching, captivating, brilliant damned eyes.

Mr. Bradshaw's voice caught her attention. "I don't believe you. With her dowry?"

"You're talking about my sister as if I'm not in the room." Jeffrey was barely audible as he mumbled. They seemed to ignore him.

"I'm not interested in her dowry," Carrington answered.

"You must be though."

"Don't be ridiculous. Of course I am. No man in his right mind wouldn't be. Which means you must be insane," Mr. Bradshaw said.

"Richard, if that's all you think of my sister, then I must ask you to stop." Jeffrey's tone sounded dangerous. She nodded her agreement even though they couldn't see her.

"The money helps. She's the perfect lady wife to come home to. Not to mention beautiful." Mr. Bradshaw didn't want a wife. He wanted a prized mare.

"Are we talking about the same woman?" Jeffrey asked. She smiled. He had voiced her thoughts.

"You don't know her as I do." Mr. Bradshaw's tone heightened to a whine. She hung her head and squeezed her eyes shut. "Lord Carrington, what do you think?"

"About what?" He sounded distracted. She pictured him staring off, his long fingers swirling a glass of brandy. A lock of midnight hair would hang over his eyes to perfect devilish effect.

"About Miss Wolcott."

Anticipation built in her chest, and the seconds ticked with wild thumps of her heart before he answered, but his response toppled her like a diving kite.

"I don't."

"Clearly you do," Mr. Bradshaw said.

"No, she's an American. So I don't."

"Miss Wolcott isn't good enough for you? It's okay for soldiers to bed American women but not to marry them, is that right?"

"That's not what I said. Which do you want, Mr. Bradshaw? For me to be interested in her or not? I'm weary of this game." Carrington's voice rang clear with a warning. Mr. Bradshaw was on dangerous ground.

Jeffrey groaned. "Please stop discussing my sister in bed."

"Then you will have to silence your servants, Jeffrey." Mr. Bradshaw's voice rose. "I don't know why they think Delia would throw herself at you, Carrington. She has always been mine."

She was about to fling the doors open and tell him otherwise when Carrington started laughing and couldn't seem to stop.

"You think that's funny?" Bradshaw's question was met with more laughter and a cough. She might have thought it was funny herself if it weren't so frustrating.

Silence.

"Quite." Carrington's voice sobered. "Give it up, man. She isn't interested." Appreciation mixed with irritation that he spoke for her.

"That's not what she told me at dinner." Mr. Bradshaw's voice was smug.

"It's like I'm not even here. Can you hear me?" Jeffrey said, but they continued to ignore him. She wanted to hug her brother.

"From what we heard, it is," Carrington said.

"Oh, you only heard her voice. She spoke in other ways," Mr. Bradshaw said. What other ways? She didn't know what dinner he had attended, but it wasn't the one she remembered.

"Right."

Mr. Bradshaw pressed on. "She couldn't keep her hands off me."

The blood rushed to her ears, and her eyes stung. Silence engulfed the men beyond the doors, and the tension seeped into the hall.

"That is—" Jeffrey began.

"She would never take you to bed." Carrington's voice tended to grow quiet when he was mad. This time, his voice rose until she flinched.

"And you think she'll have you?" Mr. Bradshaw yelled back.

"You've known her how long? I've already been closer to her than you will ever be." His voice fell quiet. He must have been at his end if he was resorting to boyhood bragging. She wanted to be angry at Carrington, but he wasn't wrong.

"How close?" Mr. Bradshaw's question hung in the air. Jeffrey must have been speechless.

"She has pretty, little dimples on her perfect backside."

Her cheeks burned. She'd heard enough. The men had too, and rustling came from inside the room. Jeffrey shouted for help from a footman as she rushed away to her room.

How could she be so stupid? He was a damned boorish British officer. The worst men of New York. And she had admired him like a heartsick fool. Had she forgotten everything she'd learned as Foxglove? Had she forgotten Arthur?

She thrust her door shut behind her. Shaking with unshed anger, she screamed at her reflection in her vanity mirror. She would have smashed the mirror but for the knock that sounded. She took a long breath and found Felix standing in the hall, brows raised. He came in and closed the door.

He nodded in greeting. "Your hand's bleeding." Her nails had left crescent moon gashes in her palms. "Your guests are also bleeding." He gave her a toothy grin.

"What do you want, Felix?" She moved to wash her hands in the fresh water in her basin.

"Fine thanks I get for checking on you. By the way, your scream is terrifying." He folded his arms.

She tilted her head back to look at him as she dried her hands. "How sweet. Were you checking on me?"

"No, but that isn't the point,"

She threw up her hands. "Well, what is the point?"

"You wanted to know about the foxgloves." He made himself comfortable, not waiting for an invitation to sit down.

She sighed. "I assumed you were busy."

"Yes but not all the time. I did leave the foxglove at the Riverton dinner. However, I didn't send you a bouquet of them, and I didn't pin one at your door. I'm not tacky or cruel."

She raised her brows. "I thought you had handed off the bouquet."

"A messenger brought the bouquet, but I was the first to suggest we throw them away. Whoever's doing this is sick. Are you planning to go on with the Marsdens' ball?"

"Now more than ever." She told him about her conversation with Helen. Felix's face shone with sweat and turned a shade of green. Arthur had been especially kind to Felix, treating him more as a brother than a servant. If he were anyone else, she would have held him, but Felix being Felix, she knew he wouldn't appreciate it.

"So you see, we can't quit now. Do you know where Arthur's things are in the attic?"

He nodded.

"Can you bring them into my room? Not all at once but a few boxes at a time. There might be something we missed. We didn't know what we were looking for the first time."

He shrugged, a frown creasing his brow. "We don't now."

"That's true, but we have a better idea of the motive for killing him." She tried to channel enthusiasm into her voice, but he was right. The boxes were unlikely to reveal anything new.

He got to his feet. "One more thing: are you planning to marry Mr. Bradshaw?"

Her eyes widened. "Goodness, no. Never."

"Can I kill him, then?" His crooked smile hinted at his dark thoughts.

"You've really gotten into this, haven't you?" She shook her head. "It would be unwise to kill him, and besides, you would have to get in line."

"It wouldn't actually be killing him anyway." His gaze became wistful. "Not a fair killing. He looked half-dead when Jeffrey dragged him out."

"Well, he deserved it."

CHAPTER NINE

T HE NEXT DAY was a long one she spent avoiding Carrington and preparing her arsenal for the Marsdens' ball. She refilled her water hemlock bottle and filled a second bottle of foxglove for good measure.

Her usual knife, she strapped on her thigh, and another two rested on her left forearm and right ankle. She tied the bottles next to the knife on her forearm for easy access. Her blush gown covered her haul nicely.

The ball was overcrowded, making it difficult to discern the decorations. The air was thick with melting wax from the ample candles burning across the rooms. From the moment she stepped in the doorway, she wished she had stayed behind. She wondered how she would ever get away with her plans.

She almost collided with Carrington waiting near the door. He wore a black eye and a jagged cut on his scalp along with his red uniform. It was fitting. Yet his injuries made him look even more appealing. A warrior returned from battle. What was wrong with her?

She flinched. "You look awful. Did you get into a fight with a rabid carriage horse?"

He closed his eyes tightly, looking as though he was counting to ten, before he opened them again. "I think I know who sent you messages."

"Really? Don't keep me in suspense." She tapped her fingers on her crossed arms, arranging her features into a mask of disinterest, though her traitorous gaze wandered over his broad shoulders.

He puffed out his chest. "It was Mr. Bradshaw."

"Did he admit it?"

"Well, no, but he has motive, and he was unaccounted for when the knife was planted at your door." She giggled, and he narrowed his eyes at her. "What's so funny?"

She continued to chuckle. "Planted."

He raised his eyebrows. "Is everything a joke to you?"

She cocked her head. "Well, yes." She frowned at him and studied his face as though for the first time. "You know, when you're angry, you have these pretty, little dimples on your perfect forehead."

His mouth fell open, and he sputtered something but finally gave up and strode off.

His investigation skills surpassed her own, and he was probably right about Mr. Bradshaw. He may even think Mr. Bradshaw was Foxglove. If Mr. Bradshaw had left the flowers, she was sure it would stop with his visits.

She cringed. He had opened her bedroom door while she'd bathed. At least he hadn't had time to linger.

She wove her way through the cramped room, and beamed when she saw Mr. Chambers heading toward her with glasses of wine punch. She thanked him and allowed herself a small sip to coat her lips and mouth. Any more and she would have the uncomfortable task of relieving herself.

Mr. Chambers named off the officers in different groups, adding anecdotes to their identities. "Mr. Granger is the prim fellow with the long nose. He likes to polish his buckles late into the night, but everyone knows he sneaks off to find company." He nodded to the man with the highest wig she had ever seen and smiled. "Mr. Gage's father is a baron. There is a bet among the men as to whether his wig is his mother's stuffed prize poodle." He gave her a pointed look.

She giggled. "No."

He nodded in quick bursts. "Yes."

Although none of the names were on her list, she began to see a pattern among the officers. The pattern was there was no pattern. All the soldiers had come from different backgrounds and had varying motives for enlisting. Most of them seemed indifferent to the colonies and needed the pay.

She wished she hadn't asked. They had become human to her, which made her job more difficult. Before, they'd been nameless enemies ruled by a crazy man thousands of miles away. Her conversation with Mr. Chambers forced her to examine her methods. She swallowed as though driving the implications deep down.

When the music opened, Mr. Chambers asked her to dance. Not feeling up to it, she almost declined. That was, until Mr. Bradshaw barreled toward her. She jumped to her feet and grabbed Mr. Chambers's arm, leading him forward. Mr. Bradshaw was either crazy or stupid to have come to the ball.

His nose looked swollen, and his arm was in a sling. She imagined those injuries were superficial compared to the one to his pride. He waited where they had been sitting, as if she was going to return to her seat and happily greet him. He probably had no idea she had listened at the door.

After the dance, she spotted Helen attempting to get her attention. She excused herself from Mr. Chambers and went to her friend.

When Delia reached her, Helen quickly grabbed her arm and led her out of the room.

"What is it? Where are we going?" Delia asked.

Helen said nothing and placed a finger over her lips. They headed down a long hall, passing closed doors. At the third such door, Helen stopped and motioned for her to come closer. She cracked the door slowly and quietly.

Delia held her mouth when her mind registered what a single

candle illuminated inside.

Her baby sister was in the arms of an unfamiliar officer, on a russet chaise. He kissed her, and his hands roamed over her dress. Helen closed the door without a sound.

"What do we do?" Helen whispered.

"We need to get Jeffrey."

A moan came from inside and then a louder yelp. Their gazes snapped to meet, and together they scrambled to open the door.

Lynette was sprawled on the carpeted ruby floor, a hand to her cheek. The officer towered over her next to the chaise but looked up when they entered. Delia shut the door with an echoing click.

"What are you doing?" Delia's voice came out calm, even.

"What does it look like?" The man's accent embodied the murderers' of Arthur. "Now get out." His attention returned to her sister. Lynette was shaking now, and rage boiled in her eyes.

Delia stepped toward him. "Get away from her."

Before she could move any closer, he grabbed Lynette by the hair and dragged her backward. To Delia's amazement, Lynette never made a sound.

"Leave or I'll break her neck. Tell anyone what you saw, and I'll make sure everyone knows I ruined her. Nothing will come of your lies, anyway." He yanked her up harder and placed a hand on her pale throat. Lynette let out a small sound, and Delia lost all reasoning.

She reached into her sleeve and threw the knife with calm precision. A thunk sounded, and the man toppled to the floor, dropping Lynette. Her sister knelt forward, gasping for air. Her dark eyes were wide as she stared at Delia. Now she had done it.

Helen paled and clasped her stomach. She took a deep breath and avoided Delia's gaze as she ventured over to the man. At last she looked back at Delia with vacant eyes. "Your aim is impeccable."

Delia expected their screams, maybe running from the room, but not this. War did strange things to people.

She joined Helen and studied the knife protruding from the man's head. It was a shame such a pretty face was ruined by so much steel. "I was aiming for the chest." She shrugged, and Helen snorted.

Lynette shivered as she rubbed her throat. "You could have hit me. Why didn't you hit me? How did you learn to throw like that?"

"I'm sorry, dear. I wasn't thinking." Emptiness had filled her like she'd been back practicing with her knives, the man made of wood. She ignored the questions.

Lynette's lips shook in an attempt to smile as she dropped her hand. "Thank you. I would rather be dead than live with what he had planned."

"Who was he?" Helen's face soured as she took in the body.

"He said his name was Lieutenant Benjamin Forrest." Doubt filled Lynette's voice.

Of course he had. Delia recognized the name from her list. "One down." She shook her head and sighed. One fewer man she could question. She hadn't realized she'd spoken out loud until Helen and Lynette turned to her and talked at once.

"How did…"

"Are you…"

She shook her head at them. "Later. We need to get out of here." She hadn't meant to reveal herself, but Lynette had needed her. She could trust her friend and her sister, couldn't she? It had only been a matter of time before they found out, and it might as well be while she had downed the man assaulting her sister.

She grasped the knife wedged in the man's head and tugged, but it refused to budge. The three of them tried, but it didn't move. Delia frowned at the knife. It must hate him more than they did. Thankfully, it was not one of her favorites.

They fell silent as Helen peeked out into the hall and opened the door wider, motioning for them to follow. They stopped in the retiring room to fix Lynette's hair and clothes. Helen and Lynette kept glancing toward Delia as she cleaned up Lynette's dark mane. Once the room emptied, the conversation was no longer avoidable.

"All right, ask," Delia said.

Lynette wasted no time. "How did you learn to throw like that?"

"Practice." She shrugged. Too many early mornings. "I'm not very good. My aim is still off." Lynette waved this away.

Helen gazed down at Delia's arm. "What are the bottles for?"

Delia hesitated. She hadn't realized they had spotted the bottles as she'd pulled out the knife. "Would you believe refreshments?"

Lynette scoffed and grabbed Delia's arm, pulling back her sleeve. She studied the thumbs of liquid and then Delia's face. "They're poison," Lynette concluded.

Helen's mouth fell open. "Why do you have poison strapped to your arm?"

"Isn't it obvious?" Lynette studied Delia as though she was some new exotic beast. "She's Foxglove."

They continued to study her. Finally, Delia lowered her eyes and pulled her sleeve back over her arm.

Helen swallowed hard. "Is it true?"

Delia nodded once.

Helen covered her mouth with both hands and backed up a step. The movement was like a fist slammed into Delia's stomach.

Helen dropped her hands, snapped them over her mouth, and then dropped them again. "It's you. I had no one to thank before. I prayed you wouldn't be caught."

Delia searched her friend's eyes, not daring to hope. "What do you mean?"

Helen regained a step closer. "You saved my little cousins." Delia blinked, and Helen gave a breathless laugh. "You didn't even know we were related. The Packards."

Recognition dawned, and she nodded. The Packards were one of her more recent successes, a father and his two young, teenage sons. Last month, she had smuggled them out, dressed as a soldier taking them to a prison ship. She wouldn't have called them "little," by any means, but she supposed to Helen, they had been at one point.

Helen suddenly hugged her, and she groaned. "Stop. I need to breathe." Helen hurriedly released her.

"They would be dead if it weren't for you. Hanged or good as dead in prison and for nothing but a rumor." Helen rested her hand on Delia's arm as though she would embrace her again if given the excuse.

"They were innocent of treason."

Curiosity shone in Lynette's expectant eyes. "Would it have mattered?"

Delia dropped her mask and allowed them to see her true self. She shook her head. "It never mattered to me."

"Well, good." Lynette sounded matter-of-fact as she took Delia's arm in hers. "We need to get back. We've been gone too long. If anyone asks, I had a fall and the two of you helped me repair my dress."

They agreed, and Helen took Lynette's other arm. Their ready acceptance filled Delia with heady warmth, like wine after an endless day.

When they entered the ball again, Abigail searched for them. When her gaze landed on the trio, her face lit, and she came to join them.

"I feel rather abandoned. The three of you are going off on adventures and leaving me. Balls are dull without friends." Abigail took Delia's other arm, unaware of the comfort she gave. Her friends were a shield against the troubles ahead.

Delia squeezed Abigail's arm. "I assure you, Abs, it was no adventure. The evening has been just as dull for us." The lie was like sour milk on her tongue. "Now, have any of you seen Mr. Baker? We have a dance scheduled."

Before any of them could reply, a shout rang out, and a lady sped out from the hall as she shuddered with choking sobs. Mr.

Marsden rushed to her, with Lord Carrington. She related a few distraught words and fainted at his feet.

Abigail frowned. "Why do I miss all the fun? I swear I don't faint." She spoke to no one in particular. Lynette shook her head.

Jeffrey approached them. "Well, the ball is over. We should get going before there's a crowd."

"What happened?" Abigail's fascination shone through her voice. She may as well be asking about a novel.

"Some poor man expired in one of the rooms."

"Oh dear." Abigail glanced toward Delia, Lynette, and Helen but said nothing further.

Carrington rushed back into the room and shouted for everyone to stay where they were. He placed his officers on the doors. Jeffrey hung his head and called Carrington over.

Panic gripped tightly around her chest.

Jeffrey rubbed a hand down his face. "Is this necessary? Can't the women at least go home?"

Carrington stiffened in defense. "They could be witnesses, and I will never be able to keep track of all these people."

Helen hastened to misdirect him. "What if the killer has already left?"

Carrington shook his head. "I'll have to assume he could still be in the house. Somebody must have seen him."

"Fine. Question us first, at least. I'd like to get home, and Delia has already had enough of a scare recently." Jeffrey mentioned her out of concern, but Carrington's attention on Delia heightened her urge to bolt.

"Very well. Consider it a favor for allowing me to stay with you." He motioned for Delia to follow, but her friends held her firm. He sighed. "I promise she won't be harmed." Lynette slowly released her, but Abigail stared him down.

"It will be all right, Abs. The captain won't hurt me." She released her arm from Abigail.

Carrington directed her to what looked like Mr. Marsden's study. He avoided the chair behind the desk and took up one of the chairs that winged it. She took the other. Dark wood paneling and deep-green leather made up the small space. The room closed in on her as though she was already in her coffin.

A tremor built at the base of her spine and burst over her. Her fists balled at her sides as she fought to remain still. She waited for him to start, but he sat there watching her. He leaned forward and rested his elbows on his knees.

"Well?" The word shot out of her as though it was alive.

He considered her a moment longer. "Can you account for your whereabouts this past hour?"

She nodded, a slow, deliberate motion. "I was with Lynette and Helen. Lynette tore her gown, and we tried to fix it."

"And before that?"

"Helen fetched me to help her with Lynette." She winced internally at her unsure tone.

He quirked a brow. "Does it usually take an hour to repair a dress?" A skeptical note laced his voice.

"No, but—"

"What else?" He interrupted her explanation, perhaps sensing her future lie.

"Lynette was upset. We were comforting her." Her words were weak, without any foundation.

He gave her a dry smile. "You're especially helpful tonight."

Her voice wobbled. "I'm trying."

His face hardened to stone. "I never get a straight answer out of you, and now you're full of explanations, so I assume you're lying." He gauged her reaction and nodded.

Her defense rallied at his assessment, and she surged forward. "I am not lying. You can ask Lynette and Helen." She crossed her arms.

"I'm sure they'll say similar things." The corner of his lips turned up. "Tell me, Miss Wolcott, where is your knife?"

Her chest tightened until she realized her advantage. "It's on my thigh." She gave him a coy smile. "Do you need me to show you?"

He swallowed and gave a short nod.

Very well. She remained seated and rested her foot on the desk. His attention was fixed on her leg. She inched up her skirts, slowly revealing her stocking to his hungry gaze. He must have gotten impatient when he reached out and revealed her thigh with the knife securely fastened.

He touched the knife as if to make sure his eyes told the truth. His hand brushed over her thigh.

A shiver ricocheted along her skin and settled between her legs. She quickly pulled her dress down, and he turned away. "Are you satisfied?"

"Yes." He shook his head. Someone knocked on the door, and Carrington sat back in his chair. "What?"

Jeffrey opened the door. "Mrs. Marsden says there's a fox-glove in the ballroom that isn't supposed to be there." Carrington swore with a colorful string of phrases she considered borrowing.

Jeffrey cleared his throat.

Carrington flinched. "I apologize, Miss Wolcott." He addressed Jeffrey again. "I will be in there momentarily."

Jeffrey nodded and shut the door.

"You have the vocabulary of a sailor," she said with a laugh, the revelation like a hidden secret.

"Of a soldier."

"Can I go now?" She moved to rise, but he pushed her back into her chair, trapping her with his arms. She leaned back and considered kicking him away. The proximity of his body was enough to unsettle her without the threat of the noose.

"I know you're lying. I just don't know why." He settled back into his chair, releasing her and leaning onto his elbow. An empty ache replaced him.

"Perhaps I don't trust you. Anything the least bit private you learn about me, you go off and tell someone."

He combed his fingers through his hair. "I'm sorry about that. Mr. Bradshaw was picking away at my patience, and what he said—" A hint of anger sharpened his voice. "It was inexcusable."

"You have no right."

His gaze dropped to the floor, and his shoulders slumped forward. "It won't happen again."

She didn't like being backed into a corner, and pushed down the pang of guilt from shaming him. She took advantage of his dejected state and got to her feet but hesitated to leave. As she walked behind his chair, she knew she could easily kill him.

Without thinking, she ran a finger along his jaw. Stubble through her glove resisted the motion. He grew still but didn't protest. Emboldened, she removed her glove and ran her fingers over a strand of his midnight hair. It was silkier than her own. She tugged on it before he grabbed her wrist. A spark shot up her arm.

Their gazes locked for a long, unblinking moment. Her senses dulled to allow only his long fingers encircling her wrist. A smile coated his features in mischief. He cupped her wrist and kissed the tips of her fingers. The caress of his lips left a tingling behind. His eyes darkened as he kept her gaze and nuzzled her hand.

Her heart flipped in her chest, and her breath left in a gasp.

She pulled back and tugged her glove on. She paused inside the door. "Are you so sure about that?"

She hurried down the hall, her face burning at her behavior. What had happened to her? He was a terrible influence. He stood for everything about England she hated. His very accent reminded her of the pompous man destroying her homeland. It was bad enough they had killed her brother; did they have to claim her sanity too?

His touch had been smooth against her skin, with a contrasting prickle of afternoon growth.

All at once, she slid across the hall floor, her legs flying out in front of her. Her head smacked against the cold tile. Her hand slapped against something thick and sleek. She brought her hand to her face. Oil.

She groaned and rolled to her side.

"Did you think I would forget you? I told you to stay away from Mr. Bradshaw," came a feminine voice. A metallic thud clanged at the back of her head.

Darkness welcomed her.

CHAPTER TEN

A SEARING PAIN like lightning flashed over her skull. She cried out blindly and grasped her head in both hands. Raised voices nearby echoed through her, bringing tears to her eyes.

She was faintly aware of a hand on her shoulder, her face. Someone said her name. She groaned again and tried to open her eyes. The sudden light was a flash of pain, and she curled into a ball, on her side. Her stomach heaved, and she vomited what little was still in it.

The hand steadied her by the shoulder and brought her comfort. She whimpered from pain, and the sound was pathetic to her. Someone shouted not far off, and the echo of footsteps thudded. The hand left, and she grabbed for it.

The shouting continued, but the noise made no sense to her head. She screamed, though it was more painful than the disturbance. That silenced the voices, and a new pair of hands touched her face and neck. The cold skin was a welcome relief. She pressed into one of the hands and released a long breath.

Another shout followed, and a lance of pain struck her. She opened her eyes again, ready to attack anyone who made a sound. A soft bright-red garment elevated her head. A group of men were shoving and restraining someone. She squinted and made out figures holding back Mr. Bradshaw.

She blinked the blurriness away further. The concern creased along Carrington's features made her eyes sting with tears.

"You have a sad face, my lord. Did your favorite hunting dog die?"

He sighed, but his mouth tugged up on one side. Carrington leaned toward her and whispered, "Your head is bleeding. I sent Mr. Wolcott to find a doctor. I'm afraid of moving you because I don't know the extent of the damage."

"Of course." She closed her eyes.

"I came running when you yelled, and found Mr. Bradshaw leaning over you."

She frowned. "I don't yell. I'm a lady." She tried to shake her head but cried out at the effort.

His steady hand on her forehead sent a flush through her cheeks. "Don't move."

"Wasn't Bradshaw." Her voice dropped to a mumble.

He inched closer, his breath whispering over her skin. "What?"

She blinked open her eyes and ran her tongue over her dry lips. "It was Gladys." What had the maid hoped to achieve by hitting her?

His gaze grew wide, but he said nothing and drew back from her face. She fought the urge to pull him close, to take solace in his capable hands. Instead, she tugged at her sleeves to make sure her arms were covered.

Carrington noticed her movement. "I didn't see any other injuries, but the doctor should be here soon." She met his eyes, and he continued, "I arranged your skirts to cover your legs properly. Yes, I saw the other knife. That's at least one thing you were lying about."

"I wasn't lying. It's not my fault you underestimated my arsenal." She grinned up at him.

"Next time I will have to have you searched." The mischievous gleam in his eyes betrayed his serious manner.

She lowered her brows. "You could try." In her state on the floor, she wished he had thought of it sooner. Perhaps the delay would have prevented the attack, and oh, would she love to see him try.

Carrington gave her a crooked smile and winked.

She laughed and groaned in the same breath, but she silenced at the approach of the doctor, who cleared her for moving. Her father went to order the carriage.

Jeffrey stepped forward to help her up, but Carrington had already hoisted her into his arms like a newborn. Her brother retrieved the officer's coat from the floor and placed it over her. As they were leaving, Carrington stopped to whisper to one of his officers, who nodded and left.

She sighed at being excluded again.

His voice was hushed. "He's bringing me a list of the guests."

"Why didn't you do that sooner?" she muttered into his chest, and her breath returned to her with the scent of cedar from his clothes. Despite the vise around her head, she didn't remember the last time she was this content. Maybe the bump on her head had addled her brain.

He repositioned her in his arms. "Because I'm a hotheaded idiot."

She snorted and gazed up at his blank expression. "I have to agree." He frowned down at her. "You said it, not me."

When they arrived, Jeffrey insisted on assisting her to her room. Carrington had no choice but to defer to her brother. She wobbled on her feet, and Carrington steadied her as he adjusted his coat around her. Her gaze locked with his. For a split moment, she wanted to tell him everything, to cry out her troubles into his arms. It would cost her life.

She reminded herself how foolish she was being, and once she reached her room, she folded Carrington's coat onto the back of her chair. The bright red was interrupted by a dark-crimson stain.

Hope tsked at her when she came in with Lynette, who took one look at her and called for a proper bath. Her maid moved into action in the methodical way she addressed all Delia's unusual characteristics.

Lynette startled at Hope's response and looked to Delia, who nodded.

They fell silent as servants brought in the tub and filled it. When they left, Lynette and Hope helped her undress, but the poison was gone.

The last she'd noticed their presence was when she'd thrown the knife. If they had simply come untied, she couldn't be connected to the bottles, and it was already established Foxglove was at the ball. Felix would have to search for them.

The warm water soothed her and lifted her to the clouds.

Hope shook her shoulder. "No dozing."

She groaned but sat up straighter. Hope lathered the soap and worked it through her hair, strand by strand. The lavender scent mixed with the coppery blood of her hair created a sharp contrast of stress and pleasure.

"This is going to take me some time to process." Lynette rubbed her arms as though chilled. "Does anyone else know?"

Delia ticked off the names on her fingers. "You, Helen, Hope, and Felix."

"Felix? You trusted the errand boy over your sister?"

Delia flinched. "I'm sorry about that. I didn't want anyone to know, but Hope and Felix figured it out on their own."

Lynette considered this for a silent moment and shook her head. "Lord Carrington's room is right next door."

"Yes, I know." She couldn't possibly forget it. The man was always haunting the edge of her mind.

"Don't you see what you've done? I could have been killed. Don't you think I could have used this information to avoid that awful man?" Lynette clenched her jaw.

"I didn't think."

Her sister shook her head, and a tear slid down her cheek. Lynette wiped it away. When Delia reached out to comfort her, Lynette held her arm out between them. The sisters weren't close, but usually Delia could be there for her. This time, Lynette refused to be touched.

Her sister paced the room until something distracted her gaze. She went to Delia's closet and bent down to pick up a box. "What are these?"

Hope answered for her. "Mr. Arthur's things."

"Why do you have Arthur's boxes in your room?"

Delia explained their investigation into his death and how she believed soldiers had murdered Arthur. Lynette slumped down on the bed and dropped the box next to her. "This is too much for me tonight. If what you're saying is true, I want to kill them."

Lynette's face was emotionless, and she gazed off for a long moment. Her eyes darted back to Delia. "When can we start?"

"You can't think I'd allow you to put yourself in trouble." Delia's bath finished, Hope patted her hair. The tub was a pinkish horror behind her.

"I already am, and I won't let you take all this on by yourself. You should've come to me. You owe me that much."

"I've wanted to tell you. To tell Helen and Abigail, but I thought you'd judge me. Call me a traitor." She slowly pulled her nightgown over her head and flinched when it caught on her scalp.

"You're a lot of things, Dee, but not a traitor." Lynette's voice lowered, and her eyes went cold. "They treat us like unruly children, taking away our privileges to punish us. I always thought we were part of them, but when it comes down to the important things, they don't see us as equals, and they never will." Her sister's declaration echoed Helen's recollection of Arthur's death and hardened Delia's resolve.

Delia nodded her agreement.

"They killed Arthur." Lynette's fists formed into tight balls at her sides. Her bald statement hung between them for examination.

"It's the most logical conclusion, but why? Lord Carrington certainly doesn't believe it."

"I'm not sure I would believe anything that man says. Get

some rest, Dee." Lynette slid her feet to the floor and exited with a soft click of the door. Delia stared after her sister, an unspoken defense of the captain still on her tongue.

Hope settled herself on the chair, making herself comfortable.

"I have first watch," Hope answered her unspoken question.

Delia yawned and slid in between the covers beside Pierre. She kicked something firm, and it dropped to the floor. Puzzled, she pulled back the covers. Lynette had left the box on the bed. Hope helped her pick up the mess, and she paused over a letter.

"What is it?" Delia took the offered letter from Hope.

"I didn't know your brother knew Mr. Hale."

"I only heard him mentioned once, but that was years ago. They both went to Yale, but Arthur was some years ahead of him. I don't know why they would write." Delia scanned the letter, but it was only a brief note about a meeting they'd had planned, probably why she had overlooked it before.

She tapped her finger against the note as she considered its origins. "Do you think Arthur was a spy? An enemy of the Crown?"

Hope took the letter back. "It looks that way, but this is too vague for us to be sure. I think I'll start going through the boxes while you rest."

Delia moved to search the box, but Hope guided her back to bed. "Now rest." Hope pulled the covers over her and gave Pierre a fond scratch behind his ear.

Arthur, a spy? Maybe she hadn't known her closest sibling as well as she thought she had. He corresponded with Mr. Nathan Hale, a spy for the rebels who'd been executed by the British years before Arthur's death. What could they have been meeting about?

Each answer brought her closer to knowing what happened to her brother but further away from her memory of him. The boxes scratched at her mind as though the answer sat in the form of a bloody dagger buried in his mass of papers and odds and ends.

As soft as her pillow was, her head made it feel like rocks, and she couldn't get comfortable any more than her mind would rest. She was going to kill Gladys. It was likely Carrington hadn't heard Delia and sent Mr. Bradshaw off to jail somewhere. Or he'd sent him off anyway out of spite.

Carrington's mask slipped by degrees. The solemn captain would give way to the handsome devil inside, and she longed to hasten his progress. A faint smile curled her lips as she entertained thoughts of drawing him out.

CHAPTER ELEVEN

THE NEXT MORNING, Delia was startled awake by Pierre growling. Felix sat on the floor, tugging a rope with him. She groaned and threw a pillow at Felix, who caught it and tossed it at her head.

"Ouch. Haven't I been injured enough?" She pushed to her feet and teetered back on the bed.

"Hope said you could rest all you like. No need to get up." Felix kept his attention on the rope as he played with the dog.

"How can I rest when you make so much noise? Did you find my bottles?"

"I've been here for hours and you didn't wake up."

She wrinkled her nose. "The bottles?"

"They're lost for good." He went back to playing with Pierre.

"Listen, you scamp, is there any other news?"

"Hmm..." He stared at the ceiling. "Hope hasn't found anything in Arthur's belongings, and she went off to bed. The doctor examined you briefly but let you sleep. Not that anything would wake you. Also, you missed the big commotion this morning."

She grew alert. He should have led with that. "What happened?"

He cocked his head at her. "It's a long story. Are you sure you want to hear it?"

"Just tell me the important points. I'd like to get out of this room."

He rested his arms on his knees. "The morning was dark and full of terrors." She gave him a death stare. "All right, fine. They didn't hold Mr. Bradshaw because you said it wasn't him and he's too well connected." She shook her head, and he continued, "Mr. Bradshaw came by and insisted on seeing you. Mr. Jeffrey made sure he knew he wasn't welcome here, but he wanted to hear it from you. Miss Lynette convinced him to leave and promised to give you a note and package from him."

He got up, walked over to the chair that still held Carrington's coat, and picked up a small box wrapped in simple brown paper and tied with string.

She read the short note first: *Dearest Delia, I mean you no harm, but I need to speak with you over an important matter, which you will understand from the contents of this package. Know this: I will not be dissuaded. Yours, RB*

She unwrapped the package and uttered a gasp. She dropped the box shut.

Felix hovered beside the box. "What is it? A dead bird? His fingers? The head of your lover?"

Her mind flashed to Carrington, and she shook the image away. "The head of...? Felix, I don't have a lover, and the box is too small for that." He only shrugged at her. "It's much worse. It's one of the bottles of poison. He must have taken them off my arm when he checked on me. He was lucky they didn't search him. I imagine he still has the other bottle."

"No, you're lucky they didn't search him. He would've turned on you the second the bottles were discovered." He tilted his head in thought. "I could sneak into his place, take the bottle back."

"I don't think that's a good idea. He may still turn me in."

Felix's face lit up. "What if we killed him?"

"That would be even worse. He's too close to the family and has already been seen arguing with half the household. They would likely blame Jeffrey or Lord Carrington—"

He interrupted her, "There's a thought."

"You fiend." She forced a smile. "It would bring down the whole family if we let the guilt fall on Lord Carrington."

He studied her, and amusement danced in his eyes. "Is that the reason you tell yourself?" He inclined his head to indicate Carrington's coat.

"What do you want from me?"

"I want? Nothing, but maybe you should consider your next move carefully. It isn't just your happiness at stake but your life." He left her alone with Pierre, who chewed on the rope.

Her restless dread festered until she decided on a course of action. She dressed in her plainest gown and donned a hooded cloak that would not be out of place in the chill spring air.

As she exited the room, Carrington spotted her from his. "Shouldn't you be resting?"

"I'm feeling much better now."

He studied her, taking in her outfit and colorless features. "Are you? You took a nasty blow to your head."

She shifted her stance. "It bled worse than it was."

He tsked, drawing closer to her position. "Do I need to tie you to the bed?"

She sputtered with laughter. "No, my lord." She sobered when he didn't move. "I have a pressing errand."

He gave her a curious grin, and she nearly told him about Mr. Bradshaw, about the poisons, and about her urge to take him back to her room. If anyone could help her, it would be him. This wasn't his problem. He was sent to stop Foxglove, not help her.

She brushed a hand against his shoulder, and he let her pass. Once she reached the stairs, she burst into a run. Carrington didn't follow her, and she neared Mr. Bradshaw's home with a regret that gnawed at her senses. Houses and soldiers flew past as she came upon the well-kept but old-fashioned three-story building nestled between twin cottonwood trees.

His butler's face remained straight through his wrinkles as he ushered her into the drawing room. The room was outfitted in the furniture and fashions of fifty years ago. Old family portraits hung over the walls, their names unknown to her. Although the room boasted lighter shades of yellow and blue, she had always found it a dreary, uncomfortable place.

She perched on an aging armchair just before Mr. Bradshaw appeared. His arm was out of its sling, and he was all smiles, though his face was still a bit swollen. He called for refreshments as he sat down on the sofa across from her. His good humor only heightened her discomfort.

"I trust you have recovered?"

"Yes, though everyone thinks I'm still asleep." Her voice came out calm or, at least, as calm as she could muster. "I want to discuss your note and what you mean by it."

His smile grew as if she had made a joke. "I mean I've found you out, Miss Foxglove." She made no reply, unable to deny something beyond her explanation. He continued in a solemn voice, "I don't know what you were thinking, but you must stop this nonsense. I will not have you strung up to the jeers of the masses."

"You will not? I'm afraid this has nothing to do with you."

"It has everything to do with me," he said as tea and pastries arrived. She absently noted her favorite lemon tarts were on the tray. He had expected her.

She hesitated until the servant left. "I free you from whatever attachment you thought you had with me. You need not trouble yourself with saving me."

"I won't accept that. You know how I care about you, and I won't be driven away because of this frivolous hobby of yours. You will desist immediately." He spoke as though he scolded a child.

"You don't care for me. The only love for me you have is the love of your idea of me." She bit down on her frustration and chose her words with caution. "This is not some activity I do in my leisure time. It's who I am and what I believe in. Why are you doing this? You can have any woman you want."

"Who? You mean Gladys? She was useful to me before, but I didn't think she would take it so far. I apologize. I hope there isn't any permanent damage to your head. The woman is mad, and I sent her off after that."

So Gladys had had other motives, but it had been for nothing. Richard wouldn't take her, and now she was without employment or a home. Delia almost felt sorry for the maid until she recalled all the trouble Gladys had put her through, or rather, Richard had put her through.

He rubbed his forehead and sighed. "You were supposed to come to me for safety, but Carrington ruined my plan, and Gladys was out of her senses. Then I happened to spot the bottles on your arm." He paused. "Foxglove isn't right. Not natural. No woman should be involved with the wars and politics of men. It's unbecoming in a wife."

She folded her arms over her chest. "I don't want to be a wife, at least not yet. I'm never going to fit this false mold you have for me, so you might as well give up the idea."

"I don't have to give up on you. No, you must give up this charade." He lifted the other bottle from his coat pocket and dangled it in front of her. She moved to grab it, but he pulled back, a catlike grin on his face. "You will stop this and inform your parents of your intentions to marry me."

She stared at him, face frozen. The bottle before her and his word against hers would destroy her entire world. If it had only been her life to consider, then she would gladly give it up, but her family would suffer as well. Her baby sister's own chance at marriage would be ruined. Arthur would never have justice.

She inhaled a gulp of air. "They'll never allow it."

"Your mother is half in love with me herself, and your father would do anything to make you happy. You will insist and plead your love for me, or I will turn you in."

The man couldn't be serious. Mr. Bradshaw's lifelong friendship with her brother, with her, amounted far less to him than this infatuation. The ugly head of betrayal turned against her at last, and it stung worse than the blackmail.

"Do you really want to force me to be your wife and deal with my sadness and hatred for the rest of your life?"

He shrugged. "I'll take what I can get. You'll come to be happy in time, and you'll see I know what's best for you."

Rage burned over her crimson cheeks. "That will never happen."

"You will obey me and be a dutiful wife." He rose to his feet.

She couldn't think, couldn't react as he pushed her against the chair. He held her shoulders back as he kissed her with his commanding anger. She protested and struggled against his arms.

Their kiss tasted of her salty tears.

When he finally let up, he placed a grossly large ruby in a gold setting onto her finger. The gold held tight and unwelcome.

She checked her tears and reined back her anger. She followed him in silence as he led her to the door with promises of a visit to her father the next day. By the time her feet hit the street, she was numb, and the ruby was a nagging weight at the edge of her mind. She walked home in a haze.

She found her father in his study, which was the size of her bedroom. It was lined with shelves of books and maps. Mr. Wolcott occupied a beast of a chair behind his desk, which took up a quarter of the room. She dropped down onto a cushioned seat across from his desk and forced a smile as she greeted him.

He didn't miss her agitation. "Are you well? You should be resting still."

She assured him of her health and told him of the events leading up to her visit. Leaving out almost everything of importance but painting a picture of a happy proposal and acceptance. She imagined that was what Mr. Bradshaw had seen and left it at that.

The frown etched in his face and the concern in his eyes revealed his disbelief, but he kept his peace. "I will consider this proposal before Mr. Bradshaw calls tomorrow."

She could no longer hide her misery, and she escaped the

room before he could comment on it. Racing her tears, she retreated to her room and found Hope tidying.

She straightened her spine and regarded Hope with unwavering eyes.

"Please tell Felix to stop investigating Arthur's death. We will stop this business with Foxglove. No more poison or rescues." Certainly no Lord Carrington.

"But, Miss—" Hope was cut off by Delia's raised hand.

"We will stop. Nothing good will come of it."

"Yes, ma'am." Hope paused at her dismissal, noticing the tears streaming down Delia's cheeks. Her maid's eyes widened as she took in the giant ruby Delia tugged on. "Where is that from?" She bent forward to examine the ring.

Delia gulped back her tears. "Mr. Bradshaw is forcing me to marry him." Words tumbled out of her as she related what had happened since she'd woken.

"You mustn't. You can't." Hope helped her pull at the ring.

"Yes, I have to. Don't you see? If I refuse, he'll turn me in. Everyone will be thrown on the streets, and Lynette won't have a future. I don't care if I die. I have imagined it a thousand times in a thousand ways, but I can't bring my family down with my principles." She would have to appease Arthur in some other way. The living needed to live.

The ring refused to budge, and Hope grabbed some soap to help slip it off. It was all to no avail. Their best chance was to cut the ring off, and under the circumstances, it was a poor idea.

Hope helped her change into a more appropriate gown. Her clothes would have to make up for her sullen mood, and while she was at it, she would bury her thoughts in the library. Fortunately, the library was deserted, and she arranged herself on her favorite pale-pink chaise with a new book on rare plants. The ruby continued to throb on her finger, and it stared at her as a constant reminder.

Once she channeled her interests into exotic ways to kill her future husband, the time passed more quickly. Lord Carrington's entrance distracted her contented state. She fixed her attention on her reading. He towered over her book.

"You're in my light, my lord."

He ignored her statement. "Is it true?"

"Considering you cast a shadow over my book and I can barely make out the print, then yes, you're in my light. Kindly move." She stared down at the pages, willing him to move away. He stayed in place and forced her to look up. "What do you want?" He glared at the ring on her finger, and she displayed her hand to him. "Now let me be."

"I don't believe it. You loathe Mr. Bradshaw. Why would you consent to marry him?"

"You know nothing of me." Her throat closed up over her harsh words.

Relief eased the cloud over her mind as he distanced his interrogation to pace the library. She went back to her reading.

He mumbled something, and she blocked him out as best she could over a passage on a particularly fascinating orchid. He reasoned to himself in a disruptive voice as though she wasn't there.

"Will you please desist your rambling?"

He stepped back into her light. "He must be threatening you with something. What is it?"

She flung her book down in exasperation. "Congratulations, but I don't want you to save me. Indeed, I don't need you to save me."

"Even if you're resigned to your fate, I owe it to your family to intervene."

She went pale. "Sir, you won't like what you find. Leave it be. You'll only make things worse. It's in everyone's best interest that you don't go digging."

He considered her, his gaze roaming from her eyes to the ring. "It can't be that bad."

"No, it's worse."

He slid next to her. "Then tell me, and I will leave it be."

"The very act of telling you will ruin my life." She covered her face with her hands, blocking him out.

"I will not judge. You have my word."

She dropped her hands. "It's not your judgment I fear but your loyalties." Her throat tightened, and her voice faltered. She wanted to believe he would keep her secret, but he had already shown he would talk.

His gaze focused on the ruby as he fell silent. At last his weary eyes met her gaze. "You're a rebel, then."

She wasn't sure how to respond or whether she should.

His voice lowered. "I don't fault your feelings there. Mr. Chambers is a decent fellow, and his beliefs give me pause, but he doesn't act on them. I don't think that's enough for you to be in any danger from Mr. Bradshaw."

She leaned her head back and tightly shut her eyes. "My views are the least of my worries."

He took her hand and examined the ruby. The thrill at his touch lodged a pang in her chest, but she couldn't pull away. Absently he tugged on the ring, and it fell off into his palm. Her eyes snapped open at his success, but he thought nothing of it and continued to examine the ring. He placed it in his pocket and rose to leave.

She grabbed his arm. "Please, don't do this."

His body relaxed in her grasp, and his eyes turned down in concern. "Let me make this right." He cupped her chin in his hand, and she stared up at him through tears.

He gave her a fond smile. "No harm will come to you."

She faltered as she tried to return his smile. Every speck of her being was on alert, and every inch of her pled with him in silence.

He answered her.

He raised her chin and bent over her. Their lips met, and air rushed past her ears. The storm flooded her pulse and surged into their kiss. His mouth was sweet, beckoning. Not commanding, as she would expect, but gentle and giving. He tasted her with a slow sweep of his tongue. The library fell away, and she melted into his touch. It was only them. No Foxglove, no war, no Mr. Bradshaw or Gladys. It was just them and the peace he offered.

Too soon he sighed into her mouth and released her. "I promise."

Breathless and unhinged, she watched after him as he strode from the room with her fate in his pocket. She shook herself from her daze and rose to stop him, but stopping Carrington was like standing in the way of a rabid bull, and she gave up before she began. It was no use. She would have to face whatever fate threw her way.

CHAPTER TWELVE

A NOOSE DANGLED over her head at dinner even as the taste of his lips lingered on hers. Nobody wondered at her dejected state, blaming it on a proposal gone wrong. Lynette took pains to comfort her at every chance, and her father made sure to include some of her favorite dishes at the table, but nothing appealed. Why did she deserve such luxury when she was about to cause their downfall?

Lord Carrington never appeared, having left with the ring and not returned. The memory of their kiss left a sour pang of betrayal in her stomach. He must be preparing a case against her at this point.

Having given up all pretense of caring, she prepared another of her drinks for sleep and poured out the poisons while she was at it. She threw the dried water hemlock and foxgloves into the kitchen fire, but she couldn't bring herself to kill the living foxgloves. They were in every household anyway.

To feel complete, she surrendered her knives to Felix to keep them safe. The loss of their presence rendered her naked to the forces around her. Unarmed, her mask abandoned, she joined the numerous vulnerable women huddled among the men.

Defeated, she lay on her bed, fully clothed, and waited for arrest.

She slept a heavy, dreamless sleep and woke late, empty and

numb. The arrest did not come that day, nor did it happen that week. Her father informed her Carrington had somehow convinced Mr. Bradshaw to call off the engagement. Carrington had left their residence shortly after and was not expected back. He would return to England, confessing an exhaustion of the war.

His retreat left a pinch in her chest. The kiss must have meant nothing to him, a whim to distract her or a brief fancy. She was a fool to believe anything else. He had fled to the other side of the Atlantic, and it was just a kiss.

And a hurricane was just a storm.

His promise echoed in her mind, and she worked to honor whatever he had done to warn Mr. Bradshaw away. She advanced into her life with caution. She occupied her days as a proper female and followed her mother's lead with zeal. She went on calls, reinvented her dresses, and danced with whoever asked. At first, her blood chilled at every sight of red, and she shook with the roar of marching soldiers.

Days passed and then weeks, and summer came.

Foxglove was presumed gone or dead, and people went back to their only concerns being the rebels, high prices, and shortages. The danger of Foxglove was forgotten, and the British roamed the streets with new confidence. The murders were pushed out of mind, unsolved and unimportant next to the rebel army.

Delia lived quietly but restlessly. Her mother dragged her through the motions of finding a husband, and Jeffrey was more watchful than ever. Yet her threats had disappeared as though Lord Carrington had brushed them away with the wave of his hand. She heard nothing of Gladys or Mr. Bradshaw.

She settled, although the nagging questions about Arthur's death and Carrington's actions remained. A deep longing she couldn't identify nestled inside her and grew roots into her life, leaving her listless and confused.

She settled, that was, until she ran into Mr. Bradshaw at a dinner party in September.

When she first saw him, she was stunned into silence, and

nobody could get more than a few words out of her. He glowed, full of health and self-regard. He met her eyes with warmth throughout the meal, which only jumbled her mind further.

He found her alone in the vibrant green drawing room after dinner. He bowed as he boasted a smug smile. "Pleased to see me?"

She hesitated and curtsied back. "More surprised."

"You needn't fear me. Your dog has warned me off sufficiently." He kept his distance, in earshot of her but out of range of the other guests.

"Excuse me if I don't believe you." Only his discretion kept her from death, and he thought she needn't fear him?

He shrugged as though unconcerned. "It makes no difference to me. I got what I needed, and I didn't even have to drag you along."

"What do you mean?"

"Your lord paid me quite handsomely and included his warhorse. Do you know how valuable that horse is? Of course, I sold him before someone thought of taking him from me."

She frowned, unable to hide her disappointment. "That's all you cared for? Money?" Could it have been that simple? Then again, he had preferred a horse to her.

"It hurts my pride, but no. I valued your friendship, something I looked forward to in a partner, but he made threats, convincing threats, to turn me in as Foxglove. He also agreed to pardon me for other crimes he witnessed, which I would rather not relate to you. I thought it best not to go through the trouble of having you. His word is good and the courts a sham. It's unlikely I would have come out well with the lead investigator naming me."

She owed Carrington more than she thought and without any way to repay him. She wondered at his naming Bradshaw as Foxglove, but he eased her doubts.

"I told him everything after he brought me the ring to end our engagement." His voice lacked feeling as if he had recited his words. "I figured you made your choice, since he had the ring. Saved me from having to go to him, and he took the poison too. One thing I don't understand—why did you want to kill off soldiers? You've never been political, and I know you don't have strong rebel ties."

"Arthur. I did it for him."

He lowered his brows. "How does that work?"

"Haven't you figured it out? The British killed him." Her words sputtered as she watched his features turn from curiosity to hilarity.

He burst into laughter and pushed away an imaginary tear. "What made you think that?"

Her hands quivered, and her heart shot into her throat. "The man who attacked him called him a traitor."

His teeth flashed in his smile, a smile her fist ached to smack off his face. "Yes, he was a traitor but not to the British." He shook his head.

"You're wrong. He associated with Mr. Hale, and he went to Yale, which must have influenced his views."

His stupid grin transformed into a smirk. "He knew Hale. We all did. When Arthur was pressured to fight against the Crown, he pushed back. Being the spoiled boy he was, he believed the rebels were ungrateful."

"You're lying." Her voice trembled over her half-parted lips.

"You know I'm not. Your little reign of terror would have disgusted Arthur more than the rebels. He was a king's man through and through." He gave her a pitying look.

"Then who killed him?" She stared forward, distant and expressionless.

"Damned if I know. Jeffrey and I have always assumed it was friends of Hale or the Sons of Liberty. I can say for sure it wasn't the British. He was one of their boys, and he had connections they wanted to use. I'm guessing they did use those connections and it led straight back to him."

Her eyes refocused as she turned her gaze on him. "Do you

plan to turn me in now Lord Carrington is gone?"

"I don't see why. I have no loyalty to either side. I'm sorry for hurting you and Jeffrey. I don't expect you to forgive me, but know I regret the loss of our friendship every day."

He studied her. "I don't care what you choose to do, but would you want to continue?" He didn't wait for her to answer but walked off after he had finished butchering the foundation of her beliefs. She didn't know what to make of his apology, and she tucked the thought away for another time.

The revelations seeped into her heart like her poison, stopping her dead. She stood alone, battling an onslaught of thoughts that haunted her on the way home and into her bed. She was a fool, a proud and misled fool.

It wasn't so much that Arthur had worked against the rebels or that he would not approve of her work as Foxglove. It was the sting of Arthur betraying his people. He must have seen the damage the soldiers had inflicted on the city, yet he'd joined them instead of fighting back. He could have at least taken the same indifference as their father and Jeffrey.

This new version of Arthur turned her stomach and soiled all her cherished memories. He was a stranger that had fed the enemy information and looked the other way as it clawed over the people.

As much as she hated the stranger her brother had become, she would find who killed him. Even if he had been a loyal servant of the Crown, he was her brother, and he had been murdered without fair judgment. He deserved that much.

Foxglove would transcend the boundaries of this war, investigating without discrimination to loyalties. Felix was right. There were no innocents in this city. She denied Arthur's murderers a fair trial, but she was repaying the favor.

Delia rubbed at her temples, fending off a headache. Why hadn't Carrington turned her in? He was a loyal British subject. It was people like him who turned in their grandmother if she committed treason. What did he care if she hanged?

She would probably never see the hateful man again, and what he didn't know wouldn't hurt him. Yet her chest ached in his absence. She pushed his haunting face and delicious figure out of her mind.

Finally, they would find closure for Arthur. She would make more of the foxglove tincture tonight and show Lynette how she did it, but they would have to find more water hemlock. The Harmons' ball would be the perfect time to continue their investigation.

The next day, Delia woke just after dawn in search of herbs but mostly the water hemlock. Lynette had agreed to go with her, but once it came time to leave, she refused to get out of bed. A sleeping Lynette was a different creature than a wakeful Lynette, and Delia decided to go alone rather than risk bodily harm.

The air was thick with moisture as she made her way along the towering trees and thick underbrush. The frequent rains had left the road soggy, and it wasn't long before her boots and hem were muddy.

The rainfall had worked in her favor, and she found most of the plants she looked for. She was some way from the house when a horse galloped down the trail, throwing mud every which way. Her hand rested on her knife as she awaited the rider's approach.

The rider slowed when he spotted her, and walked his horse to her, sparing her a mud bath.

"Ma'am, aren't you a bit far for flower gathering?" He looked vaguely familiar in his lieutenant's uniform, though he was a stranger.

She glanced around her as though she was lost. "Did I wander far? I must have failed to keep track." She gave him a wry smile.

"There's nobody for miles. If you were in any danger, nobody would hear it." He must have seen her stiffen when he added, "From rebels. You are perfectly safe from me." He dismounted, giving her a better view of the tall but lean man with dirty-blond hair poking out of his cocked hat.

He watched her with his dark eyes as she stepped back. "I'm Lieutenant Hugh Travers, ma'am. How may I assist you?"

"By getting out of the road."

He laughed, and she saw that same familiarity. She studied him but could not place where she had seen him.

His easy smile raised her suspicions. "Will you delight me with your name?" She wasn't going to answer him, but curiosity made silence impossible.

"Miss Delia Wolcott, daughter of Mr. Andrew Wolcott."

His face brightened. "Wolcott? How fortunate. I've heard much of your family."

She shook her head in confusion. "I'm sorry I don't recognize your name."

"Don't you? Maybe you know my reclusive brother, William?" She shook her head again, and he tilted his head to the side. "I fancy you only know him by his title? William Travers, Lord Carrington?"

She frowned at him, unable to make sense of his words, which made him laugh further.

"Yes, he leaves that impression."

"It seems your brother and I were never properly introduced." Her senses heightened as she gave him her full attention. What else had she missed about the man?

He shook his head. "Now that we're acquainted, would you like a ride?"

"I would rather walk." Besides, she shouldn't be seen alone with this man.

"Then I'll accompany you." He fell into step with her as he led his horse, decorating his Hessians in three inches of mud.

She held back a sigh. A stubborn family. "Why did Lord Carrington leave the service?" Did Carrington tell his brother she was Foxglove? She didn't need another officer sniffing around.

"He said the colonies could hang themselves." His smile turned thoughtful.

She eased out a breath. "You are close?"

"Indeed. Don't let his angry face fool you. He's angry all the way through." He laughed at his joke, but she stayed silent. He frowned at this. "He isn't all bad. You should ignore the rumors."

She eyed him sideways. "Then they aren't true?"

"That depends on which ones." He flashed the same mischievous look she identified with his brother, and a deep yearning to see Carrington consumed her.

"What of his wife?"

His expression turned blank, and his laughter died. "A sad business, Laura."

Her voice was a near whisper. "What happened?"

He seemed reluctant as he paused. "She died giving birth to her first child."

"I'm sorry. That must have been heartbreaking." A mass lodged in her throat for Carrington. He had lost a child and a wife in one blow.

"It was but more so, since my brother was serving His Majesty the year before." He raised his brows at his hint.

"Oh. That is…oh." She failed to find the words.

They walked in a heavy silence for a time. When the house came into view, he turned to her, and they stopped.

He appeared to be deciding whether to tell her something. "He asked me to look out for you and your family."

She paled. "Why?"

"He said you were in trouble with that Foxglove character."

She clenched her fist on her basket's handle. "I'm capable of looking out for myself." If Carrington wanted to look out for her, he shouldn't have fled the colonies.

He gave her a small smile. "He also said you would say that, which is why he didn't want me to tell you. I can see you're a sensible girl though."

She bristled. "Awful man." She escaped to the house, leaving his laughter behind her.

CHAPTER THIRTEEN

S HE PROMISED TO see Mr. Travers at the Harmons' ball the following evening, an event organized to honor the officers. Of course, the ball was a valuable opportunity for Foxglove to gather answers.

Her sister had come down with a stomach ailment and headache, and their mother stayed behind to nurse Lynette in her miserable state while Jeffrey accompanied her to the Harmons' ball. Jeffrey dragged his feet, and they arrived late. She had to threaten him with further escorts to move him along.

The ballroom opened up to reveal dozens of dancers gliding around the room. Crystal chandeliers with hundreds of candles shone from above, their light glinting off the jewels scattered among the ladies.

Those who approached her were quickly scared off by Jeffrey's displeased glares.

"Come now, Jeffrey. I have to abide by mother, or she will put me into some horrid dress and parade me around."

His lips twisted up as he considered her words and settled into a more welcoming stance.

At this time, Mr. Travers approached and asked her for the next dance. His presence gave her a sense of Carrington in the room. Carrington's phantom attendance left her oddly comforted yet alarmed.

She accepted but with little interest as he escorted her forward.

"I apologize I'm not my brother," he said.

She ignored his comment and kept her focus on the steps. Dancing with him did not require much effort. He led with a grace and skill even the Rivertons must envy.

"Why, Mr. Travers, you make it look so easy."

His smile brightened at her praise. "Of course, I'm no match for William. He has always surpassed me in anything athletic."

"I don't recall seeing him dance." She had been too distracted as Foxglove and too charmed by that damned wicked smile to ask questions.

His eyebrows shot up. "He never danced with you while he was here?"

She shook her head.

"I'm appalled by his ungentlemanly behavior, and I'll tell him so when I next write."

"Please, don't mention me to him." It was bad enough he had his brother spying for him.

"Why not? He's proud of his dancing, and this is the perfect chance to tease him. I'm amazed he didn't show off."

"There were other concerns at the time." Her voice grew quiet, her memory of his parting kiss distracting her thoughts.

"Yes and what horrible concerns."

She ground her teeth together. Lord Carrington must think the same. He hadn't even said goodbye as he'd fled the city for the last time. Now Mr. Travers was here to keep Foxglove at bay and remind her of everything she'd done wrong.

When their dance ended, he asked for another, but she pleaded fatigue, and he offered to sit the next dance out with her. He brought her some wine punch and moved to sit beside her next to Jeffrey.

Lord Carrington's sacrifices nagged at her. Surely he would realize the need to rid the world of such vermin like the womanizing officers. She pushed thoughts of Carrington aside and took a deep breath to settle the pinch in her chest. He wasn't here to judge her.

Helen approached with Mr. Chambers on her arm and another officer she didn't recognize on her other. He was an athletic figure with the build and walk of a horseman. He wore no wig but had his chestnut hair tied neatly. His icy blue eyes startled her. A chill crawled up her arms. He seemed to see through her as though consuming her essence.

Mr. Chambers introduced him as Mr. Peter Norris, and she flinched at the name. She exchanged a glance with Helen, and her friend gave her a knowing smile.

Mr. Norris ignored Jeffrey's glare and asked her to dance. Her brother could do nothing without appearing rude, and she accepted. She attempted to calm her shaking hands, in his piercing gaze, but it took all her control to make it through the dance.

The man twisted up her stomach with his towering figure and stern examination of her. Everywhere he touched left an itchy crawling sensation that made her want to scrub her skin raw.

When their dance concluded, she tugged at her hand to flee back to Jeffrey, but Mr. Norris pulled her away. Her stomach lodged in her chest as he forced her out of the room. Her feet tripped over themselves as she struggled to keep up.

"Please, sir, let go of me. Take me back to my brother." Her voice escaped in hurried gasps.

He ignored her pleas and kept his attention forward as they left through the crowd of the ballroom. She struggled with him and reached for her knife, but he grasped her hands in a viselike grip and thrust her into a broom closet.

Finally, she managed to pull a hand free when he put his back to the door. She grasped her knife, but he saw the flash of steel and clenched her wrist before she could do any damage. He smashed her hand against the wall, and she whimpered at the crushing pain. The knife flew out of her reach.

"I saw you with Mr. Gardener before you murdered him. Don't think I'm blind to what you are, whore." He spat to the side.

"I didn't see you there." Her lack of defense heightened with her meek voice.

"Of course not. I was detained by a little redheaded maid for much of the time. You'll pay for what you did to him." He growled in her face, spittle rained over her, and her head flinched back.

Her gaze shot over their surroundings as he dropped her onto her back and lifted her skirts. The brooms and mops were tucked away out of her reach. She kicked out at him, but he rested his weight on her. She couldn't move, couldn't think.

He fought her skirts, and she pulled the poison out from her sleeve. Without hesitation, she emptied the bottle into her mouth.

She almost gagged at the slosh of liquid but tried not to swallow. His task completed, he raised himself to his knees, and she lifted her head to meet his lips.

"I knew you were a whore." He forced his mouth on hers, and she opened her lips, spewing the poison down his throat. He coughed but swallowed and leaned back to catch a breath. "You had some bitter wine. Try not to mess my clothes."

His disgust allowed her to feign sickness again, since even a drop of the poison could kill her. She rolled to her side and emptied the poisoned contents of her stomach. She gasped and coughed until nothing was left.

"You think that will hamper me? I've experienced worse, and I've waited a long time for this." He reached down to open his trousers. She struggled against him and cried out, but he silenced her with a hand over her mouth.

Tears streamed down her face, and she prayed the poison would be enough, that it would work soon.

She bit his hand and released a scream, but he slammed his fist into her head to silence her. The blow buzzed through her head as she rested it against the floor.

"Stay still. You might just enjoy it."

She stared, dazed, at the darkened ceiling, the fight dying in her. She wished he would kill her soon, end her now before he violated her most private self. If only there were more poison. If only she had swallowed it for herself. She shut her eyes and waited for it to end.

The intrusion never came. A surprised grunt startled her, and she opened her eyes. He slumped forward as deadweight onto her body. Jeffrey stood over him, murder in his eyes, and pushed Mr. Norris aside.

She cried out at the sight of him. Jeffrey shushed her as he set her clothes right and helped her to her feet. Mr. Travers stood behind him, in the hall. His eyes were wide with concern.

"Did he?" Jeffrey asked.

She jerked her head from side to side.

He let out a relieved breath.

"We saw him forcing you out of the room but couldn't find you. If we hadn't heard your scream, we might have been too late." Mr. Travers swallowed as though unable to voice the possibilities.

Her tears fell unchecked as she clutched at Jeffrey, and he stroked her back.

"What do we do with him?" Mr. Travers sounded far away to Delia's ears.

"I'd like to kill him." Jeffrey's voice was a faint whisper. She may have beat him to it.

Mr. Travers moved them out of the way and kicked Mr. Norris on the side. "The man is out. I suggest we leave him here." Jeffrey shook his head, but Mr. Travers added, "At least get your sister out of here."

Jeffrey looked like he wanted to argue, but in the end, he took her to the ladies' retiring room. She stopped to breathe and steady her shaking hands. Her expression remained plastered into stark-white terror, but she would have to do.

He set her down in the ballroom and rushed to call for their carriage. She wrapped her arms around herself but couldn't stop trembling. She tried to keep her face passive, but she doubted she was successful.

After an excruciating, short time, Mr. Travers found her and sat next to her.

He frowned as he watched her shake, which put her more on edge. "The man hasn't moved. Do you want to bring in—" he began to ask, but she violently shook her head. "Very well. My brother is going to kill me."

She snorted.

"He was right. You invite trouble."

She glared at him but said nothing. Under all her fear and shock, her blood boiled. She'd been armed, and she thought she was ready. A lone man had singled her out and attacked her at a well-attended party. Shame burned in her chest. She hadn't done enough.

She could have called out sooner or brought more of her knives. She scolded herself for being so helpless, allowing herself to be a victim. Most of all, she regretted she couldn't give him a slow and agonizing death.

By the time Jeffrey came for her, the shaking had stopped and was replaced by a cold, restless ache. He led her away, and she looked back at the other guests. In place of officers, she saw fresh blood pooling through the crowd.

CHAPTER FOURTEEN

L ATE THAT NIGHT, she dressed in a simple but too-tight gown she had used in the past. Hope helped disguise her with rouge. She donned a wig that matched her dark eyebrows. She no longer looked like the fair virgin maiden.

She left the safety of her home with determination that Mr. Norris was still in the closet. He would be in the perfect state to interrogate. She barely noticed the new chill from the coming autumn or the unappreciated moon that greeted her efforts. From their back alley, light shone from a couple of blocks down, and she quickened her pace toward it.

The light grew brighter as she neared the Harmons' residence. She crept into the kitchen, where a wild-haired boy tended the fire. He startled awake from his light sleep, and a gasp jumped from his throat.

"Don't mind me, love." She tossed a bag of coins at his feet.

His face lit up, revealing his missing teeth, and he nodded quickly.

She stepped lightly past the boy and into the unlit hallway. The darkness consumed her as she felt along the paneled walls. She closed her eyes, concentrating on counting the doors.

Three, four, five.

Her hand closed over the handle, and she jerked the door open.

A moan issued from the shadows, and she kicked a booted heel toward it.

Mr. Norris grunted.

"Not so dead, are you, Mr. Norris?" Her eyes adjusted enough for her to see the outline of his body against the wall.

"Shut up, whore."

She glanced down at her outfit. Could he see more than her?

She shrugged. "I have a special treat for you, but you can only have it if you answer my questions." Her hand twitched over her knife.

"Go to hell."

"Don't be so hasty to die." She frowned down at him. "What did the Davises know? Did they know who killed Arthur Wolcott?"

He spat at her, and saliva ran down her front.

She pulled back her lips. "You're disgusting. Answer my questions, or I'll kill you."

He snorted. "You'll kill me anyway."

She tapped the blade against her finger. "How fast would you like to die?"

He grunted and averted his gaze.

"What did the Davises know?"

"Is this what your game is? Kill us all until someone talks?" He gave a dry laugh.

"Just answer the question." Her knife tumbled from her hand, and she bent to retrieve it, but instead, she met a crooked grin and a blade.

She grabbed his hand and yanked him forward while she thrust her knee into his groin. He groaned but kept hold of her. She slammed the side of her foot down on his toes, but he persisted and plunged the dagger through her dress, ripping it beyond repair.

She fumbled for the knife, catching her palms against the sharp edge. He thrust out and caught her in the side as she fell. She impaled herself on the blade.

She gasped and tumbled to the floor. His grimy hands rustled through her clothes as she sprawled senselessly.

He crawled to his knees and dropped back against the wall. Was the poison doing its job?

She lashed out and caught his hand with her heel. The blade clattered to the floor, and he slammed his head on the wall.

In one swift movement, she snatched the knife and drove it into his neck.

A choking gag forced its way from his throat, and blood gathered from the wound.

She kicked to her feet and stumbled into the hall. Her breath was labored, and she rested against the door.

She needed to go, run, but her feet dragged as she made her clumsy way through the kitchen, where the boy now slept.

The bite in the outside air hit her, and her steps slowed further. A few paces from the Harmons' back door, she dropped to the ground.

In the back of her mind, the voice of Carrington promised her no harm would come to her. A useless thought. He wasn't here, but she wished she had taken the fresh start he had given her. She couldn't let Mr. Travers write home about her dying like this.

She rolled to her knees. The sharp, twisting pain in her side grew at her movement. Her clenched teeth held back a scream as she pushed herself up. Her legs wobbled, and she forced herself to take the first step.

She ventured another step, her hand held against the wound. The blood flowed through her fingers, and she doubted she would make the short trip home. Instead of blocking her agony out, she let it surge fire through her body. She made friends with it and used the sensation to thrust her body toward her home.

She reached the street behind her house when she collapsed in the dirt. The elusive structure loomed in front of her.

She crawled. Each movement sent a cry from her throat until she gained the door. She pounded it with her fist as hard as she could, but her failing strength rendered her action insistent tapping. Several moments passed, and she tried again.

This time, the door opened, and she blinked into Felix's beautiful face. He dragged her inside and kicked the door shut. His gaze swept over her bloody outfit by the light of the kitchen fire. He handed her a damp cloth for her face and threw the wig into the flames.

Her addled mind made little sense of his actions, but she did as he bade.

Hope entered and knelt next to her. She held another cloth over the wound and asked what had happened. Delia slurred out an explanation and hoped it made sense. Hope shushed her just as voices neared them.

"What is it?" Jeffrey came into view, sleep-worn and unwanted. "Dear God, Dee. What have you been doing?" He rushed to her side and assessed her injury.

She grinned listlessly. "Midnight stroll."

He took a long breath and sent Felix for the surgeon. She protested, but Jeffrey would have none of it. "You're bleeding badly. Our simple stitching won't be enough. Can you stand?"

She dropped her head in response.

He put his arms underneath her and lifted her against his chest. "I'll have you know this is one of my favorite robes, and you're bleeding all over it."

She giggled and then flinched from the pain. He loosened his grip around her. "Hope, would you clean up this mess before someone sees?"

"That's impossible." Delia spoke into his chest. "Blood runs through the city."

He huffed and carried her upstairs.

Dazed moments passed.

Her head bobbed as he set her on her bed. Her side was soaked in a dark mess, but he managed to find the hole over her wound and ripped it wider. He gasped at what he saw and covered the wound with one of her favorite shawls, keeping the fabric in place with her hand.

He paced alongside the flickering candlelight. The movement and rhythm rocked her to sleep until he spoke.

He stopped midstride. "We can't have mother and father

know about this. Your wound's deep, but I don't think you hurt any organs, or you'd be dead by now."

Her response dragged, full of sleepy disinterest. "What would you have us do?"

His gaze caught her mirror, and he toppled it to the floor. The mirror shattered across the room in a clamor. He took the shawl from her and replaced it with another cloth from her dressing table. He pushed the broken mirror and the bloody shawl into a pile on the floor.

"Remember, you weren't in the streets." He paused. "Try not to be so clumsy next time, Dee. I can't believe you nearly killed yourself slipping around in your room." He grinned and settled on the edge of the bed.

She nodded once to him, her head dropping forward. She patted his hand but said nothing. Hope came in and stared down at the broken mirror. Jeffrey told Hope about Delia's fall, and she murmured her understanding.

Voices and unpleasant smells met her in and out of consciousness. Hands explored her side, bringing her back to the throbbing wound. She gave a desperate cry, and she pushed at the hands, but more held her down.

The pain was reinforced with each new prod. She gasped at the onslaught overwhelming her, and a burst of light ignited behind her eyelids. A rush blocked all sound as though an ocean wave had caught her, thrusting pain like torrents.

Cold hands brushed her skin and covered her with a blanket. She grabbed onto a palm and squeezed. Carrington had come back to her. Her foolishness hadn't scared him away.

A weight creased the bed beside her, and she slit her eyes as best she could. Hope was holding her hand and whispered comforting words she either didn't hear or didn't understand.

"Don't leave me," Delia mouthed.

Hope shushed her and pushed her hair off her forehead.

Delia's eyes caught on Lord Carrington's coat from so many months ago, still hanging off the chair. The sight brought fresh tears. "The blood will never wash out."

CHAPTER FIFTEEN

S HE SLEPT IN fits, waking to her screams and the living nightmare that was the realization of what had happened. Her dreams were filled with brandy and musket fire, screams, and children crying. At last she woke well enough to talk to Hope. A single candle gave off a faint glow when she opened her tear-sealed eyes. Hope was straightening her blankets when Delia stirred.

Hope let out a relieved breath. "How are you feeling?"

"Like a slaughtered pig." Her throat was raw and her tongue like parchment.

Hope handed her a glass of water from her beside. The water stung as it made its way down her throat. She took another gulp, swirling the liquid through her mouth before swallowing.

"What happened?"

"You were stabbed." Hope refilled her water. "Don't you remember?"

Delia waved the question away. "I mean with Mr. Norris. Has there been word?" She attempted to sit up higher.

Hope's gaze flickered over her as if to decide how she should continue. "I told Felix, of course."

Delia nodded her encouragement.

"He checked on the body and left a foxglove behind."

Delia's hands shook, and her stomach inched up her chest.

Her world blurred and shifted around her. Mr. Norris had bled everywhere, and the thought of the delicate flowers resting on his soaked chest raised the bile in her throat.

Hope handed back the water and settled down on the bed.

"How long was I asleep?"

Hope's voice grew soft. "A little over two weeks. You have an infection in the wound. We thought you would die." She studied Delia's face as though looking for signs of her infection now.

Delia rubbed her forehead. "Two weeks?"

"The hunt for Foxglove has exploded. Soldiers are searching houses door to door. They destroy gardens where foxglove is found. I think the only reason they haven't come here is your family's importance and connections."

She clenched her fists into the blankets. "They can't do that."

"Apparently they can. Even if they couldn't, who would stop them?"

Her mind flashed to Lord Carrington, but he was long gone. Even he wasn't a match for an entire army. Despite herself, she almost laughed at the idea of the proud English captain guarding a garden of foxgloves against a sea of redcoats. She shook the thought away.

Hope insisted she rest, and they spoke no more.

The revelations had exhausted her, and soon she fell asleep.

She awoke to the throbbing of her heart in her side. Light streamed from the edge of her curtains, and she groaned in discomfort. Sweat covered her body, and her face had a sticky coating. Lynette rushed toward her with a cloth and promptly dabbed at her face, brushing her hair onto her pillow.

Delia caught her wrist. "No more."

Lynette raised a brow, and she freed her wrist. She continued to wash cool water onto Delia's skin.

"No killing, Netty."

"Hush. You need to rest; your fever has returned." Lynette leaned in to hug her but quickly moved away. "Dee, you smell, and you're sweaty."

"How would you like to be stabbed?" She grinned, revealing her teeth. "I need a bath."

"Not yet. Dr. Thornton will be here soon to check on you again. This fever has lasted too long. At least you woke up. How do you feel?"

"Sore. Disgusting. Hungry and in need of chocolate." She sniffed and pouted.

"Of course, and you're in luck." Lynette brightened as she related the only good news. "The usual admirers have been sending you things since your accident. Abigail thought it important you were provided with ample sweets. I will ring for some hot chocolate."

Delia gave her a wide smile. "Thank you."

A thud reverberated through the wall, and Delia straightened in bed at once.

She exchanged looks with her sister. "My, Dr. Thornton knocks loudly."

A long series of knocks followed, hinting at the impatience of the caller. She'd never known the doctor to be so dramatic. The November weather must have taken a turn.

Her brows climbed up her forehead. "Do get Jeffrey to let him in so I can get this over with."

Lynette scrambled out the door and was soon replaced by Jeffrey.

"Where is Dr. Thornton?" Delia asked.

"Thornton? He hasn't arrived. I think he planned to visit later this evening."

"Then who was at the door?"

He pushed the curtain aside in her window as though to study the front of the house, which wasn't visible. "It was nobody. A trick of the wind."

"The wind?" she murmured.

He made a swift turn in her direction. "I wasn't here when Mother had you bled earlier. I'm sorry about that. Father has become even more withdrawn, or he would have stopped her."

His voice was hushed, solemn. He leaned against the chair Lynette had occupied.

"It's no wonder I was asleep so long."

He gave her a disgusted look and held his nose mockingly. She crossed her arms and rolled her eyes as he called for her bath.

She touched her hand to her chest. "Oh, Jeffrey, I'm feeling much improved. Thank you for asking. I'm touched, but don't burden yourself for me."

He frowned at her. "I have been concerned. We all have. Not to mention much of the city thinks you are the survivor of a Foxglove attack. What did happen?"

"I was mugged while I was walking home. I thought I told you that." Almost dying didn't excuse her from brotherly questioning.

"Why were you walking at night? Alone?"

"For fun."

"Fun? You were stabbed while strolling the street for amusement?" He sighed and rubbed his head. "I don't know if I believe you, but I'm not sure I want to know the truth. Just stay out of trouble."

He left when Hope entered with the bath.

The bath proved beneficial to her fever, and it didn't return. Dr. Thornton cleared her for callers, but she opted to stay where she was. A chill seemed to rest over her room like a sheet of ice. She nestled into Carrington's coat, which Hope had washed until only his masculine scent remained.

The next day, her mother found her in the coat, curled on the floor of her room. with a letter to Arthur in her hand, and ordered her dressed. Mrs. Wolcott did nothing in halves, and she would give a dinner that week to welcome Delia back to the living.

Her mother had already ordered her a gown, and for once, Delia approved of her mother's choice. It was a stunning ivory satin dress with a green sash tied in a bow at the back. The green was the same vibrant shade as her eyes.

After her mother finished dragging her around to her fitting, she headed straight to her room to rest. A vacant air occupied her space. Arthur's boxes were gone.

She called for Hope, who came down the hall. "Where are Arthur's things?"

Hope dropped her head and clasped her hands in front of her.

"Well?"

Hope fidgeted some more and answered in a low voice, "A footman came to take them away."

"Away? Where?"

"I don't know. Mrs. Wolcott ordered them taken."

"What?" Delia's scream echoed off the walls.

Hope flinched but remained silent. Forgetting her exhaustion, Delia moved past her and stormed off to her mother. She found her in the drawing room, sipping coffee.

"Mama, how could you? Where are Arthur's things?"

Mrs. Wolcott held up a hand for her to be silent and gave her a stern, unfriendly look. "It's past time you let go. The footman burned them this afternoon on my instructions."

"Why?"

"I've told you. If you insist, we can discuss this later. For now, we have guests." Her mother motioned to the opposite entrance of the room. Delia hurried to right herself as footsteps neared the door. She arranged herself across from her mother.

Jeffrey entered first in his usual easy manner, and he was followed shortly after by Mr. Travers. It had been a while since she had seen him, and she barely recognized him without his uniform. He was smiling his mischievous smile, handsome as ever. There was a pause as the two men looked back to the door, where another man came into view. She recognized his athletic stride first and then his blue-black hair that shone as he removed his hat.

She caught her breath as William Carrington met her eyes and smirked.

CHAPTER SIXTEEN

D ELIA'S PULSE RACED. Just this morning, she had been lounging in his coat, remembering his solid heat pressed against her. She willed herself silent and kept her eyes lowered as the men greeted the family and took the nearby sofa and chair.

Luckily, her mother filled the awkward moment. "It's good to see you, Lord Carrington and Mr. Travers. How lovely of you to visit us. I took the liberty of ordering refreshments."

Her hands shook at his name. Did he regret the affection he'd shown her? Would he expose her identity for deceiving him? What if he wanted to blackmail her himself? She clasped her hands tightly together to still them, and they became fists. He'd abandoned her.

Mr. Travers beamed at her mother as he slapped his brother on the back. "The pleasure is ours, Mrs. Wolcott. I found this sea-weary brother of mine at the docks and thought he would like to pay his respects."

Mrs. Wolcott's slate eyes shone. Doubtless she spun possibilities in her head. "Have you been in town long, Lord Carrington?"

"Just a few days. I was beginning to think I wouldn't make it into the city. Our ship narrowly missed being boarded by rebels." The sound of Lord Carrington's voice forced Delia to look up. Their gazes met, sending a shock through her, and she snapped her eyes away.

Jeffrey cleared his throat. "Lord Carrington was telling me he's here on business from his father and hasn't found a place to stay. I offered him his old room if that is all right with you, Mother."

"Of course, and I know your father would agree. He's being pressured to take another boarder, but with Delia's health..." She trailed off dramatically. "We didn't want a rowdy officer stomping the halls."

"I was sorry to hear about Miss Wolcott's accident." Carrington emphasized the last word.

Jeffrey narrowed his eyes at him but said nothing.

"I hope your health has shown improvement?"

All eyes went to Delia, and she studied the floor. "Thank you, my lord. I'm quite improved."

"Oh, how thoughtless of me," her mother said, nearly interrupting Delia. "Will you gentlemen be available for my little dinner party? I believe I sent an invitation to you, Mr. Travers, but I hadn't imagined your brother had returned at the time. Please join us."

Little dinner party? Delia had come across the menu that morning to find six courses. It was a gross indulgence during wartime.

Carrington's face blanched as the conversation continued. "There's no need to put yourselves out for me. I can find lodging. I would be glad to join your dinner party if it's not too short a notice." Mrs. Wolcott waved this off.

Jeffrey snorted. "Where on the street? The soldiers can't even find decent lodging. No, stay here with us. It will be just like before, and that was no trouble."

Delia held back a laugh. No trouble? Having Lord Carrington nearby could be nothing but trouble. She stole a glance at him. Did he think she would kill him in his sleep?

"Do stay, Lord Carrington." She gave him a sweet smile as he turned at her voice. He swallowed and nodded.

Mr. Travers gave him a wide grin. "Good, now I can get your

stuff out of my room." Carrington glared at his younger brother, which only amused him further.

Mrs. Wolcott sensed her chance to have the unmarried males spend time with her daughters and offered to send for his things while the brothers joined them for dinner that night.

"Delighted," Mr. Travers said, but Carrington hesitated before accepting. He must have failed to find a believable excuse to refuse after his brother so readily agreed.

Once the pleasantries were settled, Jeffrey went in search of Mr. Wolcott and Lynette. Mr. Travers did his best to engage Mrs. Wolcott in conversation. Carrington added a few words but was otherwise silent.

She wandered over to the book she had left on the window seat. The unintelligible murmur of the conversation suited her lack of interest in listening to her mother. She knew she was being rude, but it was either that or leave. Or kill her.

Delia sensed his presence before she saw him, with a prickling along her neck. She withdrew into herself while trying her best to ignore him.

"Looking for more poisons?" His voice was low, displeased.

Her heart wrenched in her chest as she fixed her eyes on the page of the book for a time, then she dropped it closed and glowered at him. "No."

He folded his arms as he stood by. "I would advise against it."

"Why? Are you going to turn me in?" She meant to sound meek, but it came out more like a growl.

He dropped his arms and sighed. He fell into the cushioned chair flanking hers. "If I were going to do that, you would be dead already."

"Then what do you want? Why have you come back?" She wasn't sure she wanted the answer. His kiss from so many months ago seemed unfinished, unanswered. Yet she couldn't imagine what he would want with her.

His worn eyes met hers. "Do you hate me so much that you wouldn't wish me to visit while I'm here on business?"

Her brows scrunched together. "No, I don't trust why you're here. Why would anyone want to come back once they had escaped?"

He lifted his shoulders in one quick motion. "Wartime can be good for business. Your father and brother see this, and I've learned I need to take the opportunity as well."

"Why, Lord Carrington, are you forced to work? Aren't your lands providing your leisure?"

His lips curled up. "I'm not afraid of work. The people are taxed to death, and profits are minimal."

"Yes, taxes from this invasion." She gestured around with her hands.

His shoulders squared. "If your people wanted to be proper citizens, they should have paid their share of the taxes for the expense of protecting them."

A strangled sound escaped her throat. "Well, your people have never seen us as equals, so why should we pay as such? Haven't we had enough of your protection?"

He appeared to rein himself in before he spoke. "They have to earn their equality." His pupils darkened his piercing stare. Eagerness stirred between her legs. She wanted to escape into those eyes.

"Oh, you mean like you did?" She struggled to contain the volume of her voice.

He fell silent, but his expression raged at her. The tension settled over them in a thick fog, and Delia found herself repeating her question. "Why are you here?"

"I thought you wouldn't be foolish enough to kill again after I left. I misjudged you." He bit off every word. "My brother told me that Foxglove had started again. He thought you were in danger."

She gave an unladylike snort. "Shows what he knows."

"No, my brother is right. You're in danger. Foxglove is going to kill you."

She froze, a wounded animal trapped before the slaughter.

"You lied. You said you weren't going to turn me in." Her pulse beat a stampede telling her to flee.

He closed his eyes and let out a long breath. "I'm not."

"Then what? Do you plan to kill me yourself?" Her hands returned to their shivering state from before. He reached over to grasp them in his. She gulped, unable to resist.

"You're already killing yourself." His tone soothed her raging nerves as his eyes changed to the warm bottle brown she saw more often in his brother.

Tears threatened to escape. She removed her hands from his and stood. "You're wrong." It took all her willpower to attempt a dignified exit, but once she had shut the door behind her, she lost control.

In a fit of blind anger, she made it to her room. How could he ask her to give up Foxglove? He didn't understand. Her mother had already destroyed her only lead to Arthur's killers. She couldn't just toss her brother aside like so much garbage, even if it meant her death.

What she would do for one more hour with Arthur, to be the sister she should have been. She hadn't known her brother the way she'd thought, and the knowledge lodged a weight in her gut. There were too many secrets between them that they would never share.

She had fooled herself into believing her work would give her a chance to find the answers she needed, and she had continued in the empty hope she could make things right.

As she changed for dinner, she caught a glimpse of herself in the new mirror on her dressing table. It had been weeks since she had really looked at herself. Her skin was devoid of color, aside from the bruise-like crescents under her eyes. Her eyes shone brightly green, not the animated green of before but the striking one of pain and exhaustion. She brought her hand up to push her hair back into place but found it to be lifeless in its pale grace.

Maybe Lord Carrington was right. She seemed to be wasting away.

She donned a gray gown with Hope's help, and her maid uttered no word of protest on her mistress's choice. The outfit was leftover from her mourning period, and it suited her mood. Hope attempted to liven up her appearance by adding jewelry, but all Delia would accept was a pearl necklace and earring set.

When she made it down to the drawing room, it was just in time to be seated for dinner. Her mother scowled in displeasure at her clothes, but Delia ignored her, raising her chin and taking her usual place next to Lynette. Jeffrey took the seat on her other side.

It was a casual meal with less fare than was usual for guests, since the invitation had been sudden. After Lynette gave a comforting squeeze to her leg, Delia maintained her habitual quiet. However, Jeffrey didn't catch on to her mood.

"Rather dramatic tonight?" Jeffrey said between bites of his roast.

She kept her attention on her food. "I'm sure I don't know what you mean." Pierre pawed her leg for scraps, and she pushed him off with her foot.

He motioned to her clothes with his knife. "Can't you be a little more cheerful? We have guests."

"Well, I didn't invite them." She didn't bother to lower her voice. Pierre whined from below the table.

Jeffrey frowned at the table over the dog. "Who let the dog in?" Nobody answered him. "All the same."

Pierre scratched at her dress more insistently. She pushed him away again.

Jeffrey eyed her roast. "Are you going to finish that?"

A disgusted grunt passed her throat, and she offered it to him. He leaned over to stab it with his knife when Pierre jumped between them, knocking his blade into Delia's hand.

She cried out as blood formed along her knuckles. Her head grew light as she gasped for air. Voices muffled around her. The flash of the blade stabbed over and over again. Her hands shook before her.

Jeffrey hoisted up Pierre and left the room.

Lord Carrington slid into her brother's place. He inspected her trembling hand and concluded it was a shallow cut that didn't need anything more than a bandage. He motioned for her to rise, and his cupped hand kept her blood from dripping to the floor as he escorted her out into the hall.

Once they were seated in the hall, Lord Carrington ordered a bandage, but already the wound was closing up. She continued to stare at the small cut on her shaking hand.

"You'll be fine." His voice took the same soothing tone as before. "I've seen worse paper cuts than this."

She shook her head and swallowed.

He forced her to look at him, guiding her chin with one hand. "You are safe. Nobody can hurt you here."

She shook her head again but with less conviction. She moaned and gave a faint hiccup.

"It will pass. Just breathe and think about dessert." He wrapped the small wound with an exaggerated amount of bandage. She looked down at it and let out a giggle when she tried to flex her hand. He grinned at her reaction.

"Are you ready to go back to dinner? If you like, I can feed you. We don't want your grievous wound to prevent you from eating the cake Cook prepared." He arched an eyebrow at her. She burst into a full laugh this time.

"Not yet." She closed her eyes and took a slow breath. When she opened them, he was calmly watching her and holding a glass of wine. He handed her the drink, and she sipped it gratefully.

"I had a sister once." His unexpected change of topic drew her attention. "She loved horses. She never saw a fault in any of them. One time, my father bought a new, untamed horse, and she couldn't wait to be the first to ride him. We should have watched her, but it didn't occur to any of us that she would be so foolish. The horse was wild and hated everyone, but she was convinced if she showed him kindness, then he would let her ride him. She saw the best in everyone, you understand."

He gazed off, absorbed in the memory. "I heard her screams across the yard and got there as fast as I could. The look of terror on her face nearly sent me to my grave. That's what you looked like at the table."

"What happened?" She breathed out, leaning toward him.

"She was thrown off the horse."

"I'm sorry." She brought her uninjured hand to her throat.

"Oh, she was fine. That wasn't what killed her, but she never trusted her instincts with horses or people again." His message shone clear in his gaze.

She skirted the hinted topic of her pain and focused on his. "May I ask how she died?"

"My sister—Catherine was her name—died a few years later from a lung sickness." His voice remained calm.

"That's awful. How old was she?"

A grave smile graced his solemn face. "Fifteen."

She placed her unbandaged hand on his. "That must have been hard."

"It was, but it was a long time ago and not what I was trying to say." He squeezed her hand. "Do you see what I mean now?"

A heavy cloud settled over her as she considered his words. "I think I'm beginning to." The person in the mirror had been a stranger. Foxglove would take what remained of her.

He raised his brows, looking hopeful. "Then you'll stop?"

"It isn't that easy." She lowered her gaze to the floor.

"Yes, it is."

She drew away. "No, you don't understand. I can't quit before I have more answers. I need to know what happened to Arthur." She had failed for months, with only a slip of paper to show for it.

He leaned toward her as though to lend weight to his plea. "At least let me help you." The concern etched at the corners of his eyes nearly undid her. She wanted to fall into his chest and cry until her tears ran dry. Maybe he did see her.

She bit back her sorrow. "How? It isn't like you're an officer anymore."

"That only means fewer restrictions. I'm a viscount and my father's heir, which gives me certain advantages. Plus, I am, as you once told me, male and British."

She rolled her eyes, but her smile betrayed her humor. "Don't remind me."

His gaze flicked over her shoulder, and she turned to Jeffrey, minus Pierre, walking toward them. "We'll talk later." He spoke in hurried syllables and distanced himself from her. They hadn't been sitting too close, but the distance brought a chill as he moved away.

Jeffrey glared at Carrington, and she wondered how long he had been there.

Carrington returned Jeffrey's attention with a calm gaze. "Don't look at me that way. You were the one who stabbed her."

She covered her mouth to hide a laugh. Jeffrey glanced down at her bandaged hand. "I'm sorry, Dee. Does it hurt?"

"Only a little. You're forgiven, but next time I get to stab you." She cracked a smile.

"I wouldn't go that far."

Her gaze fell on Carrington. "Don't you think it's fair I get to stab Jeffrey next time?"

Carrington gave Jeffrey a solemn look. "You'll have to wait in line." Jeffrey scowled at him, but she erupted into a delighted laugh and accepted Carrington's arm as they stood.

"Come, my lord." She let him lead her back to the dining room, where he promptly took Jeffrey's chair. Jeffrey gawked at him but resigned himself to sit next to Mr. Travers, who looked on, amused.

"Jeffrey, if you can't keep your cutlery to yourself, you should go back to sitting in the nursery." She glanced at him from the corner of her eye. "Mr. Travers may need to mount a defense."

Like the overgrown child he was, Jeffrey aimed a kick at her beneath the table and narrowly missed her. She was forced to retaliate and kicked out toward him, but Carrington caught her foot under the table. He brushed his hand over her stocking, and a sharp awareness settled between her legs. Her breath caught in her throat.

Their eyes locked, and a wordless message played between them. He let out a breath and slowly released her foot.

Her face grew hot, and Lynette giggled beside her. The awkwardness drew her attention to her mother's voice as she droned on to her father, who didn't appear to be listening. Her mother seemed to become aware of this and turned to their guests. She brightened when she saw Lord Carrington seated next to her daughter, but she frowned at Delia's hand as if the wound had been her fault.

Delia tried to hide her thoughts in her cake as she became increasingly aware of Carrington's leg resting against hers. He was unnervingly composed, and she suspected he was trying to distract her from her earlier ordeal. She conceded to herself it was working.

When her mother rose to leave for the drawing room, Delia jumped up, to the amusement of Mr. Travers and Lynette. She squared her shoulders, but her quick exit betrayed her flight from the rogue staring after her.

CHAPTER SEVENTEEN

L YNETTE DREW DELIA aside in the drawing room while their mother took up her needlework. They sat flanking a window on a view of fat snowflakes settling across the ground in a clean carpet. She gazed out the window a bit longer before Lynette got her attention.

"What happened?" A wicked smile spread over Lynette's face.

"Nothing. You have too much of an imagination." Her mouth straightened into a thin line, not giving anything away.

"Jeffrey thought something had."

She gazed up at the ceiling. "Netty, Jeffrey would think I was being taken advantage of if a man so much as looked at me."

Lynette inched closer. "True, but you were in the hall for some time."

She groaned. "Yes, in the hall where the servants were wandering by every minute. We were just talking."

"Oh?"

She took a quick breath. "About Foxglove. He wants me to quit."

"And are you?"

Her eyes met her sister's. "I think I may have to."

Lynette surprised her by nodding. "I've been thinking the same thing. As much as I want revenge..." She took a breath. "I can't go through that again. I haven't slept well since." Her sister reached out to hold her uninjured hand. "You've been through more than me, and I don't want to lose you too."

"You won't lose me, Netty."

Yet she needed to finish what she had started. She needed Carrington's help. Alone, even with Felix and Hope, the answers eluded her.

When the men entered, Mr. Travers hurried to meet Delia and Lynette. While her father joined her mother, Jeffrey and Carrington came in separately, the tension between them a living thing.

"As interesting as this situation is, they may kill each other," Mr. Travers whispered to them. He took the other part of the sofa with Delia.

She huffed and folded her arms. "Jeffrey's unreasonable."

Mr. Travers met her eyes, and his lips quaked on the verge of laughter. "I don't think he is. If you were my sister, William would be bleeding on the floor. I think he's showing remarkable restraint."

She scoffed at that.

"You don't know him like I do."

Lynette laughed at Delia's wide-eyed expression.

To Carrington's credit and her disappointment, he remained with Mr. Wolcott. They gestured toward an article in her father's paper, and she assumed they discussed either business or politics.

She smoothed her features into a calm expression. "Should I be concerned?"

"Well, as long as you keep good company, you should be safe. Being alone with my brother is the number one cause of spinsterhood in *The Debutante's London Season Handbook*." His face was stern, but his eyes danced with merriment.

"You're making that up. There's no such thing." Her grin split her features.

Mr. Travers dropped his voice dramatically and leaned toward her. "Are you sure? London is a terrifying and mysterious place. If there isn't a handbook already, there should be."

"Any woman with half a brain would know not to be alone with either of you."

"With me? I'm hurt." That mischievous smile sparked up to his eyes.

She tilted her head, studying his face. "Mr. Travers, you look much like your brother when you smile."

He inhaled a quick breath. "I'm shocked."

She giggled. "Why is that?"

His brows inched up comically. "That he smiled. No wonder you find me so handsome."

"Handsome? You're both hideous." She bit her lip to steady her laughter.

Lynette made a garbled noise and coughed. Delia peered over her shoulder at her sister and saw Lord Carrington and Jeffrey coming toward them. They were both frowning at Hugh, who looked at them innocently.

Delia waved them off as if to dismiss them, but Carrington took the seat closest to his brother and Jeffrey next to him.

"Hello, brother." Mr. Travers beamed at Carrington. "I was just talking to the lovely Miss Wolcott, and she was admiring my smile." Delia grinned at Mr. Travers. That was, until she heard the low growl coming from Carrington.

She decided she'd had enough and got to her feet. The men, taken off guard, barely had the chance to stand before she left the room. Her sister followed her out the door. Once they made it to Delia's room, Lynette erupted into full belly laughter.

Lynette panted while holding her side. "You handled that well."

"Did I?" She dropped onto her bed.

Lynette nodded in a quick burst and spread out on the other side of the bed.

"They deserve it. Jeffrey will turn us both into spinsters, and the Travers brothers are only after one thing. Where have all the nice ones gone?"

"Oh, the nice ones are at war, dead, or married. All we have is

British rakes." Lynette turned onto her side to face her. "Do you think we will come out of this?"

"Out of what?" Delia turned to her.

"This war."

"Of course. It can't go on forever. There are only so many men on the earth, and who would let the women do the fighting?"

"They keep saying it will be over in a few months until the time comes and they say it will be another few months. I have doubts it will ever stop."

Delia nodded against her pillow. "And we aren't getting any younger. Mother will marry us off to corpses on the battlefield soon."

"Oh my, Dee, that is morbid. She would too." Lynette frowned. "As interesting as this conversation is, I have a novel to get back to." Her sister rolled off the bed and left without another word.

Indeed, Delia had reading to do as well. She was lost in her new book when footsteps came from the room next to hers. The servants had brought in Carrington's things while everyone had been at dinner, so it must be the man himself. She toyed with the thought of seeing him and wondered what he would do if she knocked on his door in only her thin nightgown.

She laughed to herself and heard the steps stop at the sound, which only made her laugh louder. A knock echoed through her room. She flinched.

"What do you want?" An appropriate question given the late hour and her state of undress. In response came another knock.

"Really." She stomped to the door and threw on her robe before opening it a crack. She startled to find Felix there with a crooked smile on his face. He held out a rose to her and a note. She raised her brows in question, but he only bowed and skipped off before she could say anything.

She shut the door behind her and examined the rose. It was a pale yellow, a gesture of friendship. She inhaled the sweet floral fragrance and opened the note. It read, *Dearest Miss Wolcott, I have behaved no better than that horrible man who will remain nameless. Please forgive me. Your friend, William Travers*

She picked up a quill and wrote a quick note back: *Dear Barbarian, you will have to make it up to me. The Honorable Queen Dee*

She rushed out into the hall and pushed the note under his door, knocking just before she ran back. Footfalls sounded next door and moments later, a deep laugh. She dropped back on her bed, satisfied when a slip of paper peeked out under her door. A lazy smile tilted her lips, and she retrieved it from the floor.

Dearest Honorable Queen Dee, I will endeavor to seek your forgiveness to my dying breath. Your servant, Barbarian

She giggled and reclined back in her bed, her novel forgotten. Her mind wandered to Carrington's broad shoulders and eager lips. A horrible, frustrating, and yet tempting idea. Foxglove and a loyalist? They didn't even have anything in common. He could only be after one thing, and she wasn't about to give him one of the few choices she had left.

⟫⟪

THE DAY OF her mother's dinner was a disaster from the start. Everything that could go wrong happened, and to make matters worse, heavy clouds loomed overhead, threatening a nasty storm. They could only hope the snow would wait until after their guests had come and gone.

She tried to avoid her mother at all costs, but Delia and Lynette ended up doing one tedious task or other. She barely had time to dress before the guests arrived. Hope fastened her into her new ivory-and-green gown and her matching heeled shoes.

They pinned her hair partially up, with a thick lock curled to rest on her shoulder. She completed her outfit with emerald-and-pearl earrings and a large emerald pendant necklace in white gold. She blinked at the ethereal being in her mirror.

Standing next to her family to greet the guests was an exercise in patience. Of course her mother had invited more eligible men than desirable women, though the numbers were even if one counted dinner partners.

Mr. Chambers escorted Helen inside. Her options had become limited after her romance with Arthur. Besides, Mr. Chambers was a good man. She had no doubt they would make each other happy. She expected there would be an announcement of their engagement soon.

Before dinner was announced, the snowfall returned outside the drawing room window. The flakes were slow at first but gradually increased as she watched. Still, the outdoors appeared more welcoming than the crowded drawing room, where every male was forced to make conversation at her mother's behest.

By some strange twist on her mother's part, Delia was seated next to Mr. McCabe and Carrington at dinner. The two were the most eligible men in the room, though her mother knew Delia preferred New Yorkers (ruling out Carrington) and she had a strong dislike for Mr. McCabe.

It was not that Mr. McCabe was outright rude, but he had just enough arrogance that Delia always appeared inadequate when he was in the room. He was handsome in a way that it seemed an afterthought: Mr. McCabe was a second son, but he was handsome, or Mr. McCabe was an avid drinker, but he was handsome. He sucked the joy out of any conversation, and Delia cursed her mother.

"You look beautiful in that color, Miss Wolcott. Your mother must have found a new dressmaker," Mr. McCabe said between sips of soup. His hazel eyes slit beneath his carefully powdered wig.

A frown creased her brow. "Thank you?" She didn't know if she should feel appreciated or insulted that he implied her previous gowns were lacking.

Carrington cleared his throat. "It is a becoming shade." She nodded her thanks to him. Maybe Carrington would balance Mr. McCabe out.

Mr. McCabe stared at her from the corner of his eye. "It's certainly better than the dull clothes you wore the last I saw you." That would be at Arthur's funeral.

Her fist clenched under the table, and her features slid into an emotionless mask. "Yes, I'm sure. That was a difficult time."

"Of course. Dear Arthur. I miss him. It isn't the same without him causing trouble with the rebels." Mr. McCabe sniffed, the extent of his emotions.

"A noble pastime." Carrington paused and studied the other man. "I'd like to know more concerning these exploits I hear so much about." She nearly jumped into his lap and kissed him. It would be improper for her to have such conversations with Mr. McCabe, especially at the dinner table.

Mr. McCabe regarded him and checked to see if anyone else listened. "Later. It's not a subject for ladies." Mr. McCabe tilted his head to Delia. She held back a groan.

Carrington only nodded and turned his attention back to his food. He had a healthy portion of gammon to work through. How did he eat so much?

"Miss Wolcott, you must have more of this spiced wine. My mother swears by it for a healthy complexion." Mr. McCabe poured her more before she could respond. She thanked him through clenched teeth. "Never be afraid of too much wine."

She squeezed her eyes shut. Surely he didn't mean women needed to drink more?

"I'm sure Miss Wolcott has much experience with wine. Haven't you?" Carrington gave her a wide smile. Her cheeks burned as she looked away. "I've found hot water is best for good complexions."

Mr. McCabe brightened. He must have thought Carrington his kindred spirit. "Oh yes, hot water is rather extraordinary for the skin. Now, taking your wine with your bath is doubly beneficial."

She restrained herself from ducking under the table. Was this a suitable conversation? Of course, everything seemed appropriate to Mr. McCabe's vanity, but talking about Arthur was off-limits. She didn't know where Carrington was going with this, but he seemed to enjoy her embarrassment.

"Yes, baths." Carrington sucked in a breath. "Invigorating." Delia shifted in her chair. Why wasn't dinner over with already?

She cast a glare at Carrington. "I've found that wine is especially good with certain flowers."

His eyes shone as he gave her that mischievous smile. "Really? I think flowers are more suited to the bath. The skin."

Mr. McCabe waved his hand, knife in his grasp. She flinched and scooted away from him. Her movement seemed to both concern and delight Carrington until she lowered her brows, and he reluctantly moved his chair away a bare inch.

She was spared from further discussion for the rest of dinner, as the musicians chose that time to begin. When the ladies left for the drawing room, she spotted Pierre lounging on a sofa. Of course, he was supposed to be absent tonight. She sat next to him, hoping to curtail any unruly behavior, and ran her fingers along his coat. The constant snowfall claimed her attention.

Abigail moved to join her, but Delia just shook her head and gave her an apologetic smile, wanting to be alone. Her friend nodded her understanding and went to join Lynette and Helen. Delia needed more information from Carrington and couldn't very well get him to talk about his conversation with Mr. McCabe if they were surrounded.

After many drawn-out minutes, the men rejoined them, but Carrington wasn't alone. He spoke with Mr. Chambers and Jeffrey, whom he led to her side. She tried not to sigh but failed. Carrington picked up Pierre and settled him on his lap as he sat next to Delia.

Jeffrey scowled at him. "I swear that dog will be the death of me. Why is he in here?"

She scratched behind Pierre's ear. "I don't know, but Mother won't have him outside, or he will disappear."

Jeffrey shrugged. "Good riddance, if you ask me."

She bristled. "Nobody asked you. Pierre is part of the family. At least he's cleaner than you." Carrington and Mr. Chambers checked their laughter behind their hands.

"That's because you women bathe him in all sorts of perfumes and oils. He's a dog and should be outside with the other rodents and mud." Jeffrey gripped Pierre behind the neck. Pierre yelped and flinched away.

She grasped for Pierre in Carrington's lap. "You're hurting him."

"Nonsense, he's tougher than he looks. Here, I'll prove it to you." Jeffrey picked up the dog, dodging Carrington's hands, and opened the window, through which he tossed him into the waiting snow.

With a startled cry, she jumped to the window and watched with growing horror as Pierre rushed off into the snow and disappeared into the storm. She turned on Jeffrey. "How could you?"

"He'll be fine. At this time tomorrow, he'll be begging at the kitchen for scraps." He dropped back into his chair, spreading out his limbs.

She turned back and forth between the window and Jeffrey, her mouth wide. She darted to the door that opened to the yard and jerked the frozen lock open. Without hesitation, she ran out into the winter night.

CHAPTER EIGHTEEN

"**P**IERRE."

Delia rushed headfirst into the blinding storm. She shielded her face from the onslaught, but Pierre was nowhere in sight, his gray fur hidden in the shadowed snow. She trudged forward toward the outline of neighboring homes, the snow already to her ankles. Her thin shoes soaked through in the first few moments outside.

The door clicked shut behind her, but she ignored it, hugging her body for warmth as she called for the dog once more.

"Miss Wolcott."

Instead of responding, she took another step, searching for footprints leading out from the window. "Pierre, where are you?"

Carrington caught up to her. "Miss Wolcott, come inside." He pulled her toward the door.

"We can't just leave him. He'll freeze in this." She blinked away the offending snow.

"I'll look for the dog. Just get inside. You're not dressed for the storm."

She looked down at herself. She hadn't bothered to grab so much as a shawl, and her thin gloves were no match for the New York winter. Already her fingers and nose were numb from cold. "I should look for him. He barely knows you." She jerked her arm away from him.

"I assure you, I'm capable of finding him and I will not rest until I bring him back. Now, please, go inside." He grabbed her arm once more and tugged her toward the house.

Instead of following, she struggled to release her arm. He let go just in time for her to slip in the snow and land on her backside. As she fell, she kicked out in front of her, toppling Carrington to the ground.

He groaned from on top of her. "I'm going to kill your brother."

She struggled as she became aware of their situation and looked back to make sure they weren't visible from the house. The snow made the house a blurry mass behind them. He put his hands out beneath him and faced her.

"On second thought, I did fall on a comfortable surface." He grinned wickedly. She placed her hands against his chest and pushed at his solid mass. Someone could come searching for them any minute and he wanted to play games with her reputation.

"At least you aren't lying in the snow. Now get off me. It's no wonder you eat a lot. You weigh as much as a horse." She shoved at him, but he simply raised himself on his hands to lift some of his weight.

"Is that better?" He grinned down at her.

"Yes. No." She colored. "Get off. I'm freezing."

He raised an eyebrow. "That's your only objection?"

She tilted her head away from his searching gaze and bit her lip. This was madness. He nestled on top of her, where anyone approaching could see. His leather-and-brandy scent entranced her.

He nudged her to face him, and a primal need sharpened the deep-brown pools of his eyes. Warmth flooded her body.

His breathing quickened as he took her in. A heart drummed between them, but she couldn't tell whose.

She grasped his shirt in her hand and pulled him down to steal a kiss. He responded at once with a kiss of his own. He was gentle but needy, pressing her deeper into the snow. She opened her mouth to him, a tinge of wine on his breath. He explored her, possessed her. His warmth made her forget the downy chill beneath them.

She moaned from her body's response, and the sound startled him into pulling away. He rolled off to his side and regained his feet. A breath of frozen air replaced him. He reached down to help her up, and her arms encircled his waist. He pulled off his coat and wrapped it around her, holding it about her shoulders.

She missed the raw need that had flared from his ungiving weight.

He led her back inside, eyes never leaving her face. When he opened the door, there was a chorus of voices, and Jeffrey intercepted them just inside.

"What were you thinking, rushing out there over a stupid dog? And you—" Her brother pointed to Carrington, who cut him short with a stern glare.

"This wouldn't have happened if you had left the dog alone."

"But—"

The viscount held up a hand. "It was cruel to throw a dog into the snow to prove a point." Delia shivered into his side, and he reinforced his grip on her shoulders. "Don't blame Miss Wolcott for having concerns for a dear pet. Your sister was without a coat, and she fell in the snow. She could catch her death from your foolish actions."

Lynette rushed forward and took Delia into her arms before draping a shawl around her shoulders. She closed Delia in a protective embrace and rubbed the chill from her arms.

"Now, Mr. Jeffrey Wolcott." He waited for the other man's attention. "Get your coat and come with me to find the dog."

Jeffrey shook his head. "I hardly think it is necessary. You can't expect me to go out into that." He shrugged toward the window.

"Jeffrey." The stern voice of their father brought silence. "Lord Carrington is correct. You have behaved abhorrently, worrying your dear sister like that. You will not come back until you find the dog, and you'll do it alone." All heads turned to the elder Mr. Wolcott, who was a man of few words, but when he spoke, he did with purpose and people listened.

Carrington regarded the elder Mr. Wolcott. "I'll help find the dog."

"If you insist, but it's my son's responsibility to bring him back."

"I do insist. The only way I could get Miss Wolcott to agree to come back was if I promised to find the dog. I keep my promises." Carrington's gaze locked with hers as though reminding her of his promise months before.

He sent for his heavy coat and gloves and then bent at her side. "Rest assured, I will find him." His whispered words tickled her ear. The sensation sent a bolt echoing through her body.

With that, he strode outside, and Jeffrey followed grudgingly behind him.

Lynette escorted Delia to her sister's room, where a fire burned. Delia's body shook as Lynette and Hope helped her change into a thick nightgown and bundled her into bed. Her maid left to get her some warm milk while Lynette sat beside her.

She sucked in a deep breath through her nose. "Netty, what do you want? You can return to our guests at any time."

"Can't I be concerned for my sister?"

"Yes, but I saw the way you were flirting with Jeffrey's friends."

"All right, fine. I wanted to know what happened. Why is Lord Carrington acting like a mother hen?" Lynette's voice was accusing, her never one to be left out of a secret.

Irritation crawled over Delia's skin. "He's not a mother hen."

"Oh? He stood up to Jeffrey. Nobody stands up to Jeffrey. Father barely bothers to contradict him. Carrington was lucky he wasn't thrown out."

"Father would never have thrown him out."

"No, but Jeffrey might have if Father hadn't spoken up. I've never seen Carrington so commanding. It was…" Lynette pursed her lips. "Thrilling."

For some reason, her sister's words sent an itch along Delia's spine. Lynette was not supposed to admire Carrington. Though, she did admit she had enjoyed watching Carrington take control of the situation.

He was every bit the earl's son in those moments and was probably a sight when managing his men. His steady confidence drew her, and if she wasn't careful, he would command her heart.

Delia cleared her throat. "I'll agree with you there. It was nice to see Jeffrey humiliated for a change."

"You still haven't answered my question."

"There was a question?" Her mind wandered, lost to a certain kiss in the snow.

"Yes. What happened?"

"When?" She blinked at her sister in confusion.

Lynette threw up her hands. "I don't know. Something has happened, and I want you to fill me in on all the details. He had an interest in you before, but he's become increasingly obvious about it, and when you came back from your jaunt in the snow, he was downright possessive."

"He was? That will have to change."

"But why?" Lynette's heightened voice made Delia flinch.

"I'm sure I don't know." She smiled in gratitude at Hope as she entered with her drink.

"This isn't over." Lynette cast a sharp glare at her as she slammed the door behind her.

Hope handed her the glass. "Dare I ask what that was about?"

"Just Lynette being Lynette, wanting more than I will give her." She sipped the milk, and the sweet liquid slid along her tongue. "Have they found Pierre?"

Hope shook her head. "Not yet, though the storm seems to be clearing up enough for some of the guests to leave."

"Well, that's something." Her words fell hollow between them. What if they never found Pierre? What would her mother do to her brother? Delia wondered if Jeffrey had been right and the dog would simply reappear the next day, and she regretted sending Carrington out into the storm.

She didn't know what had possessed her earlier when Carrington had pinned her down in the snow. She had wanted to get up, but at the same time, she hadn't wanted him to move. Delia was on dangerous ground and shouldn't be alone with him if she cared anything for her reputation.

She didn't sleep, not for lack of trying. Her mind raced through thoughts of Pierre, Arthur, and Carrington. Were Pierre and Carrington safe? What had happened with Mr. McCabe? Once she recovered fully from her ordeal, a dark weight rested in her stomach as she entertained thoughts in the comfort of her room.

An eternity passed before the door to the room next door opened and shut. Frantically, she threw on her robe and went to the door, but Hope met her there.

"They found Pierre, and he'll be fine. Though he was soaked through with cold and Cook said he probably would've died out there if he was out much longer." Hope ushered her back to bed.

"What of Lord Carrington and Jeffrey?"

Hope's eyes crinkled in amusement. "They seem to be fine too, though they're both in a foul mood. I suspect they fought while searching for Pierre, though neither of them has said anything."

Delia pushed toward the door, but Hope blocked her way.

"They're bringing him a bath now."

Delia's gaze narrowed at the door.

"I can have Felix take him a note if you like." With a nod from Delia, Hope readied the writing instruments.

Delia wrote, *Dear Lord Carrington, Thank you for locating Pierre. I am sorry to have put you to so much trouble. I have many questions that need waiting, since you are unfairly indisposed. For now, I am in your debt. Miss Delia Wolcott*

Hope called for Felix, who assisted with the bath. Felix eyed the note and disappeared into the next room. It wasn't long before Felix returned with another page. Doubtless, the errand boy had read the response too. If she didn't allow the liberty, he would find a way.

Dearest Miss Delia, It was my pleasure to assist in finding Pierre. Jeffrey, on the other hand, may turn up dead soon. As for your questions, you are welcome to join me if you wish, though I doubt you will get many answers, since there will be no talking. I would like to begin your penance. I am yours, William

Her jaw dropped under Felix's glee-filled gaze. She read it a second and third time, not believing his words. Her face turned redder with each reading. Finally, she picked up a quill and wrote without salutation, *You cad. D*

As surprised as she had been by his note, she couldn't help but laugh at his boldness. She handed her own to Felix, who glanced at the message before delivering it to Carrington. Luckily, the boy wasn't a gossip.

When he returned with another and bowed, presenting it to her in his hands, she slapped him on the head with it before reading. The paper ran with ink from droplets of water.

Madam, I am tired, wet, and sore from my breeches being too tight. If you would like to relieve some of my discomfort, then it would be most welcome. Otherwise, I will talk to you at a more suitable hour and in a more proper way. I wish you a good night. William

Felix was beside himself with joy when instead of writing another note, she sent Carrington back one of her gloves. She smiled as echoed laugher filtered from his room, and her smile lingered as she drifted off to sleep.

For a change, no nightmares haunted her as they often had since she'd been stabbed. It was a dreamless, deep sleep, and she woke later than usual, excited and refreshed.

Hope dressed her in a green gown and tied up her hair simply. Delia didn't have the patience for any more, and she hurried to the breakfast room.

The guests had all departed after the storm had let up. When she entered for breakfast, her father had already come and gone. Everyone else was scattered around the table. A blinding light hit her off the snow just as a servant closed the curtains. The remaining light was gray and vacant.

"We were wondering when you would appear. It's a miracle you made it to breakfast. I assume you've recovered from your little adventure?" Her mother didn't wait for an answer. "Poor Lord Carrington and your brother went through a lot of trouble for you. We are grateful to them, aren't we?"

"Yes, Mama." Delia lowered her head.

"I said, aren't we?"

"Yes, Mama." She raised her chin. "I'm grateful to Lord Carrington and Jeffrey for going to so much trouble on my behalf."

"Quite." Her mother paused, a command for her full attention. "Now that you have ruined your dress in the snow, I insist we go to the dressmaker and get you a new one for the holiday. Lynette takes such care of her things that she has decided to make do with what she has."

Her sister gave her an apologetic look. Delia shrugged and asked Jeffrey to pass her the toast. He reached out for it but released a full-bodied sneeze that showered the plate. Delia gawked at him.

"I'm sorry, Dee. I've been sneezing since last night. I have it worse than Carrington." He sneezed again off to the side as though to emphasize his words.

"You're sick?"

He sniffled, the sound caught in his voice. "My only consolation is that Carrington is too." He grinned at the former captain, who watched him.

Carrington favored her with a lazy smile. "It was worth it."

Jeffrey drew his brows together. "I hate you."

"Too bad." Carrington tilted his head to Delia.

Jeffrey folded his arms behind the table. Mrs. Wolcott sighed and excused herself from the room, presumably to get ready for their shopping trip. Lynette leaned on her elbows, watching the two argue.

Delia's sigh echoed her mother's, and she added more bacon to her plate to make up for the discomfort. They ate in silence for a while, aside from the occasional sneeze. Lynette lost interest and left the room. Jeffrey and Carrington continued to stare each other down until Delia rose from the table.

Her brother came to block Carrington from following her out but was waylaid by their mother calling to him. Carrington gave him a triumphant smile before Jeffrey stormed off. They sat back down at the table, to the irritation of the servants.

She poured herself another cup of tea. "Well?"

Carrington stared after Jeffrey. "He's impossible."

She watched him through her lashes, willing him to pay attention to her words. "What did Mr. McCabe say?"

He hesitated before speaking, watching her hand drop the sugar into her cup. "Arthur didn't exactly share your views."

"Yes, I know." She kept her gaze on him as she sipped her tea.

"Well, he was working on both sides. You see, with his school connections, he was a perfect spy. A jewel to the Crown, so to speak."

"Go on."

"Arthur was a member of the Sons of Liberty. A loyal member, by all appearances. He fed them information, most of it useless, and he reported back to us. Your brother betrayed his comrades for the Crown and your family." He inched his hand to grasp hers. Distracted by his accounts, she allowed his touch.

"They killed him for secrets?"

Carrington ran his thumb along her knuckles. The sensation made her heart somersault. "They killed him for betraying a friend, an important spy."

"Who?" She already knew the answer.

He squeezed her hand as though he sensed her discomfort. "Nathan Hale."

"Are you saying Arthur is responsible for the execution of Mr. Hale?" Her fingernails bit into his hand.

He released her nails from his skin. "It appears so. At least, according to Mr. McCabe, but it makes sense." He brought her hand to his mouth and kissed her wrist. She shivered and pulled back her hand. What if the servants saw?

"Then who killed him?"

"If I had to guess, I would say his friends in the Sons of Liberty or another spy. If that is the case, he must have been good at his job, since it took them so long to find him."

"I need to be sure."

He sighed. "I can ask around about his work if that's what you want. It's possible the killers are already dead and gone." He found her hand again.

She jumped away, glaring at him. "What are you doing?"

"I'm sorry. I can't help it." His eyes were half-closed as though he had just finished a delectable meal.

"Yes, you can. Why are you set on ruining me?" And in the breakfast room of all places.

He pulled back at her accusation and released her hand. "That's not my intention."

She shot to her feet. "Really? That's what it would amount to. I'm not going to be your mistress, Lord Carrington. It would destroy all my hopes for the future."

He stood, and his face fell into a wooden expression as she raced from the room.

CHAPTER NINETEEN

DELIA DIDN'T SEE much of Carrington for the next week. He was absent for most of each day, and he avoided conversation with her at meals, sitting next to Mr. Wolcott and Jeffrey. Her brother had made peace with him but still eyed him with suspicion.

His silence told her he was respecting her refusal of his advances. What reason did he have to help her now? As willing as he had been to talk to Mr. McCabe, Carrington's aid came grudgingly. What would she have to pay for his assistance?

She had given him no reason to keep her secret either. Carrington was a gentleman, and she believed he honored his promises, but he had also tried to use her in the same way as Mr. Bradshaw. It didn't help that she couldn't escape the man in her thoughts and dreams. How could she forget the hard weight of him pressing her into the snow for a passionate kiss?

She lounged in the library with the worst novel cradled on her lap. Abigail had lent the book to her, and she had to agree with her friend that it was scandalous. It was captivating and maddening, and she hadn't put it down since opening it that morning.

Jeffrey came into the library to speak to her, never mind she was nose-deep in her book. She glared at him when he spoke and reluctantly set it down. If this was his way of making amends, he was off to a bad start.

He sat across from her, on the edge of his chair. "I need to talk to you."

"Oh?"

He twisted his hands in his lap as though he wrestled with his words. "I'm sorry about Pierre. I shouldn't have thrown him out."

"No, you shouldn't have."

His brows angled up in an inverted *v*. "He could have died in that weather, and I'm beside myself with guilt. I've been a heartless monster. Can you forgive me?" He leaned forward and rested his hands on his knees, a silent plea in his dark eyes.

"That depends. Why did you do it?"

He shook his head and ran his hands through his hair. "I don't know. I was frustrated and angry but not with Pierre. He's not a bad dog, really. He was just there."

Her nose scrunched up. "About what?"

"I'm worried about you. I was almost too late already." He dropped his gaze to study his hands.

"That's ridiculous. You can't always be there."

He met her eyes, and his voice became determined. "All the same, it's up to me to protect you. Father is never around, and Mother doesn't concern herself with keeping you proper. I think she would find it advantageous if you were compromised."

He took a slow breath. "Now you just seem to be inviting these situations, and I'm completely powerless to help you. Do you know how scared I was when I saw you bleeding all over the kitchen floor?"

His hands shook, and he rubbed them over his legs. "All I could think of was losing you the way we lost Arthur. It was happening again. I can't lose you too, Dee."

She leaned toward him and squeezed his hands, but she remained silent, unable to make any promises.

He squeezed back, and for the first time, she saw the gray at the edges of his temples, nearly masked by his white-blonde hair.

"Then Lord Carrington came back. I'd hoped he'd lost interest in you and settled down in London.

"It was different with Richard." His gaze was mournful.

A pang throbbed in her chest. She hadn't realized her brother missed Mr. Bradshaw. "I don't see your point."

He shook his head. "You aren't leading Carrington on, are you?"

Delia frowned. She knew she hadn't led Mr. Bradshaw to believe there was anything between them, but Carrington? She sighed, which was answer enough for Jeffrey.

"You aren't making my job easier."

She slumped into her seat. "I know, but the man brings out the worst in me. I don't know what it is, but it's difficult to refuse him."

"You did just fine the other day."

"Perhaps." Sure, she had done well then, but how long would she be able to keep her better judgment around him? It had taken all her willpower to refuse him. She silently thanked him for avoiding her and, at the same time, hated him for his absence. She had to keep space between them. No more kissing.

Jeffrey rose and leaned in to peck her forehead. "You'll have to marry eventually."

"What? You won't support me as a spinster?"

"If it came down to it, you know I would. But I know you, Dee, and not having your own family would kill you." He paused a moment, lost in thought. "You will never need to worry about money, so don't concern yourself with marrying for it. The same goes for Lynette."

She grinned up at him.

"Now go back to that horrible book, but please don't emulate the behavior in it."

Her grin widened. "Oh, I will."

His lips twitched down in an attempt to frown but failed and shot up instead. "What will I do with you?" He shook his head all the way out the door.

She knew he was right. She couldn't afford to dally with men who had no intention of making her an offer of marriage. Unless Jeffrey stared Carrington down the length of a pistol, Carrington wouldn't consider her a suitable candidate. She was an American from a mercantile family and not the lady he needed as a wife. She repeated this to herself, but her body refused to believe it.

These thoughts would creep up on her at the most inconvenient times. She was consumed with such musings at the bookstore days later. She wandered the dusty shelves with her gaze, not seeing the titles in her reverie. The space was crammed with books in no noticeable order and with no regard for customers who didn't wish to trample them.

She collided bonnet first with Mr. McCabe of all people.

"Mr. McCabe, I'm so sorry. I didn't see you there." She raised her hands out in front of her to steady herself and straightened her hat.

"It isn't a problem, Miss Wolcott. I can't imagine what your mind was on. This is a miserable selection of books." He frowned at the titles.

Seeing her chance, she dove headfirst. "I'm afraid I was lamenting poor Arthur again." She sighed melodramatically.

"I'm sorry. Arthur was so dear. I understand." He appeared sincere as he patted her arm. Maybe she had misjudged him? "If it makes you feel any better, Arthur died a hero. His services to the Crown were not in vain."

She placed her hand over her heart. "Oh, thank you, Mr. McCabe. That is gratifying to hear. I only wish I knew what he had done that was so honorable." She failed as an actress, but he didn't seem to notice.

He hesitated as if he considered his response. "Your brother caught the rats running through this city. Without him, the rebels would have a stronger foothold in New York. He doesn't get the credit for fear of rebels going after his family." He gave her a steady smile. "Be assured he's a hero among those who knew him."

She doubted their safety was the reason he hadn't gotten credit. Spying was a dishonorable profession. As for him being a hero, she knew at least those who killed him would disagree.

"Surely that would mean his death was avenged?"

Mr. McCabe appeared uncomfortable as he shifted from foot to foot. "Well, from what I know, there were three attackers and at least two of them are dead."

Improper indeed. He must have been putting on a show in front of Lord Carrington for her sake. Why hadn't Carrington told her this? What else was Carrington holding back?

She gasped for effect. "Three? How do you know?"

He lowered his voice. "I was in the group that hunted them down. They weren't too hard to find, since they were bragging about killing him at a tavern. It was an idiotic thing to do, considering soldiers occupy the city. I suppose they thought the Sons of Liberty were indestructible. Unfortunately, we only found two of them after they left the tavern. We think the other man fled."

"What happened to them?" Dread dropped her stomach like a stone.

"They're gone. That's all you need to know." So Mr. McCabe did have a limit.

"Gone?" She tightened her lips.

His voice went flat. "Dead."

"That's comforting, Mr. McCabe. You've set my mind at ease, though I do fear the third man may come for my family."

The news sent a bubbling itch across her skin. No closure came at hearing they had been dead all along. Her fingers twitched to squeeze their throats as she screamed into their faces. They had murdered her brother, and she needed to see them pay.

"He's long gone." His eyes shifted over the patrons of the bookstore, and he lowered his voice. "But do lock up as always."

She widened her eyes in alarm. "He sounds dangerous. I hope the military is aware of him."

"You can be sure they are, but I'm not privy to their information. We acted independently to hunt the killers down." Pride rang clear in his voice.

She raised a brow. "We?"

"Arthur's friends. We left Jeffrey out of the planning, since he was still in shock and none of us thought he would go along with it. He refused to let us tell him about it afterward. Fancy, his sister has a stronger stomach than he does."

She knew he meant that as a compliment to her, but it came out as an insult to Jeffrey. At least Mr. McCabe had trusted her to know what she could handle. Lord Carrington had only skimmed over the details. He'd given her a black-and-white sketch when she wanted a full-color portrait.

Her teeth set as she thanked him and exited the bookstore. The nerve of Lord Carrington. He had some explaining to do. She would strangle the information out of him if she had to. That was, if she could find him.

As luck would have it, she spotted the man who could make that happen. Mr. Travers walked past as she exited the bookstore. He was in uniform and accompanied by another officer, but he stopped to greet her, while his companion left before they could be introduced.

"I apologize for Captain Danvers. He's in a bit of a hurry, thinks he has a tail on Foxglove." He took her arm.

The color drained from her face. "Really?"

"He's the man replacing my brother. Took them forever to find someone willing to do the job. I think they were hoping Foxglove would just disappear." They walked to her carriage down the street where Hope waited.

"Are you a part of the investigation?"

Mr. Travers chuckled. "I'm just a secretary. As curious as I am about Foxglove, it's beyond my pay. I saw what the investigation did to William, and I'm not getting involved. Captain Danvers has taken on a daunting task."

"You don't think he will catch him?"

The merriment vanished from his face. "He may, but at what

cost? The price of failure is high, and success doesn't necessarily mean reward. The pressure alone is enough to kill a man."

Her face fell. "I didn't realize the stress was so great on your brother." An uneasy knot tied her stomach.

"William excels in high-stress situations, which is why he made an excellent officer. He got far enough into the investigation that he found it futile and recommended they don't expend valuable resources on the hunt for Foxglove. They originally agreed, but the incident at the Harmons' ball changed everything." He met her eyes. "It wasn't the only factor in his leaving here, but it was one of them."

"What do you mean?"

They reached her carriage before he responded, and she offered him a ride. He accepted with gratitude, and Hope scooted over to accommodate Delia. When they settled, he was ready with his response.

"Our mother desperately wanted him home. She doesn't understand why her firstborn would want to join the military. Anyway, she thought it was past time he remarried and had an heir. With so many men away at war, she thought it was a great opportunity for him to find a suitable wife. She's furious he came back here."

"Then why did he?" She frowned, irritation she couldn't place spread over her like a rash.

He gave her a lopsided grin. "Why do you think?"

She gazed out the window at the passing buildings. "He's insane if he likes this city."

"He loathes this city. I know he enjoys the countryside, but the city is a latrine."

She turned her slit eyes on him. "I'd imagine London would look much the same if an army occupied it." Their conversation was fast approaching the end of her tolerance.

"Indeed. I do feel the London balls resemble military occupation." He paused. "I don't fault William running away from them. This country is like a vacation from society."

She tsked. "Your poor mother." A vacation from society and a departure from civility.

He raised his brow. "Yes, poor Mother. Two dashing, unmarried sons escaped across an ocean."

Her brows drew together. "Well, your brother is ignoring me. He's going back on a promise he made me."

His eyes widened. "Is he? That's rather strange. I'll have to talk to him."

"Please do." She moved her gaze back to the window.

"I will certainly tell him. I'm going to meet with him soon, and it will be my pleasure to carry your message."

"You're a strange man," she said as they reached his stop.

"No, I just live for tormenting him." He stepped out, waving her goodbye.

Carrington was going back on his word to share information, and she wanted to hurt him any way she could. She would send Mr. Travers to him just to vex him. When Carrington came to her, she would berate him for withholding information.

Yet he didn't respond the way she thought he would. Instead, he ignored her further. He used her parents and Jeffrey as shields, and it frustrated her to no end. She waited to find a way to talk to him, but an opportunity never presented itself. Instead of giving up, she simply grew angrier as each day passed. Until she finally encountered him at the Rivertons' annual masquerade ball.

CHAPTER TWENTY

T HE RIVERTONS HELD a masquerade ball every winter, which allowed people to don costumes and masks while making fools of themselves. Mrs. Wolcott trusted Delia and Lynette to choose their outfits this year. A welcome change they celebrated between themselves.

Lynette went as Queen Mary, a curious choice that sent Delia into fits of laughter. Inspired by her decision, Delia dressed as Queen Elizabeth. They both wore big, flowing skirts, and crowns, but the similarities stopped there. Lynette opted for a red velvet dress in a modest cut. Delia chose a white dress with gold floral embroidery and a low, straight neckline that hinted at cleavage. They had to dust Delia's hair a redder hue, but the sisters' costumes suited them otherwise, and they had mock battles over custody of England while they were getting dressed. They finished off with matching demi masks.

The ballroom was an enchanted affair of glowing candles and garlands of pine and holly. The resulting scent and low lighting gave a mysterious outdoor feel to the gathering. The Rivertons themselves had decided to wear costumes from Greek mythology. Abigail made a stunning Aphrodite.

The hosts' costume choices, however, did not reflect the guests'. The only requirement for the Rivertons' ball was wearing a mask; each guest arrived with one or one was forced on them.

Delia's costume must have served her well, because she snuck up to Lord Carrington. His navy suit was formfitting, making it difficult to look away from his sculpted figure and commanding stance. His mask was a solid black velvet affair that only set off his midnight hair.

She caught her breath and greeted him in a haughty voice, "Papist, I will have your head. Denounce your false queen at once."

He jumped when he recognized her and did a poor job of hiding his laugh. "I'm no papist but a loyal subject of yours, Your Majesty." He bowed low and kissed her hand, lingering over her touch.

Her heart leaped in her chest. "I don't believe you. I hear you abandoned me and joined your Scottish kin. I ought to throw you in the Tower and cut off your head."

"You would like that, wouldn't you." He grinned below his mask.

"It's not what I like but what I must do for the sake of my country." She gave him a determined smile. She had waited long enough for updates.

"Then, if you must threaten me, I'll be forced to send my Scottish barbarian family to invade your country." He caught her stare.

Her answer was interrupted by a large man she thought was Jeffrey coming to spoil her fun, but on second glance, she recognized Mr. Bradshaw.

"Good evening, Your Majesty." Mr. Bradshaw bowed low. He gave Carrington a curt nod. "Would you do me the pleasure of the next dance?"

What could Mr. Bradshaw possibly want? If he had new information on Arthur's killers, she had to see it through. She knew she shouldn't, but the red hue ruining Carrington's face reminded her she would be safe enough on the dance floor.

"With pleasure, peasant." She took his offered arm. Carrington's mouth fell open, and she grinned at him. Mr. Bradshaw's eyes lit up through the slits in his mask, and he waved at Carrington as they left.

Mr. Bradshaw watched her. "My days have been empty without you and Jeffrey. Tell me, are you all well?"

"Indeed, we are." She paused, measuring his motives. "We've missed you too." Jeffrey hadn't been the same since Mr. Bradshaw had left their lives. He had lost an irretrievable sum gambling with officers without his friend to restrain him, and his clothes had grown tighter.

Mr. Bradshaw's solemn eyes followed her. "I've failed you both. You were two of my oldest and dearest friends, and I ruined it. I can't take back my actions, but I will try to make up for them if you allow me. Can you ever forgive me?"

She considered her words while studying his appearance. He did look much like her brother tonight. It was a reminder of how similar the men were. The almost brothers were broken apart.

"I think I have. You no longer make me want to hurl you across the room, so that must be in your favor."

He chuckled. "Indeed. I can't say I blame you if you hate me, but I regret the loss of your friendship. I've missed your family greatly. Do you think it's too late to start over?"

"It may be difficult. I think you'll have to talk to Jeffrey about this. You've caused me a great headache. If you can get it through your head I don't want to marry you, I may forgive the rest. It will take time, and I can't promise you anything." She lined up with him and waited for the dance to begin.

"I do apologize for my actions. I no longer consider marriage with you, and I made a deal with Carrington not to pursue the matter anyway." His voice lowered. "I want to make amends with you. My behavior haunts me."

They danced in silence for a time. She caught a glimpse of Carrington standing next to Jeffrey as they watched her with matching stony expressions. She gave them her widest grin, causing Jeffrey to tilt his head, and Carrington tightened his jaw. When the dance ended, Mr. Bradshaw led her back to them.

Jeffrey's eyes flashed toward Mr. Bradshaw. "I should kill you for approaching my sister."

"There's no need. We've called a parley." She released Mr. Bradshaw's arm. Carrington's eyes burned into the place where she had touched Mr. Bradshaw.

"Are you sure?" Jeffrey studied her face.

"I'm sure. Out of respect for our long friendship with Richard. It will mean nothing if we can't at least entertain forgiveness."

Carrington nearly choked when she called Mr. Bradshaw by his given name.

"Dee, you're a better man than me." Jeffrey's face lit up with a boyish grin. He turned to Mr. Bradshaw. "We have a lot to discuss, and I have no expectations, but I think Dee has a point. I've missed my best friend." Jeffrey nodded to Delia in gratitude, and he led Mr. Bradshaw away.

Carrington stepped in front of her. "Is that it?"

She placed her hands on her hips. "Is what it?"

"After all the trouble I took, you're going to run off and marry him anyway?"

"First of all, I never asked for your help. I do appreciate you getting him out of my way during his time of insanity, but I'm a believer in second chances and he has earned one. Secondly, who I marry is none of your business."

"Like hell." He grasped her arm and hauled her out of the ballroom.

"What are you doing? Let me go." She tugged at her arm, but his grip fastened tight.

He shut them into a cramped, dark room, which happened to be the Rivertons' study. At last she freed her arm. She stumbled over to the short window and pushed aside the curtains. A ray of light shot through the unsettled dust.

She brushed her hands down her skirts to straighten them, collecting her thoughts. "What is your problem?"

"You're my problem. A fine thank-you this is." His pupils

eclipsed his irises as he stared her down.

"Thank-you? I have thanked you." She stepped toward the door, but he placed his back firmly against it. She clenched her fists. "I have no intention of marrying Mr. Bradshaw. Ever."

He frowned down at her, and she raised her chin in defiance.

"This is about him and Jeffrey. What happened between them has never sat right with me. What is it to you, anyway?" Her eyes slit, and her fists spread to her sides. "You've been ignoring me. Not to mention going back on your promise."

"I was trying to do what you wanted, and no, I haven't given up my promise. What is it you think I do all day?"

She told him about her encounter with Mr. McCabe and what he had said. Her account left nothing out, and her frustration, fueled by the memory, altered her tone.

He listened, arms folded as he leaned against the door. When she finished, she was ready to take off his head.

"Why didn't you tell me?" she asked.

He frowned below his mask. "His story was exaggerated. It seemed like so much talk, but I learned much the same on my own. He got one thing wrong."

"What's that?"

"The third man is here in the city."

"Where? When were you planning to tell me this?" Or had he planned to tell her?

He hesitated a moment, drawing out the information as though he enjoyed it. "I talked to some men I served with, who said his name was Mr. Bryant Gilbert. They've been looking for him but without any enthusiasm."

Her mouth dropped open. "I know him. Or I used to know him, anyway. He went to Yale with Arthur." Mr. Gilbert had visited once on a school holiday, a joker with a wandering gaze.

"Then would you know where he is?"

She tapped a finger on her lower lip. "I haven't seen him since Arthur died, and I know nothing about his family."

"Then I'm ahead of you there. His family fled the city, but my friend tells me they've had sightings of him. At first, they thought he was a spy, but his activities would give him little information of value."

"Let's go, then. I can recognize him on sight."

He shook his head. "There's no way I'm taking you with me."

"Why not?" She moved to push past him.

He straightened his considerable height, a wall blocking her exit. "Because it's dangerous and you shouldn't be seen there."

"I can disguise myself just fine."

His face hardened. "I'm aware of your disguise, and I think you would fit right in. That's the problem."

Her eyes widened. Had he been in her things? "How could you possibly know about my disguises?"

"Your friend, Felix, is an interesting fellow. A smart kid. He's taken a liking to me."

"The traitor." She rubbed at her forehead. What else had he told him? "What do you mean, my fitting in is a problem?"

"One of the places he was spotted the most is a brothel."

She waved this away. "I'll be just fine." A rush of excitement went through her at the anticipation of investigating with Carrington. And to a brothel at that. What woman would pass up the chance to see what happened in the men's domain?

His forehead wrinkled as he raised his brows. "Have you ever been to a brothel?"

She wanted to lie, but he would sense it when they went. "Well... No... But it can't be that bad."

"It's worse than bad, and I won't have you dressed like a whore in a brothel."

"You won't have me go?" This man was impossible. Who was he to say where she could and could not go?

"A poor choice of words. I can't take a respectable woman into a brothel."

"Then take a man. A whore isn't my only disguise." She crossed her arms in stubborn determination.

"I'm not taking you." His words hissed through clenched teeth.

"If they're so bad, then why do you visit them?" Her voice sharpened as she channeled an impression of her mother.

"I don't visit them."

"Then you haven't been to one?" Her lips quivered together, holding in her laugh. "How would you know how bad they are?"

"No. Yes. Damn it."

In one swift movement, he grasped her shoulders and pushed her against the door, silencing her with a rough kiss. She placed her hands against his chest in a half-hearted protest, but he persisted. Her body melted into him, and she returned his kiss with equal urgency. He smiled into her lips.

He pulled her wrists above her head and pinned her to the door. She yelped in surprise, and the sound faded into his mouth. He transferred her wrists to one hand and used the other to cup her chin. He parted her lips with his tongue, possessing her.

She moaned into his mouth. Her body was a tingly, flaming mess, and she resented that he could so easily reduce her to this. She tugged at her hands, wanting to touch him, but he only gripped them tighter. His head drew back from hers as they caught their breath, and he searched her face.

When she made no further protest, he leaned in to nuzzle her neck, using his free hand to tilt her chin. He started behind her ear, trailing a line of fire down her skin, to her collarbone. She gasped, and he returned to her mouth, stealing her breath.

His palm slid to her chest, stroking her breast through the fabric. A whimpered plea poured from her, and he dropped her hands. His relentless mouth returned to her neck, alternating between soft kisses and frantic nips.

An inferno coursed between them as he pushed his hips into hers, his desire apparent through their clothes. He groaned into the sensitive flesh of her neck.

"Oh God." He breathed out the words.

"Carrington." She grasped his shoulder. "We can't do this."

He groaned and planted her more firmly against the door with his hips.

Her fingernails dug into his shoulder. "What if someone saw us leave? Or found us here? I need to go." Every inch of her craved him, but his kiss would have to suffice. She couldn't let him ruin her.

He sighed and stepped back from her.

"Thank you." She straightened her appearance as best she could without a mirror.

"No, I should apologize. I lost my head." He dragged his hand over his hair as if it would push the sense back into him.

"Does that mean you'll take me with you?"

He startled, taken off guard. He must have thought she had forgotten. "What? No, absolutely not."

She stepped up to him, pressing her breasts against his chest, and looked up at him with a coy smile. "Please."

He sputtered, using his hands to put her a safe distance away. "You're driving me mad."

"Then take me with you."

He moved farther into the room, avoiding her touch. "That will only make it worse. Why do you think I have been avoiding you? I can only guarantee your safety if I'm not in your presence."

"That's ridiculous and backward." She folded her arms under her breasts.

"Really? What do you think Jeffrey would do if he found out we were alone here?"

She sighed, dropping her hands. "I see your point. I better head back." She turned to the door, wishing she had forgotten her self-control for once.

"You go along first, and I'll follow in a few minutes. I need to dive into the snow." He scanned the room as if to distract himself.

"Oh, you poor thing."

"Don't make me run after you. I won't take responsibility for my actions when I get ahold of you. I don't care where I catch you either." His threat was solid steel. She believed every word of it.

She caught his gaze and blew him a kiss. Her lips tilted in a coy smile.

"Out, you hellion." His voice came out a low rumble from deep in his chest.

She burst into laughter and giggled through the hall. By the time she made the ballroom, she had settled into a wide smile. To her amazement and annoyance, nobody seemed to have noticed her absence. She wondered at what she might have gotten away with.

She headed to the refreshment table, where a footman handed her a glass of spiced cider, and she spotted some empty chairs. The current dance ended, and she made eye contact with Lynette before sitting down, a silent invitation.

Carrington entered the ballroom, back straight and proud. She frowned at him as he found her sitting alone and came to her side. Lynette and Mr. Travers beat him there, and Mr. Travers promptly asked her to dance. They left before his brother reached them.

"Are you having fun?" He winked through his mask.

Her face warmed, but she didn't know how he could know.

"Oh, it's written all over his face and a bit of yours as well." He guessed her thoughts as they lined up to dance.

"Do shut up."

He either didn't hear or ignored her words. "I thought I would make a nice distraction. Give you both a chance to look less obvious."

"Is that why you're tormenting me?" She fell into the steps as the dance started.

"Goodness, no. I'm tormenting him. We generally stay clear of each other's, er, interests, but there has been a time or two where we've stolen from each other as well." He gave her the Traverses' mischievous smile.

"Does that mean you plan to seduce me?"

The skin on the edge of his mask reddened. "No, but he

doesn't know that. I wouldn't want him to think he has succeeded. You see, it humbles him."

"How do you know he has succeeded?"

"More the better. He pranced around like a peacock when he came into the room though. Something has pleased him, and I want to be the one who splashes cold water on his face."

She puffed out a breath. "He can do that on his own."

Mr. Travers screwed up his face and tilted his head, making her giggle. "Oh, you are the very devil. I'm going to rub this in his face. Please, tell me more."

"I'm not telling you anything. Besides, there's nothing to tell."

A deep frown transformed the visible half of his face in disbelief.

"Fine." She couldn't believe she was doing this, but she had to get back at Carrington for keeping her out of her investigation. "If you want to get a rise out of him, then I suggest you mention my glove. Maybe ask how it's suiting him."

Her words coaxed his smile back. "Should I ask what it means?" He glanced over to where Carrington stood.

"No, I think it would be funnier if he had to explain it."

He patted her arm in agreement. When their dance ended, they moved apart, and true to his word, he headed directly to his brother. Delia made for Abigail, who sat along the side between dances.

She drew Abigail's attention to the Travers brothers, and she leaned into her friend's ear to speak over the din of the ballroom. "Watch." They stared together in anticipation.

Mr. Travers said something in an offhand way, and the visible half of Carrington's face bloomed bright red. Mr. Travers laughed and slapped his brother's shoulder, but instead of looking ashamed or amused, Carrington swung his fist into his brother's face.

Delia gasped, her lips frozen apart.

"Oh dear." Abigail turned an accusing stare on her. "Dee,

what did you do?"

"Mr. Travers was playing a joke on Lord Carrington. I had no idea he would react so violently. If I had known, I wouldn't have told him anything."

Abigail giggled. "I've always wanted men to come to blows over me. You're living out my dream, dear." She squeezed Delia's hand.

Mr. Travers's nose streamed blood. He had a wide grin on his face as he met her gaze and gave her a reassuring nod. Carrington caught the gesture and started toward her. Mr. Travers held his hand to his face as he left to clean up the blood.

"Abs, please don't leave me." She gripped her friend's arm to keep her in place.

"I wouldn't miss this for anything." Abigail shook with laughter.

To her luck and Abigail's disappointment, Jeffrey and Mr. Bradshaw intercepted Carrington on his way. He tried to get past them, but they resembled a fortress. His shoulders slumped as they spoke, and they ushered him away. The man had the worst luck.

"My, my, Dee. You'll have to tell me what dreadful things you've been up to."

"Of course." She loved Abigail like a sister, but there was no way she would tell anyone about what had happened in the Rivertons' study. Besides, it was so out of character nobody would believe her.

CHAPTER TWENTY-ONE

WHEREVER JEFFREY AND Mr. Bradshaw had taken Carrington, she didn't know, but she didn't see any of them for some time. Delia and Abigail danced with the usual good humor with whoever asked. After a half hour of waiting for Carrington's return, she took a break from dancing, and Abigail dropped down next to her.

"Don't you think Mr. Reyes is a fine dancer?" Abigail asked.

"Mr. Reyes? I don't think we've ever danced." Her gaze roamed the room for the thousandth time.

Abigail gave her a pointed look. "You really should instead of letting your shoe do all the dancing for you."

She looked down at her foot, which drummed a mindless beat into the floor. She stilled her leg with a steady hand and sighed.

"Do have some fun, Dee. They can't very well kill him, as much as they might want to. Your brother and Mr. Bradshaw are usually levelheaded enough when they aren't acting like children."

"Am I that transparent?" She released a long breath when Abigail nodded. "I would rather he didn't suffer on my account. It would be a pointless exercise. Besides, I already got him into a fight with his brother."

"Pointless? Why is that?"

"You know there couldn't be anything of it. We have nothing in common. He's titled and from one of those old English families. You and I, we're new money from unknown families."

Abigail's nose scrunched up. "I wouldn't say unknown. At least, not in New York. Besides, that didn't stop Mr. Chambers from proposing to Helen."

Her heart swelled at the thought of Helen married but shrank when she considered her own prospects. "That won't matter in England. A relationship with me would only end in my damaged reputation." And what was left of her heart.

"Then he has no business bothering you."

"Yes, I tried to tell him that. I'm afraid his reputation as a rake won't allow me to see this any other way." A prickling danced along her neck, and she glanced up to see Mr. Travers beside them.

"As you should." He nodded to them in turn. "I don't know what my brother is about, but I would stay clear of him. For a time, at least."

Delia's mouth dropped open. "He's your brother."

His voice lowered. "Exactly. You need to tell me what it was I just did to anger him so I can do it again in the future."

Delia's cheeks reddened, and she shifted in her seat.

Abigail tilted her head. "Yes, Dee. What did he do?"

She cleared her throat. "It's a long story, and I don't know if I could bear to repeat it. Suffice it to say, Mr. Travers, you mocked his lack of success with me. He may think you have had more…er…advancement than he has."

Mr. Travers beamed at her. "That's too perfect. I'd like to pay him back for that brotherly display of affection you witnessed. For now, Miss Riverton, I don't believe we've danced this evening. Shall we?" Abigail's eyes lit up as she took his arm, and Delia couldn't help but wonder if there was something between them.

She suspected her scowl frightened away any dance partners, which suited her mood. Her feet throbbed, and she didn't much feel like pretending her heavy costume could fly with her across the room. She wanted to escape and fling off her constricting clothes, but she had begged off too many events recently. Delia could sense her mother's impatience more every day, but how could she explain to her that she needed closure with Arthur's death before she could even consider getting married? She could be wrong, but she suspected poison making and knife throwing weren't ideal for family life.

She wished she could be content with knowing what had happened to Arthur and that most of his killers were dead. Instead, a nagging wound that she couldn't abandon or ignore eclipsed the memory of her brother. The more answers she found, the more persistent and festering the wound became.

Her thoughts were interrupted by the quick arrival of Abigail and Mr. Travers from their dance. She widened her eyes in question.

"We noticed them enter the ballroom and thought it crucial we return," Abigail explained, sitting down in her previous chair. Mr. Travers took Delia's other side. She rolled her eyes at their protective gesture. It was too much.

Delia held her breath and cast her gaze about the room. Sure enough, Jeffrey and Mr. Bradshaw with Carrington in between them advanced toward her. She clenched her teeth, not because the men were bleeding and bruised. They weren't. Not because they were scowling and throwing each other murderous glances. They hadn't been. No, they were laughing and appeared to enjoy one another's company.

Mr. Travers sighed beside her. "I don't even have the satisfaction of William getting injured. Of course not; my brother could charm the skirts off a nun."

Delia and Abigail let out a collective gasp.

"Well, it's true. It's no wonder he was able to escape our mother's matchmaking aspirations. I doubt I'll have the luxury. Maybe I'll get lucky and Washington will have me shot first."

"You have to leave the city to be shot by rebels. Unless you can die by paper cut." Carrington grinned at his brother, his arms around the shoulders of Jeffrey and Mr. Bradshaw.

Mr. Travers scowled. "Well, maybe I can have one of you gentlemen do the honors."

"Gladly." Carrington pulled away from the others.

"I said 'gentlemen,' William." Mr. Travers emphasized his brother's name.

Jeffrey and Mr. Bradshaw both shrugged, but Jeffrey gave a quick nod to Mr. Travers.

Delia lowered her brows at the men as she studied them. "What were you fools discussing?"

"I'm hurt, Dee. You don't believe we were sharing our intellectual pursuits?" Jeffrey gave her a playful frown.

"I know you weren't. Jeffrey, dear, you don't have any intellectual pursuits. I'm sure whatever you were talking about was far more entertaining than our conversation." Irritation crept into her voice.

Mr. Bradshaw proved the most accommodating. "Carrington, here, was telling us a story from jolly England. Nothing you need to hear."

Mr. Travers groaned. "If it's anything like the stories he usually tells, then it's unfit for a lady's ears. It's unfit for humanity's ears." He shot his brother a glare. "You're lucky Mother hasn't overheard any of your stories. She would disown you."

Abigail huffed. "You know, telling us we shouldn't hear these stories only makes us want to hear them more." Delia nodded in agreement.

"And they know that I, Richard, my father, and the three Riverton males will have their heads if they tell you." Jeffrey jabbed Carrington in the ribs, sending him into halted laughter.

"They're no fun, Dee." Abigail sighed and took Delia's arm.

"No fun at all." She stood with her friend and headed toward the ladies' retiring room.

Abigail spoke once they were out of earshot, "That was rather anticlimactic."

"At least nobody was hurt."

Abigail giggled. "Don't tell me you don't want to hit them yourself. All four of them need a sound beating."

"True. It would have been satisfying to see at least one black eye." She glanced over her shoulder to them and found Carrington in the hall, not far behind her and Abigail. Delia pretended not to notice him and continued, a little louder, "Yes, a black eye and maybe a broken nose. That Carrington has it coming to him."

Abigail continued to laugh, catching on. "Only? What about a broken arm? Or a bloody lip? I'll bet he would hate to be any less pretty." A groan came from behind them, but they ignored it. They hastened their footsteps.

"Pretty? Abs, you're mistaken. He's about as pretty as a bridge troll." They both erupted in laughter and fled for safety behind the closed door. Delia pictured the subject of their discussion, grasping out at them and cursing their insolence. The image at once transformed into him capturing her in a passionate embrace and his wicked lips exploring her in hungry abandon.

She took a quick breath.

"That was fun." Abigail tugged at her already perfect midnight hair.

"I'm afraid I'll pay for it." She grimaced at her reflection. The powder in her hair was nearly gone, and she appeared to be a deceased young Elizabeth. "I dread leaving this room."

Abigail tilted her head toward her. "I'll leave first and see if I can get him to invite me to dance." If anyone could drag Carrington off, it would be Abigail. "At least then I can get a better idea of what his intentions are."

"All right. I need a minute to straighten my skirts, anyway. I don't know what I thought when I chose this monstrosity."

"You thought you would look splendid, which you do." Abigail pecked Delia on the cheek and sauntered out of the room. Delia tugged at her dress for a few unsuccessful minutes before throwing up her hands. She peered out into the dim hall, seeing no one, and took a slow step out.

She let out an unladylike squeak and jerked in surprise when a hand grasped her shoulder a few feet from the door.

"A bridge troll?" A thin hint of amusement trickled through his tone.

"An angry, dirty bridge troll." Her heart lodged in her throat, beating in frenzied bursts. She pushed away his hand without turning around.

"I know I'm not a dirty bridge troll."

She peered back at him, favoring him with a deep frown. "Yes, and that's the problem. I imagine you eat small children and helpless women too."

His brows shot up. "Only helpless women." Oh dear, she'd walked right into that.

She gulped. "What do you want?"

"My brother has pointed out to me on more than one occasion that we haven't danced. I would like to remedy that." He bowed gracefully in front of her.

She eyed his offered hand. "What do you want?" she repeated.

"That is one thing, but I would also like to talk to you. Shall we?"

She hesitated a moment and took his hand. A current rushed through her body, and she gazed breathlessly into his eyes. He stiffened as though he had grown uncertain from her reluctance, but led her back to the ballroom.

They moved silently, each daring the other to be the first to speak. An unfamiliar nervousness thickened between them, which distracted from the conversation.

The music erupted like a challenge, and they moved together as though they were the only two people in the room. His possessive stare embraced and consumed her all at once. His attentions flared desire through her, and she cursed herself for leaving the study earlier.

His skill at dancing was not exaggerated. For them, it was an effortless sweep across the floor, and she forgot the press of her shoes and the weight of her costume. The heat ricocheting between them did nothing to clear her addled brain, and she surrendered to his guidance.

He flew her through the steps as though they were a part of him. Her breath caught when he added his own flourish to the moves, bringing her even closer than was proper. Touching her with a quick brush of his fingers whenever and wherever he got the chance. All the while, he devoured her with his eyes.

When the music ended, he bowed over her hand, calm and serious as ever. The fire that licked between them had melted her into putty. Her movements were languid as if he had made love to her in the middle of the Rivertons' dance floor.

She ached for more and allowed him to lead her into another dance. This time he was more deliberate, subdued. She held back a whimper of frustration.

He broke their charged silence. "What did you say to my brother?"

"You're going to lead with that?" She let out an exasperated breath. "Well, when you refused to let me accompany you to the brothel, I thought it best I move on to better prospects."

His brows shot up. "You did what?"

"Nothing, bridge troll."

"It isn't nothing." He stepped closer in their chaste dance. "Don't you know my brother's reputation?"

"Is it any worse than yours?" she countered as they separated briefly.

He paused until they rejoined. "Well, no."

"Then why should you be concerned?" He made little sense, and all she wanted to do was go back to the previous dance. Why did he have to ruin things by talking? They said women talked too much.

"Because I can account for my behavior, not his."

Except he didn't seem to have any more control over himself than he did his brother. The man had come close to ruining her on more than one occasion and relied solely on her judgment. Dancing with him had been a mistake. He didn't need help entertaining foolish notions about her.

"That makes perfect sense for you but not for me."

He let out a long breath. "This is going all wrong."

"What is? Surely this dance isn't as good as the last one, but it isn't a loss." With any luck, he would take the hint and let them enjoy the dance while it lasted.

"This whole conversation." He trapped himself in his dilemma, and each plunge of his shovel dug his grave.

She shot him a pinched look. "We've done enough of what you call talking unless you want to tell me you've changed your mind and want to take me with you."

"I'll never agree to that."

"Then the conversation is over." She focused her attention back on their dance.

"Can you just give me a chance for one second?"

She noted the plea in his voice and softened to him against her better judgment. "Fine. Talk. Get it over with so I can rest from this wretched costume."

"I can help you with that." His lip curled up, but she only glared at him. "All right, did I mention you're dressed as my favorite queen?"

"Oh, really? How droll." Boredom etched her expression as her attention shifted to the musicians. She darted her gaze back to him when she realized he grasped for words. He appeared more nervous than she had ever seen him. It was delightful.

"You aren't making this easy."

Her eyes widened at him. What had happened to the hedonist she had danced with minutes before? "Why should I?"

"I deserved that. I've been wondering." He paused, and then his words rushed on into a heap. "Against my better judgment, I've decided I would like to speak to your father." He studied the other dancers shyly, unaware of her glare. "I know it isn't what's expected of me or what my mother would want. Your family is respectable but not what I should marry into. It doesn't help that, no offense, your manners are atrocious."

She applied a false sweetness to her voice. "Let me guess, your family's title goes back to the reign of Queen Elizabeth and your mother wants you to wed a duke's daughter?"

His head bobbed at her words. "Then you understand." He finally turned and met her gaze, unprepared for her red-faced fury.

"Yes, I understand, and no, you may not visit him." Her voice fell quiet, but inside she screamed at him. Her fingers flexed in his grip, a silent plea to lash out.

"Why not? It's the proper thing to do."

She blinked at him in alarm and puzzlement. Could he believe what he was saying? "Are you mad? Do you think this is what women want to hear? I don't know what women are like in England, but if this is the kind of talk you get by with, then they're fools. Why don't you go home and let your mother wed you to some duke's daughter and spare me from your insufferable presence?" Her words left a pinch in her chest.

"You're refusing me?" His stare widened in disbelief, and he slackened his grip on her hand.

She snorted. "That's right. Amazing that such an ill-bred woman could refuse such a catch as you." The dance needed to end. Now.

She ignored people's stares as she extracted herself from the dance midstep, sending him off balance. She made it halfway down the carpeted hallway before he caught her by the wrist. Luckily, most of the guests were too far in their cups in the ballroom to notice. Otherwise, they were naked in the deserted passageway.

"I'm sorry. I worded that badly." Concern lined his eyes. "I can make whatever grand gesture you prefer and do any manner of convincing while I court you."

She gawked at him. She couldn't grasp what possessed the former captain. A nervous schoolboy had replaced him. He would have done fine if he had kept to the dancing.

She pulled her wrist away from him and stepped back. "You will not, and I have plenty of reasons not to wish to marry you." And the list seemed to grow every day.

"Such as?"

"For one, I like my atrocious manners, and I wouldn't trade anything to join London society. Secondly, I don't want to live in England and leave my family, so marriage to you would break my heart. Courting me would be pointless. Thirdly, I wouldn't be able to trust you to remain faithful, and I'll have nothing but a true marriage. Finally, you're demanding, possessive, and on the wrong side of this battle."

Charming, caring, tantalizing, achingly handsome.

"You can't deny there's something there," he said under his breath.

She thought back to their seductive kisses and the suggestive dance they had shared. Her face burned in shame, and her frustration only kindled the inferno inside her.

"I deny nothing, but that doesn't mean I need to act on it." Her words served to convince herself as much as him. It had all been harmless fun.

"You're willing to ignore that I've kept your secret and I haven't yet ruined you? How have I not earned your trust?"

"What do you mean, 'yet'?"

Carrington grasped her face with both hands and pulled her into an answering kiss. Delia squirmed at his attentions and gained enough room to push him away. She rewarded his efforts with a stinging slap to his grinning face.

He rubbed at the growing red spot on his cheek next to his wide grin. "That hurt." How was it he was enjoying this?

She planted a fist on her hip. "You're lucky I can barely move my legs. It's a pity I stopped carrying my knives."

"You have? I thought you merely liked me."

She frowned at his words. "It's not too late to hire a food taster. I do have access to most of your meals."

"Aw, but you would also have to poison the rest of your family."

He had her there. Instead of answering him, she turned away and headed back to the ball. He caught up to her and put her arm in his.

"What are you doing? I'll be ruined if I'm caught returning alone with you." She hissed the words through her teeth and attempted to pull out of his hold.

He held her arms firm. "More to my advantage." Would he force her hand now that she had refused him?

"You fool. I'll make you miserable until your dying day, which will not be far off." She stomped unsuccessfully at his dodging feet.

"Idle threats." He laughed, now leading her to the ballroom.

Her face flushed as she grew overheated, sweat trailing down her spine. The dance had been bad enough, not to mention that he had chased after her, but now he would be seen bringing her back from whatever imagined tryst they would be presumed to have had. She hoped for a fire or a hurricane, anything that would disrupt her descent into this mad future.

Relief came but not in any way she imagined.

As Delia and Carrington stepped into the ballroom side by side, all attention focused on a small circle on the far side of the room. A hushed murmur in the air accompanied the desperate sounds of Mrs. Riverton weeping into Mrs. Wolcott's embrace at the edge of the group.

Carrington turned to Delia with a questioning look.

"It wasn't me." Her brows creased together. "I know nothing about this."

Finding the safest avenue to join the group, Delia tugged Carrington toward Abigail and Lynette, not far off. He eyed the larger group and sighed, reluctantly allowing her to lead him where she wanted.

"What happened?" Delia whispered to her friend and sister. Both turned to her with wide eyes. Abigail smirked at Carrington's hold on her friend's arm but said nothing.

Lynette gave them a bored look and waved dismissively at the other group. "It's nothing. Where were you?"

Delia ignored the question. "It's not nothing. Why is Mrs. Riverton crying?"

Abigail caught her gaze. "Mother tends to overreact. She's had one too many ruined plans this year."

Carrington leaned forward into the group. "Then what's everyone staring at?"

"Someone put a foxglove in a vase. Just nonsense. A sick joke someone must be playing, since nobody is dead or dying." Lynette studied Delia with knowing eyes.

Abigail shook her head. "We don't know that. One of the victims wasn't discovered until the next day." She wasn't wrong, but the rest of them knew better. Lynette, Delia, and Carrington exchanged glances.

"Is everyone accounted for?" Carrington scanned the room again as though he would tally the guests.

"Yes, but one never knows if some unintended guest arrived. We're all wearing masks, of course." Abigail's voice filled with doubt.

Delia gave Abigail a patient half smile. "As long as nobody eats or drinks anything, I would imagine we're all perfectly safe. Wouldn't you agree, Lord Carrington?"

He cleared his throat. "Yes, of course. Unless Foxglove used a less potent version of his poison; then we may not know for some time." She glared at him, and he shrugged back. "I'm not going to lighten the possible meaning of this flower. From what you've all witnessed—" He paused to stare at her. "—I wouldn't put anything past Foxglove."

"That's just what I was telling my husband." Mrs. Willoughby stepped into their tight group. All interesting conversation died at her arrival. "I said, 'Mr. Willoughby, that Foxglove will be the death of us all. Never mind the soldiers surround us. He has no mercy, mark my words.'"

Carrington gave the woman a pitying look and patted Delia's arm. Mrs. Willoughby caught the gesture, and her eyes widened. That couldn't be a good thing. He was as good as courting Delia now, with or without her say.

"Quite without mercy, Mrs. Willoughby. I would bet no man can capture him while he poisons their hearts." Carrington's voice turned grave, his eyes alight with the mischief vacant from his face.

"I do believe you were quite close, Lord Carrington." No doubt Mrs. Willoughby attempted to encourage his usual reluctant talk.

"I can only hope I've made some advancement of the cause. It would wound me if I haven't made some progress where other men have failed." He gave Delia a meaningful look, a hint of his intentions to come.

"And continue to fail." Lynette gave him a half smile.

His gaze flickered over Delia's features. "Indeed. Perhaps this is another man's battle."

Delia gave away nothing with her blank expression. Internally, she couldn't help but laugh at his jokes.

Oblivious, Mrs. Willoughby grasped at his attention. "Lord Carrington, we all know you were the best man for the job. Whyever would you quit?"

"Quit? I never quit. I merely decided what was more important to me, my sanity or my pride." Carrington grew quiet as he gazed off.

Delia bit her lip to ward off a laugh. "And which won?"

"Hmm…?" He seemed lost in thought.

"I said, which was more important to you?"

He gave her a worn look. "Oh, damned if I know. I seem to be losing both at the moment."

"Well, then." Mrs. Willoughby peered over her shoulder. "I think I hear Mrs. Perry calling me." Delia thanked whatever gods existed as Mrs. Willoughby made her escape from their group. The woman must have grown bored with the conversation, since

Carrington wasn't giving anything away.

Abigail heaved a sigh. "At last she's gone." She looked to Carrington and then Delia. "Mind telling us what that was about?" She didn't get her answers, because Jeffrey and Mr. Bradshaw joined them.

"I thought she would never leave." Jeffrey indicated with a tilt to his head where Mrs. Willoughby had gone. "Anyway, we need to be off. That flower killed no one but this party. Mother is staying behind to comfort Mrs. Riverton." Jeffrey looked to Abigail in sympathy.

"All right, I'll go see to her." Abigail hugged Delia and Lynette before giving the men a thin-lipped stare. She turned back to Delia. "You'll fill me in?" At Delia's nod, Abigail humphed and left to find her mother.

"I better go with her. Maybe I can help Mother leave." Lynette walked away without saying goodbye. Delia stared after her sister longingly.

"Your Majesty, I would be happy to escort you home." Lord Carrington bowed over her hand.

Jeffrey groaned. "You don't need to inflate her vanity any more than she already has."

She narrowed her eyes at Jeffrey as Carrington continued over her hand. "He's merely acknowledging my superiority as you should too, peasant."

Mr. Bradshaw laughed and bowed to her, pushing the other man aside. Carrington grunted as he nearly toppled over.

Carrington straightened and offered to escort Delia. Instead, she took Jeffrey's arm and turned up her nose dramatically at Carrington and Mr. Bradshaw.

She couldn't imagine what had happened with the three men to create such a fraternal bond among them, but she wasn't sure she liked it any more than when they'd been enemies. It reminded her of what she had read about wolf packs. An apt description of their behavior. She would have been amused by it if she didn't believe she was the sheep.

CHAPTER TWENTY-TWO

T HE DAY AFTER the ball, Delia's body ached in protest from carrying around her costume. Felix, Hope, and Lynette all swore they had nothing to do with placing the foxglove. It must have been some cruel joke. At least nobody had been found dead.

She meant to go with Carrington whether or not he gave his permission. What was he going to do? Lock her up? Nobody would allow that. Plus, she had Hope and Felix to help her.

For now, she would bide her time. It was unlikely Carrington planned to visit the brothel during the day. After spending the morning avoiding him, she idled away in the library. A snowstorm had raged since this morning, and she couldn't even consider leaving the house.

She was left with books or needlework, and she wasn't about to do anything constructive today. Lynette was in a cheerful mood, and she took up her needlework in the library while Delia lounged on a chaise, reading the latest installment in the series Abigail had loaned her. She should stop reading these books. They were awful but so delicious.

Their mother had returned late last night. Today she complained of a headache and stayed in bed, relieving them of her presence. Even their father was home, but he'd barricaded himself in his study.

Jeffrey was the first to break their peace, creating all the noise of a giant bear. She scowled at him from over the top of her book but said nothing, curling her legs under herself on her seat.

"What are you reading?" Jeffrey asked without much interest as Carrington opened the library door. Pierre rushed in from Carrington's side and settled at Lynette's feet.

"A novel from Abigail."

"Another? Why do you read such drivel?" He stretched out on the seat next to Lynette, across from Delia. Why did he need to ruin their peace?

"I like this drivel." She blinked down at the book. "At least, I think I like it."

"You read so much of it you must." Jeffrey motioned for Carrington to sit.

"I don't read nearly that many. This is the..." Delia counted on her fingers and frowned, "...twelfth book? My, I must like them."

"What are they about?" Carrington took Jeffrey's other side.

"You don't want to know." Jeffrey rolled his eyes. "It's always about a kidnapping or a robbery, and then some foolish woman falls for the villain."

Carrington raised his brows at Delia.

"It's not always about a kidnapping or a robbery, and the women aren't foolish. They're brave and caring, unlike you." She cast a sharp glare at Jeffrey.

Jeffrey returned her look, blinking rapidly. "Then, pray tell, what is your book about?"

She drew herself up and hardened her spine. "A kidnapping, but that's not what they're all about."

"I swear, if there's any truth to those books of yours, then all of England must be awash in crime and prompt marriages." Jeffrey smirked, leaning back and crossing his legs.

"They take place in England?" Humor danced in Carrington's eyes.

She hid her face in her book and attempted to ignore them.

"Do they, Dee?" Jeffrey asked, laughter coloring his tone.

"Not all of them. One was in Scotland." Her answer was muffled in the book's pages.

Carrington and Jeffrey fell silent, and suddenly they both erupted in full-body laughter. She lowered her book, closing it on her bookmark. She looked away from them, refusing to accept her embarrassment.

"Netty, I think I'll ring for some refreshments. The only thing this book needs is some warm chocolate and pastries." Lynette humored her, smiling and nodding her agreement. Delia pulled the bell to call for their snack.

"Wonderful." Jeffrey rubbed his hands together.

Delia turned a scowl on him. "You don't get any." Pierre barked in agreement.

"What about Carrington?" Lynette asked.

"He only gets some because he's a guest and Pierre likes him." Delia gave Carrington a faint smile. A small olive branch to encourage answers.

Jeffrey crossed his arms. "Really? He's as bad as I am. All right, I know when I'm not wanted. I'll see to my food." He got up and stalked out of the room, Pierre growling as he passed.

Lynette patted Pierre's head. "Good dog."

"We all know who the man of the house is. Jeffrey should learn that." Delia leaned in to scratch behind Pierre's ears.

Lynette nodded, an exaggerated lift and drop of her head. "I don't know what is taking them so long. I'm going to see about our chocolate and maybe some biscuits."

"Don't forget lemon tarts," Delia called after her. Lynette waved her hand back at her as she shut the door behind her.

Carrington stared after Lynette, a smile sliding over his face. "You seem to have a great fondness for lemon tarts."

"And chocolate."

"Is that so?"

"There is just something so comforting and rich about chocolate. When it's just the right temperature, it's like a caressing hand soothing away your troubles in a lover's embrace." She studied him with lowered lashes.

"Yes?" He moved to Lynette's vacant chair, which was closest to her chaise. He leaned toward her.

"Of course." She inched away from him. "Chocolate and lemon tarts solve all worldly problems."

"Surely not all problems?" He favored her with that mischievous grin that caught her breath.

"All problems." Her voice held firm, but laughter bubbled inside her. "Only tea has the same potential."

"Then it's a shame the rebels destroyed so much."

"I agree. If only something less enjoyable were taxed, such as brothers or men's shirts." She bit her lip.

"You don't think men's shirts are useful?" His eyes crinkled at the corners as he chuckled at her fancies.

"Oh, I'm sure they're useful. To the men."

"It's a shame your sister's coming back." He reached out for her arm.

"Is she? I'm not so sure." She dodged his hand. "When do you plan to go to the brothel?"

He dropped his arm and fell still at her unexpected change of subject. "Why?"

So I can follow you, she wanted to say. "I would like to know if you find him."

"You'll be the first to know."

She huffed. "Then you're just going to make me wait? That's rather rude."

"It is, isn't it?"

Her mouth dropped open. "This is important to me."

"You think you're not important to me?"

"No, I think you want an excuse to get into my bed. You talk about being proper and acting honorably, but you contradict yourself with your actions and words. When it comes down to it, how am I to know if you'll run back to jolly England and forget I exist? I would just be another conquest of yours. You may not have anything to lose, but I do."

"What about your behavior?" His voice dropped to a low growl.

She averted her eyes. "Mine? I know there isn't much excuse for my flirting, but that's all it is. Your conclusions are imaginary."

He analyzed her with his gaze, which pierced her until she was transparent. "I don't believe you for a second."

Her skin blazed. "Believe what you want. I'm done discussing this." She rose to her feet. She would find somewhere else to read.

"Fine. Next time you're worried about what you have to lose, consider the decisions you made as Foxglove."

Her feet locked in place, and she whipped her head toward him. "Foxglove is completely different. I was helping people."

"Perhaps at first, but in the end, you may have destroyed more lives than you saved." His eyes shone with fury and disappointment.

She dropped back onto her sofa. "That can't be true. The New Yorkers I saved would disagree with you." She stared forward, away from his wounding glare.

"New Yorkers, yes. Did you stop and think about the soldiers whose families suffered? You've made many a widow and orphan."

Was this truly what he thought of her? Surely the men she had killed had known what they'd been getting into? But their families, had they a choice? She pictured a wife waiting by a window for any chance at seeing her husband's return, not knowing he would never come and she would be destitute. The image refocused, casting Delia as the widow, gazing grief-stricken at a portrait of Carrington. She halted the line of thought. She already fought the tears that swam across her cheeks.

"I'm sorry, Delia. I didn't mean to upset you. You're an amazing, caring woman, and I know the deaths you caused torment you." Carrington forced his bulk next to her. "I'm sure you're aware I've killed men in battle. It's never easy. War is never easy."

She looked at him then as the tears blurred her vision. He put his arm around her shoulders and squeezed. The small gesture took the sting out of his chiding words.

"As much trouble as the soldiers cause in this city, and as much as it may seem that killing them will help to end this war, they're still human beings."

She brushed away a tear from her cheek. "Then why did you do it?"

"I didn't. Not after my first battle. I couldn't stomach what we were doing. Why do you think I was reassigned? I know you didn't always see the aftermath of your work, but I experienced every shot I made and every wound I inflicted. Battle is chaos. You have to live outside your body to come out of it sane. Unfortunately, I didn't learn that early enough. Most of the men here are doing it for paychecks, but I'm one of the few who saw it as an honor. I can tell you now. There's no honor in the slaughter of war."

Maybe he understood her more than she thought.

They remained silent for a time aside from her sniffles as she leaned into his chest and inhaled the scent of him. She needed this, needed him. He offered a sanctuary others lacked. His body remained still except for the occasional gentle squeeze of her shoulders.

She didn't want to move, didn't want to think, but their conversation had awoken guilt she hadn't realized she possessed. She had lied to convince herself that what she was doing was right, was just.

She wouldn't have much of an impact on the overall outcome of the war. Thousands of men were dead or dying. Some not from battle but from cold and disease. She was a tiny player on a chessboard of carnage.

Beneath the guilt and the regret, anger tugged at her senses. Arthur was just a number to these men. He was a man who had betrayed his peers, but he was still a man, and he deserved the same justice all men deserved.

She pulled back from Carrington. "What about Arthur?"

He studied her face, gauging the meaning of her words. "I will find Bryant Gilbert." He leaned down to kiss her forehead.

"We'll find him." She met his gaze. "And I'll kill him."

Concern shone in his eyes. "Are you sure?"

"I must finish this. Arthur demands justice."

"All right." He sighed, and his face grew worn. "If you think it will help you find closure."

After all their arguing, that was all it had taken. She thought she knew him, but at every corner, he revealed something that intrigued her. He was like a spring flower full of hidden blooms.

"Thank you." She tilted her head up to show her appreciation, but they jerked apart with the click of the door latch.

Jeffrey pushed the door wide. "What idiot left the two of you alone?"

"You did." Carrington twisted his face up, giving an impression of annoyance and amusement.

"Lynette was here when I left." Of course, Lynette never stayed anywhere long. His watch seemed to fail when he needed it most.

"She doesn't count."

Delia let her shoulders drop. Carrington's inviting presence called her to rest, but she didn't comply.

Jeffrey ventured into the room. "I suppose you're right."

"And I thank you." Carrington's eyes gleamed.

Her brother threw him a hard stare. "I suggest you move a safe distance from my sister before I disembowel you." He pointed at Carrington's chest.

Carrington shielded it with his hands and moved to where Lynette had been seated.

"Not nearly as far as I'd like, but it will do." Jeffrey's eyes fell on Delia's face. "Have you been crying? Why has she been crying? What did you do?" He turned back to Carrington. "Explain yourself."

"It wasn't him." She struggled to find a plausible explanation. "I'm just overemotional."

"Overemotional? I don't believe you. Why are you defending him?"

"You're the one that says I cry too much." Maybe he would believe her courses had started. "I just hate being trapped in this house all day."

"Fortunately for you, the snow has stopped, and most of it didn't stick. Let me guess: he sought to comfort you in your emotional state and then he was going to use that to his advantage to ravish you?"

"Of course not."

His sharp stare bored into Carrington. "Let him talk. I'm sure that's just what was happening before I returned. As much as you may think I am, I'm no fool. I've used that trick myself. I should call you out."

Carrington sat up and leaned toward her, his hands resting on his knees. "Delia, did you believe I was going to take advantage of you at any time?"

Clearly he'd had some intentions after Lynette had left the room, but he hadn't acted on them. True, he must have known they would be interrupted, but this was nothing like the kissing and touching she had allowed while her mind had been more in order. He'd had ample opportunity.

She shook her head. Carrington nodded to her and turned to Jeffrey. "As you can see, she is unoffended and unharmed."

Jeffrey glanced between them with wide eyes. "It's Delia now?"

In her muddled state, she had failed to notice Carrington using her given name. On his lips, her name sounded natural, comfortable. She considered him among her friends now, as strange as it was. Why shouldn't he use her name?

Carrington's face held a question, but she only shrugged at Jeffrey. The gesture seemed to irritate her brother further. He grunted, grasped Carrington by his shirt, and jerked him to his feet.

"What are you doing?" she squeaked.

Jeffrey ignored her. "We need to talk." He fists still clenched the other man's shirt.

"Then talk." Carrington nearly spit in Jeffrey's close face.

"Alone."

"Why?" She glanced between them. "Jeffrey, let him go." They both ignored her protests. Their gazes waged a battle she could not join.

"Fine." Carrington pried Jeffrey's hands from his shirt. Seeing she had no intention of leaving, Jeffrey led Carrington to the door. When they noticed her following, Carrington stopped and took her hand.

Carrington's tone lowered. "It's nothing we haven't already discussed before, and I'm still living. This time will be no different."

"Discussed before?" Her voice rose as her eyes darted to Jeffrey.

"Yes, your brother likes to scare your suitors off."

She frowned at him. "Of course he does."

Carrington shook his head.

"What did he do?"

"He's been trying to get me to stand aside since I met him. It's no wonder you don't have any serious suitors other than Mr. Bradshaw."

"Why?" An iron bolt shot through her chest as she turned on her brother.

"He's only going to hurt you." Jeffrey shifted under her stare. "He will run home after he ruins you. I can't let that happen."

Her jaw went slack as she internalized the full weight of his actions. "Can't I judge that for myself? Haven't you already done enough to coddle me? I could have been married years ago, before this war even happened." Before she had become Foxglove and pushed aside marriage herself. She would have avoided helping the patriots then, since family meant everything to her.

She had lost Arthur, and Jeffrey would keep her from having a family of her own in the future.

"None of them were right for you."

She ached to lash out at him, to wound him in some way for taking control of her future. "That's my choice. Of course, I must consult Mother and Father, but you're stealing the most major decision of my life away from me."

Jeffrey said nothing. No explanations could excuse his behavior in her mind.

"It's one of the reasons I returned to England," Carrington began, but Delia hushed him.

She centered her fury on Jeffrey. "Get out." He hesitated to leave, and she continued, "I'm going to talk to Lord Carrington for a moment. You wait in the hall until I'm finished."

When Jeffrey tried to protest, she held up her hand. "You're not Father. You will not argue, you will not threaten, and you will not continue this intrusion into my life. Get out, and I will send Carrington to you when I'm done."

Jeffrey kept his peace, hanging his head as the door shut behind him. It was the only thing that kept her from physically harming him. He was almost twice her size, but she wasn't afraid to throttle him anyway.

Carrington chuckled, a broad grin on his face.

She raised an accusing brow at him. "Is this amusing to you?"

"More arousing, but I see your point." He cleared his throat and straightened his face.

"You were saying?"

"Your brother and Mr. Bradshaw, might I add, saw my interest in you before I knew I had any. I think it's one of the things that gave Mr. Bradshaw the final push he needed to try to get you to marry him. They both saw me as a threat but for different reasons."

"You let them scare you off?" It seemed an outlandish idea, since he had taken such aggressive actions toward them recently.

His voice fell to a hush. "It wasn't just that. When I first learned about Foxglove from Mr. Bradshaw, I couldn't believe it. The more I considered it, the more likely it seemed. Imagine my humiliation and distress when I found out the woman I longed for was also the killer I sought. I would go out to hunt an unknown by day and come back to sleep feet away from her. In the end, I decided I had to flee like the coward I am."

"Then why did you bother to come back?"

He combed a hand through his hair. "My mother was over-joyed when I returned. She dragged me along to every party and dinner in London. It became obvious I wasn't going to find a wife. I was just going through the motions." He looked into her face, and his intent eyes settled on hers.

"Oh?" Her breath caught as she listened, not daring to hope.

"You see, every dance and conversation I had was never enough. My mother nearly arranged a marriage for me when I told her I was uninterested in her choices. She's much like your mother in that respect. Luckily, my father had my best interests at heart. I told him everything, and he left it up to me to decide who I would marry."

Her voice became a breathy whisper. "What was it you told him?" Her heartbeat pounded louder than her words.

He smiled, a bit self-consciously. It was an unfamiliar look from him, and it made her uncomfortable to see him less confident. She took his hand to reassure him, and he squeezed it.

"I told him about you. Not about Foxglove but about the woman whose family I had stayed with during my time here. I told him about how I wasn't ready to give you up. My father doesn't care much for titles or lineages. My mother's line is fairly new by anyone's standards, though sometimes she forgets that. He agreed I should return and see if anything came of it."

He raised her hand to his mouth to kiss her wrist, a favorite spot it seemed. The brush of his lips sent a shiver up her arm and down her spine.

"I was preparing to leave when I received Hugh's letter. I can't tell you how frantic I was to get back here. In my mind, you were hanging from a scaffold. Sometimes you were bleeding in the streets. There you were dead or dying, and I was weeks away from you. It was the longest, most terrifying trip I've ever experienced. When I arrived and found out one of my nightmares came true, I nearly died from the shock."

"How did you even find out it was in the street?" Could nobody keep a secret in this house?

"When my ship landed, I came directly here. Nobody would let me in to see you, and I nearly beat the reason out of Jeffrey. He tried to lie to me at first. I'm amazed anyone believed you could accidentally stab yourself with your mirror. He told me you were fully recovered but still weak. It was the only news that kept me from pounding down your door like a crazed animal."

"That was you?"

She grew dazed. Jeffrey had said it was the wind, but Carrington had come to call. He really did care for her and for so long. All this time she thought he only wanted her in bed. He had spoken to his father about her, across the ocean.

"Yes. You can ask Hugh. It took him some persuading and a fair bit of alcohol to calm me."

A grin played over her lips. "I think I would have rather liked to see you break down the door. It would have been wonderful entertainment in the dull state I was in."

He gave her a faint smile and kissed her wrist again, lingering. "I will keep that in mind," he said into her skin. He peeked up at her. "Are you ready to let me court you? You're beautiful, and when you open your mouth, you drive me out of my mind. For some reason, the madness only draws me closer. I only ask for you to give me some chance. Is there no hope for me?"

"Lord Carrington—"

"No, call me William."

"Lord Carrington." She emphasized his title. "As far as I can tell, you're already courting me and have been for some time. You'll have to talk to my father and make peace with my brother. As much as my brother aggravates me, he's still important to me, and I don't want to marry anyone who can't get along with my family."

"William." He pulled her closer.

"You had better go. You have a great deal of work to do. Don't forget about Mr. Gilbert."

"How could I possibly forget?" He nuzzled her neck. She knew she should push him away or, better yet, slap him again, but she tilted into him instead. This couldn't continue.

Her confident voice distorted into a squeak. "You know, Jeffrey is right outside the door. Go meet your doom."

He inhaled the scent of her hair, sending sparks down her neck before moving to her ear and whispering, "I will make you scream my name."

Just then, the door latch clicked, the worst sound she could imagine. This time, Carrington didn't move away. She didn't want him to.

Jeffrey peered in. "I heard my name." His eyes grew to twice their size when he saw them. "What's going on? I've waited long enough."

"I was just telling your sister what I was going to—" Carrington choked on his words as her elbow slammed into his stomach. A playful spark shone in his eyes, and he leaned into her ear. "This isn't over."

Carrington straightened his back and turned to Jeffrey. "Is your father still in?"

Jeffrey's stony face matched his hardened voice. "He's in his study."

"Wonderful. Shall we?" Not waiting for an answer, Carrington moved to the door. Jeffrey gave a resigned nod to his back and followed him out.

She shivered at the loss of his embrace. He had sent her through a breathtaking whirlwind, and she no longer knew up from down. She had no self-control around him, no possibility of refusing his advances. Her foolish needs had taken over. Why had she agreed? The man must have charmed her out of her senses.

CHAPTER TWENTY-THREE

DELIA DIDN'T KNOW what she was doing. She had been attracted to Carrington from the beginning, as had half the women in New York and some of the men, but she had trouble imagining anything coming of it. She still couldn't see herself moving to England, away from everything she knew and loved.

It had started as a game of sorts but had quickly gone beyond her control. There was truth to their jokes and lies to her denials. Could she go into a marriage with their opposing loyalties? How did Carrington overlook their differences?

As she considered her possibilities, her mother entered the room in a whirl of excitement. Mrs. Wolcott dragged Delia to sit next to her on the sofa. She held both Delia's hands in an unusual display of affection.

"Your father informed me of Lord Carrington's intentions toward you." Her mother gave her a pleased smile. That was fast. She must have been in the room or listening at the door. "You will, of course, accept him. Your father would have you play this out, but it has become obvious you may not get another offer."

Her mother frowned. "You've already thrown away your chances with Mr. Bradshaw. I still haven't figured out why he gave up on you, but I imagine it was something you did to discourage him. You will not make the same mistake with Lord Carrington. I forbid it."

Delia removed her hands from her mother's grasp and dropped her clenched fists to her sides. She couldn't form the words to speak, and her mother barely noticed the change. She had been pushed and pulled from all sides today. Jeffrey would make her a nun, and her mother would force her into a hurried marriage. She was done being under their thumbs.

"Goodness knows what you did to attract such a good match. You have your father to thank for inviting Lord Carrington to stay with us." Her mother took a deep breath. "Now then, I have decided there are several scenarios we may use to ensure he does not change his mind."

"Are you suggesting I trap him into marriage?" Delia's fists shook at her sides. Of all the controlling schemes, this was her mother's worst.

"Trap him? He already wants to marry you. We would merely be steadying his course."

"I can't agree to that."

Mrs. Wolcott gave her a puzzled frown. "Agree to what?"

"Any of it. I haven't decided if I wish to marry him, and if he wants to back out, then that is his decision. There will be no forcing either of us. If I chose to marry him, it will be because I have deemed it the best choice for my future happiness."

"You can't be serious." Her mother studied her with her lips stretched in a thin line. "Marriage isn't about happiness. It's about safety and starting a family. You don't have the luxury of choice here. Turn this one away and you will face a future of childless spinsterhood."

Nothing would convince her she should marry for the sake of marriage. As much as she wanted a family, her children would be miserable with her. "Then so be it." Delia found her feet and bolted out of the library.

"If you ignore my warnings, I will never speak to you again. Delia Madeline Wolcott, you will be dead to me!" her mother shouted after her.

"Good!" she shouted back as she slammed the library door

behind her.

She stomped back to her room. Her first urge was to seek out Carrington to refuse him and defy her mother, but she would never forgive herself for such a move. It wasn't Carrington's fault her mother meddled in their lives.

In all other decisions, Delia had never openly questioned or refused her mother's whim, but her marriage would send a ripple effect throughout her life, and she refused to let anyone steal that.

AFTER TAKING DINNER in her room, Delia sat on the edge of her bed, listening to the room next door. Carrington had returned earlier, presumably to sleep, but she needed to be ready in case he decided to hunt down Gilbert.

Felix had obliged her wishes and found the men's clothes she now wore, all-black attire from the slightly loose coat to the snug, formfitting breeches. Felix had even included a new set of knives that she now carried on her belt. Hope had tied her hair up to fit under her new cocked hat.

As she waited in the dark, she held her breath, allowing only for the controlled intake of air. Her body ached of wanting to lie back, but she ignored the pleas and shifted her weight to relieve her discomfort.

At last, just after one in the morning, came the soft sound of his door clicking shut. Ever the people pleaser, Carrington was heading out tonight. He must not have confidence in their relationship.

A faint shuffle of feet settled in front of her door, as though he listened.

After an excruciating period that seemed to last forever, the quiet steps retreated. He must have decided she was asleep. At last she was able to relieve herself with the air she so desperately wanted. She allowed several minutes to pass before creeping to the door to peer into the empty hallway.

She entered the street through the back door in the kitchen and scanned the road to the east. The moon gave off just enough light for her to make out any figures lurking along the way, though it would be challenging to identify anyone's features. Her breath momentarily obstructed her view as she scanned her path.

The way clear, she took the opportunity to sprint forward across the mud-colored snow. She halted at the first intersection and surveyed the area. Families slept in the homes lining her way, and the only sound came from her rapid heartbeat.

Reassured of his absence, she repeated the process three more times before she neared a shadier part of town where drunks teetered through the street in the now frequent lights. Laughter seemed to echo over her as she progressed.

She spotted him then.

He was almost unrecognizable in his worn clothes. However, she could not mistake that familiar, self-assured gait. She smiled to herself and walked forward with more determination.

No longer alone on the street, she would be unrecognizable among the young men. If Carrington sought her face there, she had worse problems than his discovering her. His suspicious nature would leave her no freedom.

Carrington made an unexpected turn into an alleyway, and she hesitated before following him. Her reluctance proved beneficial when she heard his voice.

"Are you ready?"

"I've been ready my whole life. What took you so long?" came a familiar male voice that she couldn't place.

"I wanted to make sure Delia had gone to sleep," Carrington replied.

"It's Delia now?"

"Can we do this later?"

"Fine. Do I have time to enjoy the establishment's services?"

Carrington grunted. "Do you really want to? The whole city is a disease." Well, at least she knew he had reservations about using brothels.

"Has that stopped us before?"

She flinched. The other man must be his brother. A mark against them both.

"No, but it's different now."

"Good God, you aren't even married and she's already got you on a leash." Mr. Travers sounded outraged.

"It isn't like that at all. I've lost all interest in other women."

She couldn't help but sigh with relief. Maybe she could trust him. He wouldn't lie about that to his brother, would he?

"I can't say I blame you. What about other men?" Amusement trickled through Mr. Travers's voice.

"No one, and you keep your whoresome hands to yourself." The last part came out a low growl.

"What about my mouth?"

She slapped a hand over her gasp.

"Do I need to thrash you before we've even started?"

Yes, please do get on with it. The cold had caught up to her, and she shivered from standing in place.

"You're touchy this evening. Come to think of it, you've been touchy since your ship landed. Could it be you're questioning your chances?"

An annoyed grunt answered, presumably from Carrington.

"You are. How splendid. I've never known you to lose confidence in a conquest."

"This isn't a conquest. Now stop wasting valuable time. I still have my hopes set on a nap before breakfast."

Mr. Travers must have made some inaudible response, because footsteps shuffled toward her hiding spot. With a frantic dash, she hid in a darkened stairwell that led to somebody's basement. She pressed into the shadows as they came out of the alley.

They gave no indication of noticing her as they passed, and she watched as they made their way further east. She waited for them to make it halfway down the street and followed their lead.

The streets became crowded with off-duty soldiers and loud laughter. It made her task a challenge, and she pushed ahead to keep up with them. They passed by worn taverns and cramped lodgings, never stopping but allowing the clinks and shouts to fade in and out.

All at once, Carrington and Mr. Travers disappeared.

No brothel came into view, only darkened, boarded-up buildings interrupting the well-lit nighttime entertainment. She turned in place, at a loss for where they could have gone. At last, she sighed and continued east, hoping she hadn't completely lost them.

As she took her first steps, her feet slid out from under her. A yelp jumped from her throat as she smacked her bottom on the stone ground. Her hands shot back and caught her descent just in time to save her head, scraping her palms in fire.

Two dark forms loomed over her. Oh dear.

"Why are you following us? Do we look like easy targets?" Anger laced Carrington's voice.

She shook her head, not knowing how they didn't recognize her. It was mostly dark, of course, but the truth was painfully obvious to her.

Mr. Travers folded his arms. "Are you a pickpocket? I can't see a runt like you robbing the two of us. You're either very brave or very stupid. My guess is stupid."

She took her chances with a short nod and lowered her head in feigned shame. Maybe she could get away with a bit of pity or a quick beating.

"He must be one of the city's orphans. Should we take him to the patrols?" Mr. Travers sounded as if he wanted nothing to do with her.

She shook her head with such violence that they paused to study her.

Carrington tilted his head. "Where do you live?"

She shrugged at him.

"I don't think he can talk. Homeless, I would guess."

Carrington held out his hand to help her up, but she scrambled back. "Don't be silly. We won't bite you. At least, I won't."

Mr. Travers snarled comically at her.

She hid her smile as she allowed Carrington to help her to her feet, but he misjudged her weight, and she stumbled forward into his chest. He stilled as he steadied her fall, his hands on her shoulders. Then he leaned forward and inhaled.

She stood paralyzed.

He slid his hands around to her backside, where he appreciated the tight fit of her trousers. She stiffened at his ministrations, his touch creating a curious need low in her belly.

"I thought you said you weren't interested in young men. This is disturbing, William." Mr. Travers took a step toward them, meaning to intervene.

Carrington gave his brother a hard look that stopped him short, and with a tight grin, he dipped Delia into a passionate kiss.

Her arms dropped back as he embraced her, and all his frustration and anger pressed into her lips. His uncompromising mouth served as a chastisement for her actions. When he finished, she held back her whimper for more. It had almost been worth getting caught.

As he straightened her, he pulled off her hat, and her unruly hair tumbled out of its plaits. Mr. Travers gasped as he studied her. His gaze wandered up and down her form before resting on her legs. He smiled approvingly, his mouth partially open. Carrington cuffed his brother's head.

"As much as I appreciate the view"—he gestured to her tight-fitting trousers—"you were supposed to stay at home. What were you thinking, coming out here? A young female alone in the middle of the night?" Carrington's voice held an icy bite.

She gave him a smug smile. "But I didn't go out as a female. Even you couldn't tell the difference."

"That doesn't mean you're in any less danger. Men are not any more immune to these streets than women. Criminals would see a small, lone male wandering the streets. An easy mark."

"It was the loose shirt that fooled me. You know where my priorities lie." Mr. Travers stroked his chin, still examining her. "That, and I had no idea she had…" He paused as he turned to see his brother's glare. "…other assets."

"I should have noticed sooner, but I was under the impression you had better sense. You were stabbed earlier this year, remember?" Carrington held her shoulders, his fingers digging into her skin.

She lowered her gaze, saying nothing.

"What do we do with her?" Mr. Travers asked. "We can't take her with us, and we can't leave her here."

"Take her home for me. I'll continue our search."

A jolt of disappointment landed in her stomach. She was already here. Couldn't he give her some credit? Foxglove had been active for months, and the stabbing had been an exception.

"Alone?"

Carrington nodded. "I'll be fine."

"Wait," she said as Mr. Travers pulled her away from Carrington's grasp.

Carrington had already turned toward his task. "Now, Hugh." The command held all the force of an older brother.

"Wait, Carrington."

"I can't deal with you now. Wait for my return." Carrington moved off with forceful steps.

"But—"

Hugh pushed her forward, startling her into silence. "As much as it pains me to agree with my brother, I have to say, coming out here was extremely foolish." He took hold of her arm and guided her along.

"You aren't helping," she huffed. "How could you let him go alone?"

He let out a long, impatient breath. "Did you know I was going to be with him?"

She shook her head, unable to mount a defense.

"Then why does it matter now?"

"I was with him at the time." Her mouth stumbled over her words.

"You would have been a distraction. Why do you think he wanted you to stay behind? It wasn't for any lack of respect but his need to protect you. He would have been too busy watching out for you to have any success."

He waited for a reply, but when none came, he patted her arm. "He'll be fine. The man is angry as a bull, and you should worry about the safety of anyone who crosses his path, which is why he sent me with you instead of bringing you home himself. I suspect he will break some teeth before the end of the night."

"Why is he so distant of late?"

Hugh paused, considering his reply. "My brother worked hard to get back to you, and he is not used to losing control of his emotions. When he gets angry, he can make rash decisions. It's my guess he wants to avoid doing something he will regret."

Her hand went to her mouth as she held herself in check. If she had lost Carrington to this disagreement, she didn't know what she would do. With that thought, she realized how much she cared for him. If they didn't marry, she would rather they at least part as friends.

They finished their journey in silence, but once they reached her home's back door, he promised to rejoin his brother. He watched as she closed the door behind her, assuring himself of her compliance.

Upon entering the kitchen, Delia gave a start when she spotted Felix sitting idly by the fire. Sparks floated around him as he poked at the flames.

"How did it go?" He favored her with a mocking grin from his stool.

She scowled back at him. "You know the answer to that. Thank you for not giving me up though."

"Where would the fun be in that?" He laughed and set more fuel on the fire.

"Here I thought you were on my side. Are you Carrington's

man now?" Her hands settled on her hips.

He shrugged. "I'm my own man, but you can never doubt my loyalty. This is what you wanted, after all."

She couldn't fault his reasoning. Delia had made her bed, and now she had to crawl back into it. Her body was sore from the shock of her fall, but it was her injured pride she would have to drag behind her.

She nodded in resigned agreement. Then she surprised herself and Felix by hugging him. He froze in her grasp and then hugged her back. His small frame relaxed into her.

He smiled uncertainly as she released him. She wondered if anyone ever hugged him and decided she would make a habit of it whether he liked it or not. Too much of his life centered on hatred and blood.

"Don't get any ideas. Carrington is a good sort, and I'd hate for you to break his heart." His voice went flat, but a spark of humor remained in his eyes. "Besides, I'm too much man for you."

She couldn't contain her laugh, and she nodded her thanks to him for lightening her mood. He waved her off and gave a playful kick toward her backside as she left him for her room, to await Carrington's return.

CHAPTER TWENTY-FOUR

ALL THE WORRY and uneasiness in the world could not have kept her exhausted mind awake. She slept a light, dreamless sleep that was only hindered by footsteps in the hall and the subsequent sound of a door opening and closing.

She bolted upright and paused only to throw her robe around her thin nightgown. She made her way with her bare feet and tapped lightly on Carrington's door. A loud, bark-like curse came from inside before the door opened.

His hair was disheveled, the shoulder-length dark strands falling into his eyes. He stood with the door ajar, leaning against the doorframe minus his boots, coat, and waistcoat, his shirt partially unbuttoned.

She stared at the small triangle of skin on his chest, a few unruly curls peeking out, and took in a deep breath. How did he look even better when he was a mess? It wasn't fair. She wished she had at least straightened her hair before leaving her room.

He smirked, appearing to note her reaction to his appearance. "What?" His voice came out a whisper. Was he afraid of being heard? Since when did he care about being caught with her?

"I assumed you wanted to talk." She fiddled with the belt of her robe.

He let out a long, impatient sigh. "Not right now. I'm exhausted, and I still need to think."

She drew her brows together. "If you weren't already doing your thinking, what were you doing?"

He rubbed a hand over his face. "Releasing my anger so I would be able to think."

Leaden guilt filled her chest. "I hope you didn't hurt anyone."

"I appreciate your newfound concern for strangers, but the only ones I hurt were myself and the supply of whiskey in your fair city."

Her mouth fell open as her eyes scanned him anew. "Are you drunk?"

"Not as much as I was when you knocked and not nearly as much as I would like."

She craned her neck to peer along the hallway and back to his flat stare. "Can't I come in?"

"No."

"I'm sorry about before. Won't you let me explain?" Her plea sounded more urgent than she intended. Whatever remained of her dignity, she laid it at his feet.

"Are you going to tell me you were held at gunpoint to follow me? Or were you possessed by demons to hinder my progress? Or maybe you just accidentally wandered alone into one of the worst parts of town in the middle of the night?"

She closed her eyes tightly and rubbed at her temples.

"No?" He grunted, a low, guttural noise. "Then go back to bed, and I will speak to you later. The only reason I'm back here and not piss drunk in the street is that my brother insisted I be cut off. You can either blame him or yourself for my mood. Now go back to bed."

His words hit like the memory of the blade stabbing into her flesh, but this was worse. Her stomach jerked as though kicked by a mule while the ground fell out from under her.

She backed up from Carrington, her lips parted as she searched for words, but nothing came. Her body locked up as he shut the door on her. Somehow, her feet numbly walked the void that should have contained the floorboards.

She stared forward with a vacant gaze, and an empty cavern resided where her chest had been. The bed rose to meet her as she dropped, not bothering to remove her robe or get under the blankets.

His hard eyes loomed behind her eyelids, so full of anger and worse, disappointment. The tears never came. Instead, she curled on her bed with her arms clasped around her knees.

Finally, her dreams took her but gave her no relief.

She was buried from the chin down in her garden. Her body was immobile, encased in dirt. Only her gaze remained free. The summer sun beat down on her face, almost blinding her. Her tongue, swollen and parched, tasted like sand. Laughter surrounded her, and she squinted to see who it was.

Her mother sat laughing with Jeffrey. They lounged sipping tea with Arthur, Lord Carrington, and Mr. Bradshaw. None of them seemed to mind her state in the ground.

Arthur offered her a cup of tea, and he poured it for her, where she could just glimpse it on the table. Her mother smiled a wide, lopsided smile and poured milk into her tea, though she knew Delia did not usually take it with milk.

Delia whimpered, unable to speak through the dryness of her mouth.

"Drink your tea before it gets cold, dear." Her mother's voice held its familiar chiding tone.

"She doesn't need tea, Mother. She needs biscuits." Jeffrey laid one next to her cup on the saucer.

Mr. Bradshaw brought the tea over to her head but spilled much of it down her cheek.

A scream ripped from her throat as the scalding liquid poured down her face. She groaned, wanting to rub it off, but her limbs remained still in the hard-packed dirt.

Mr. Bradshaw looked down at her in adoration but did not release the cup. He poured the tea down her throat, but Carrington stopped him, took the cup from his hand, and pushed him aside.

Carrington poured her some more tea from a different pot and added two sugars, just as she liked it. He stirred with an odd-looking spoon she couldn't quite make out through the glaring sun.

When he set the cup before her on the saucer, he pulled out the strange spoon and tapped it on the lip of the cup. It wasn't a spoon at all but a stem. The foxglove dripped as he set it on the saucer, where a small puddle of blood formed.

She pitched her head to and fro as he lifted the cup to her tightly sealed lips. He attempted to force her mouth open.

"What's wrong? You don't like it?" Carrington frowned in concern. "It's your favorite, the same brew you made for me. What's wrong?"

She jumped awake to a hand shaking her shoulder.

"What's wrong?" His voice echoed out of her dream.

She blinked up to see Carrington standing over her, the same frown of her dream on his face. She rubbed at her eyes to banish the thought. Her body was wound tight in her robe, and she struggled to remove it before remembering she was not alone.

He had shut the door behind him.

"You were screaming." He shifted from foot to foot. "I waited, but nobody else came to check on you. I couldn't just leave you to whatever horror you were facing. It sounded like you were dying or being attacked. How anyone slept through it is a mystery to me."

"They're used to it." She tugged at her robe in an attempt to straighten it. "The nightmares stopped before you came back."

"They don't appear to have stopped." He shook his head in wonderment. "I've never heard you scream like that."

She sighed. "This was different. It wasn't about being stabbed."

He raised his brows in question.

"I don't want to relive that dream, and it will be easier to forget if I don't talk about it."

"If that's what you wish." He stepped toward the door.

"Don't go."

He must have heard the fear in her voice, because he turned back, though reluctantly. She rushed to him then, her arms embracing his chest like a frightened child's. She buried her face in his warmth and breathed in whiskey and leather.

Her cheeks flushed when he didn't return her hug. At least he had managed to put on his shirt and trousers before checking on her.

"It felt so real. I thought it was real. I hurt you terribly, and I was powerless to do anything. I'm sorry."

He wrapped his arms around her then and held her for a long minute. Slowly he released her and put distance between them with his arms on her shoulders. She peeked up into his stern face and wide eyes.

"You must never do that again. Never put yourself in danger."

She shook her head in quick jerks. "Never."

He pinched the bridge of his nose. "Don't lie to me either."

"I'm not lying." Her gaze dropped to hide her shame at his distrust. Was it so difficult for him to imagine she could tell the truth?

"You'll excuse me if I'm unconvinced. I didn't think you were lying about staying behind either."

She paused, giving herself time to harden her voice. "I promise I'm not lying."

He caught her eyes, reading them. "We'd better talk about this in the light of day, which, I'm afraid, is not far off." He rubbed a hand over his face. "I need sleep and food before I'll be ready to have this discussion."

"You don't believe me." Hurt sharpened her tone.

"It's not that I don't believe you but whether I should."

"Is that it, then?" Was this the one action where he drew the line? "You'll abandon me like I always thought." She crossed her arms, drawing into herself.

His gaze darted to hers. "How can I abandon you if you've

already shut me out?"

She cast her gaze away, unable to match his stare.

"You're so obsessed with avenging your brother that you close everyone out, never trusting anyone. I assume letting people in on your secret was an accident?"

"I never meant to tell anyone. Felix was especially impossible."

"He would be, but I doubt you've trusted him either."

As much faith as she had in her friends and family, she hadn't confided in any of them. The sudden unexplained death of Arthur had led her to shut out anyone who tried to see the pain whittling away her soul. Since she had nobody to blame, she blamed everyone, and her trust fled with her suspicion.

"I can't live like this, always on the outside. This can't work if you don't trust me." His body slumped in as though his whole life weighed on him.

"But I do trust you." The words escaped her lips, and with a swelling certainty in her chest, she realized they were true. Imagine she had come to rely on the one person she would never have believed capable of keeping her secrets.

"Then why did you follow me?"

"It had nothing to do with your ability. Your investigation skills are excellent, admirable even. I needed to see the truth. Too many times, I've been sheltered from it. I couldn't take the chance you would finish the task without me."

He closed the distance between them and steadied her face to meet his eyes. "I'm never without you."

Her heart skipped, and she tried to look away, but he only strengthened his grip.

"Every moment of my day is spent with you in my mind. Your captivating green eyes linger, reminding me of home. Barely a thought passes without my wondering what you would think of it. When I hear something amusing, I look around in hopes of sharing it with you to get your witty response. I often talked to you at my home in London and imagined you answering me, but it was never quite enough. So you see, you've never left me."

He brought his lips to hers then, softly as if asking a question. She moaned in response. Encouraged, he cupped her face in both hands, taking his time to tease her mouth with his tongue before exploring.

She met his tongue with hers, the bite of whiskey still on his lips. The taste emboldened her, and she pressed her hands to his chest, running her fingers over the hard muscle beneath his shirt.

A new urgency seemed to ripple through him, and his hands went to her robe and tugged at the belt. He drew away from her, breathless.

His eyes searched her face and widened the distance between them. "Are you sure? I won't draw back after this. There will be no getting rid of me."

She nodded, her eyes half-closed as she attempted to meet his lips again, but he stilled her with a hand and tilted away from her as though to withdraw.

"Say it."

She blinked away the fog as she met his eyes. "I've never been surer of anything."

Carrington hissed out a breath he must have been holding. He folded her back into his arms, and his lips joined hers. His hands roamed over her arms to her back. His fingers trailed over the bottom of her spine, and she shivered at his touch.

She tugged at his shirt, ready to rip the fabric if it didn't move.

He chuckled into her mouth. "Relax."

Her frustration mounted when he whispered kisses along her chin and down to her throat. A low moan lingered on her breath as she yanked his shirt apart, buttons and thread flying before her wide smile. Carrington stared down at her handiwork, shaking his head.

"I was rather attached to that shirt." His hands returned to her robe.

"I'll buy you another. I'll get you a mountain of shirts just to rip them off you." She explored his newly bare skin with her hands, marveling at the power in his chest and forearms.

His breath caught at her touch. "Why waste shirts? I'll be happy to stop wearing them if you stop wearing everything."

Their limbs tangled as she pulled the rest of the shirt's fabric off his body while he finished removing her robe's belt. "You'll agree the effect is worth the shirt." She gave him a playful smile. He laughed and retook her mouth, silencing her.

His hands caressed over her hips. He cupped her bottom and lifted her in his arms. She gasped into their kiss and grasped his shoulders while wrapping her legs around his waist, her nightgown riding up.

He settled her gently across the bed, and she dropped her arms above her but kept her legs holding him in place. He tickled the backs of her thighs until she squirmed and released him but not before rubbing at the bulge in his trousers. He groaned, causing Delia to giggle.

"You will pay for that," he said through his teeth.

"Will I?"

In answer to her challenge, he brought his head down to kiss along her neck and teased a line of fire to the thin fabric covering her chest.

His hand wandered underneath to rub her nipple with his palm. A cascade of pleasure ricocheted under her skin and down to her toes.

A moan burst free from deep in her throat. He used his other hand to pull the fabric down, baring her to his greedy gaze.

He covered a nipple with his mouth and sucked, sending waves through her body. She gasped and shamelessly arched her chest to his mouth.

He nipped and teased the sensitive skin, and his hand fondled her other breast. Her eyes fluttered closed, and she allowed the waves of pleasure to lift her away.

His tongue wandered over her flesh, to the other nipple. Her hands found his hair, fingers grasping as the intensity overwhelmed her.

She brought her legs around him again, but this time he pushed them down. His attention diverted, she blinked at him in annoyance. His fingers found the bottom of her nightdress at her thighs. He pulled the fabric out from under her and up over her head.

"That's better. Not one rip either."

She glared at him until he brought his mouth back to her breast, effectively rendering her mute. He smiled lazily, and his eyes held the hint of a secret.

Separating her legs with his knee, he tickled along her belly as he moved his hand between them. Her body jerked as his fingers danced along the eager skin between her thighs. Nobody had touched her there before. The sensation in her belly grew, and she ached for more. She whimpered in protest as he moved his hand away.

Her face grew crimson when he laughed at her response. To appease her, he kissed her lips lightly and showered kisses down her belly as he lowered himself.

With firm hands, he spread her knees wide and slid his tongue along her inner thigh. She cried out, her hand catching her mouth before she made too much noise.

When he stroked the sensitive nub of skin with his tongue, she bit into her hand to keep herself from screaming. Her other hand gripped his hair to hold on.

Her breath caught as his finger joined his mouth and entered her as he sucked. A frantic race beat in her chest, and she panted behind her hand.

Her legs tried to close on his head, but he pushed them open as he continued to torment her with his insistent licking. He used his finger to penetrate her again and again until she thought her heart would erupt.

Just when she couldn't take any more, he drew his mouth away. She tried to guide his head back, but he only grinned and stood. She sighed and lay back onto the bed. A throbbing need consumed her. Through the haze, she trailed her gaze over his body as he stepped out of his trousers. A devilish grin spread over his face as he returned to her.

He stroked the area between her legs, releasing mewling sounds from her throat. He nudged himself at her opening, and his eyes settled on hers for final confirmation. She nodded and lifted her hips encouragingly.

"This might hurt, but I promise it will be over quickly." Carrington plunged into her without hesitation. The swift movement brought a sharp, burning pain inside her. He had given her his full length without warning, leaving her no chance to anticipate the discomfort.

Her groan turned into a moan as the discomfort settled and he moved in and out of her. Her body adjusted around him as the pain melted into pleasure.

His mouth took hers, consuming the sounds of her wanton cries. His forehead rested on hers, and their eyes locked. They exchanged breath as he worked faster. She raised her hips, taking him deeper.

"Please." She breathed the words over him.

"Please, what?"

"Please, Will."

"Close enough."

Their pace became frantic, and her eyes rolled back behind her lashes. Her legs grasped his bottom, clinging on as she shook around him.

He covered her lips as she cried his name. He thrust into her again before crying out himself, spending himself inside her.

Her body shook with his release, her hands digging into his shoulders as she erupted.

He rested his head on hers as ripples of pleasure went through her again and again. She closed her eyes, catching her breath.

He stayed inside her and cocooned her body protectively. Surprisingly, his weight didn't bother her so much. His heartbeat and breathing coursed through her own body, melding them as one.

"Is it always that good?" Her breathy voice was almost a whisper.

"It has never been that good for me." He nudged her head over to catch her lips and then rolled off her, onto his back. Already she missed the touch of his skin, and she crawled over to rest her head on his chest.

"What now?" She trailed her fingers through the hair on his chest.

His arm went around her. "Now we sleep."

"No, I mean after that."

"We eat. If I weren't so spent, I would eat your whole pantry. Oh wait, I did that already." He grinned, catlike.

She tilted her head away. "You know what I mean, Carrington."

"William." He stressed the syllables of his name.

"Carrington, are you going to answer me?"

"I intend to make you my future countess, but that won't be for a while, since my father is in excellent health. Until then, you may call yourself Viscountess Carrington or Mrs. Travers, whichever suits you."

Her mouth twisted down in distaste. "I would rather not be called Mrs. Travers. I associate your surname with your brother."

"Wonderful point. Wouldn't want to give him any ideas." He kissed her forehead, the gesture strangely comforting.

"Carrington, did you find Gilbert?"

He sighed at her return to the topic. "Must you bring every man's name into our bed but mine?"

"I did say your name. You were too busy kissing me at the time." A laugh vibrated inside her at this obsession of his.

"Was I? Well then, I'll have to get you to repeat it." He tickled her sides until she begged off. "Delia, I'm half-dead from making love to you, and already I'm aroused. I'm going to go back to my room and sleep this off."

She groaned as he moved out from under her.

"It wouldn't do if someone walked in on us like this," he said.

"Come back. You're warm." She reached for him.

"Don't tempt me."

She sighed, her body like jelly against the covers. "Did you answer me about Gilbert?"

"I see I've made you senseless. No, I didn't find him, but I know where he is."

She rose to her elbow, but he silenced her with a stern look.

"We can discuss this later. That will have to be enough for you for now." He bent down to kiss her hair and tugged on his trousers. He retrieved what was left of his shirt and shook his head as she gave him a wide grin.

"You're a menace." He took in her naked form as she lounged across the bed, devouring her with his gaze. Reluctantly he let himself out, the door closing lightly behind him.

CHAPTER TWENTY-FIVE

DELIA MOURNED THE loss of the intimate closeness of Carrington's body. She would have to dress and get under the blankets, or she would freeze. Before she could move her puttylike limbs, a light tap sounded on her door. Maybe he'd changed his mind?

"Go to bed," she called.

The tapping continued. Looking down at the state of herself, she pulled a blanket over her body as best she could without getting up. "Come in."

Hope poked her head in the door, appearing scandalized with her wide-eyed gaze. She hurried into the room and shut the door behind her. Delia tried to summon the shame at what Hope must be thinking, but it was slow to come in her muddled brain.

"Ma'am?"

"What is it?" Delia buried her head in the pillow.

Hope cleared her throat. "I was coming to arrange your clothes for the day, as I do when I first rise." Of course, Delia knew this. Hope must be stalling for time. "I crossed paths with a rather proud and half-nude Lord Carrington in the hall."

Delia groaned. At least she could rely on Hope not to talk.

"I won't judge you, but could you be a little more careful? At least let me assist you in the future." Hope stepped closer to the bed. "It will be some time before a bath could be ready, but let me help you wash and"—Hope eyed the patch of blood Delia had overlooked—"change the bedding."

Delia's jaw slackened as she stared down at the offending evidence. Hope must have seen her distress when she'd rushed to sit next to her.

"I expect you will marry him?"

Her widened gaze jumped to her maid. "But what if I don't want to marry him?"

"Don't you? It appears to be a little late for that." Hope met her eyes with a look of patience and concern.

"I don't know." Her attention wandered back to the blood. Still there. "Can you imagine me, a noble lady? In England? The very idea makes my stomach turn. We're completely different people."

"To me, you're already the noblest of ladies." Hope's good opinion soothed her. "I've been fortunate to serve you, and I'd miss you deeply if you moved to England."

"But surely you would come with me?" Her voice bordered on panicked.

"I'd be honored. You know, I haven't any family here."

"That's a comfort, at least, but I still don't wish to leave. It doesn't change the fact Carrington and I are devoted to opposite sides of this battle." She clutched the blanket to her chest as if she could ward off the dilemma with the thin barrier.

"I'll admit I'm surprised you're siding with the men who killed Arthur." Hope gasped in surprise at her own words. "I didn't mean that, ma'am."

"Yes, you did, and you're right. I've always sided with my neighbors. Those men who killed Arthur were just one small, misguided group."

"Excuse me, ma'am, but can't that be said about the soldiers in this city? Indeed, some of them don't deserve to breathe the poisoned air of New York. Then there are those like your Lord Carrington and his brother. Good, honorable men who don't deserve to be grouped with the ruffians."

Delia cocked her head. "Why, Hope, I never knew you were so passionate about this subject. You're calling Carrington honorable after tonight?"

Hope's cheeks colored an attractive pink along her dusky skin. "It was a momentary lapse of judgment from him. I'm sure he will have many of those where you are concerned. It's not fair to judge him by the actions of his countrymen. I believe he's loyal because his character demands it. In that, you're much the same. It's a shame you were born on opposite sides of the ocean."

She regarded Hope with fresh eyes. Her maid had stated her situation more clearly than Delia could ever hope to achieve on her own. Her emotions had clouded her opinions. She hadn't been capable of seeing things for what they were. She did admire Carrington's steady loyalty, as much as she resented where his loyalties lay.

Yet he had shifted his loyalties.

Carrington had put her before his countrymen, before his king. He could hang for keeping her secret. He hadn't just ignored her sins but had actively covered them up. It wasn't just his neck at stake, but his family could be disgraced and his father could lose his title.

It tore her up inside to think she had treated him as poorly as she had. Carrington loved his country, and he had shown a devotion to her she couldn't hope to match. Where did that leave her?

Dawn peeked in from the edge of the curtains. She needed sleep but knew it would not come. To her relief, she was the first and only person in the breakfast room. She took full advantage of her good fortune by loading her plate with freshly cooked bacon and eggs. Her brother and Carrington tended to eat most of the house when they dined, and she relished a sick pleasure in denying them what she ate.

Her luck continued into the library, where she whiled away her time finishing the book her family so frequently interrupted. The book left her yearning for more, and she rose to find another, knowing there was nothing of interest. She lingered at the shelves when the library's door opened, and Carrington entered.

"How did you sleep?" The well-known titles distracted her gaze.

"Like a corpse, though bacon would have rounded out my morning nicely. Your brother took the last of it before I could, and the servants had already started on dinner."

She glanced at him with a bright smile. "Bacon does round out a good morning. I rather thought so myself."

He returned her smile and walked toward her, but he stopped just in front of her. "Do I have anything to do with your good mood?" His voice fell to a near whisper.

She tilted her head to the side, pretending to consider his question. "Hmm, maybe."

"If you have to think about it, then I didn't do a good enough job."

She let out a dramatic sigh and shrugged.

"You wound me." He placed a hand to his chest. "I'll take this challenge to heart, hopefully tonight?"

"Is that what you think?"

He leaned into her and tickled her sides. She slapped away his hands, but he pulled back as they heard the unmistakable sound of the door. "There needs to be more locks in this house."

Mr. Henshaw cleared his throat. "My lord, there's a Mr. Danvers here to see you. Would you like to meet him in the drawing room?"

Carrington frowned at the butler. "The library will do."

Mr. Henshaw paused, eyes toward Delia. "He asked to speak with you alone."

"Well, that's too bad. This is Miss Wolcott's home, and she has every right to be here."

"As you wish, sir." Mr. Henshaw bowed as he left.

"Thank you," she whispered, squeezing his hand once and releasing it.

He winked. "You can thank me later."

She laughed into her palm. "Is that so?"

Carrington frowned. "This day needs to get on with it."

She snatched a book from the shelves at random and settled on her favorite chaise, and Carrington followed her lead. To her relief and disappointment, he sat a safe distance away just as the door opened to admit Captain Danvers.

He strode up to them with the keen determination of a hunting dog and stood before Carrington, who examined his replacement with amusement in his eyes.

Mr. Danvers waited for him to speak, shuffling in front of him uncomfortably.

At last Carrington obliged him. "What brings you here, Mr. Danvers?" Carrington didn't bother to greet him.

Mr. Danvers glanced toward Delia but decided against asking for privacy. "I've narrowed down the identity of Foxglove, and I wanted your opinion on the matter." Mr. Danvers stood as though presenting his prey.

She made a small sound in her throat. "Won't you sit down, Mr. Danvers?"

In answer, the man took the edge of a chair off from Carrington.

"How, may I ask, did you narrow it down?" Carrington sat erect, as poised as ever. She wondered how many of these situations he had been in to perfect such calm. Already she barely managed to keep her features in place.

"It was rather simple. I placed the foxglove at the ball and watched the reactions of the party." Mr. Danvers's dark eyes lit up with pride at his cleverness.

Her face fell. Had she given something away in the moment? She hadn't been in the room at the discovery of the flowers, but surely he'd watched them after they'd returned. And he must have seen their return. How humiliating.

"What conclusions did you draw from such an exercise?" Carrington still appeared unaffected, acting as though he spoke to a child showing him a drawing he was proud of.

"While I was observing the guests' behavior, I first wondered if Foxglove might be you."

Carrington stiffened. "Me?"

"Yes, but that isn't possible, since you were only in New York for part of the events. Then I decided you must know who Foxglove is. Why you haven't turned him in is a mystery to me." His voice dropped, low and threatening.

"A dangerous accusation, but if you must know, I'd planned to visit you this afternoon with some information."

Mr. Danvers's brows jumped. "Really? Then you do know?"

Delia's gaze jerked toward the door as the urge to flee nearly overwhelmed her. Could he be turning her in now, to save his own hide? She didn't want to believe it.

Her word carried little weight next to his sex, family, and authority. She tried to straighten her face as she waited for his damning words. He deserved that much of her trust.

"May I assume you've already told some of your lady friends as well? Or are they also involved?" Mr. Danvers's gaze strayed to Delia's pale face.

"I did discuss it with some of the ladies of Miss Wolcott's acquaintance before the ball."

What was Carrington playing at? If he was going to turn her in, he should get it over with.

"And you didn't bother to consult me? The leader of the investigation?" The captain's voice rose in indignation.

"Watch your tone." Carrington glared at him. "I haven't had time."

"Foxglove could be roaming the streets, plotting his next victims, and you can't spare the time away from your dalliances." Mr. Danvers waved toward Delia.

She lowered her head to her chest to hide the shame spread over her features. She wanted to cry and crawl under her seat.

Abruptly, Carrington came to his feet, looming over the shrinking form of Mr. Danvers. "You will not speak that way about Miss Wolcott in my presence or otherwise. That is, unless you want to exit this house on a stretcher or, more preferably, a box."

"I'm sorry, my lord. My tongue got away from me." Mr. Danvers immediately offered his apologies to Delia through his terror of the viscount. She nodded in acceptance, in awe at Carrington's defense of her. Carrington resumed his seat as if nothing had happened.

Mr. Danvers cleared his throat. "But, my lord"—he attempted to smooth his way—"I fail to see why you hesitated to speak with me."

Carrington studied his hands. "That is my business, but if you must know, I didn't see any rush."

"Any rush?" Mr. Danvers squeaked.

"He's already in jail." His voice was offhand.

"In jail? Why was I not informed of this?"

"An unrelated crime but equally damnable. Treason. Didn't you find it odd when Foxglove suddenly stopped killing people?"

"I hadn't thought." Mr. Danvers paused. "I assumed he was injured or maybe dead, but never imprisoned. How did you come by this information?"

He sighed. "I overheard some interesting talk in a brothel. It was fortunate I knew enough of the case to make the proper connections."

"Who is he?" Mr. Danvers stumbled over the words.

"A former member of the Sons of Liberty, Mr. Bryant Gilbert."

She flinched at the impact of the revelation. Gilbert was in jail? When was Carrington going to tell her? He must mean to prevent her from going there.

Mr. Danvers studied him, disbelief marring his features. "And you told a group of ladies you overheard information in a brothel that indicated Foxglove was in jail and no longer a problem. I don't buy that."

"Of course not," Carrington scoffed. "I told them they would no longer need to worry about Foxglove and when the flower appeared, it was likely a sick joke. It's bad enough I'm forced to speak of such things in front of Miss Wolcott now."

Mr. Danvers came to his feet in a rush, bowing. "If that is the case, I must interrogate him immediately. Where is he being held?"

Carrington gave him a tight-lipped stare, unmoved by his enthusiasm. "I will send you the information when it is ready. I was already writing up a report for you out of courtesy."

"This evening, then?" Mr. Danvers's voice was a hopeful plea.

"Tomorrow at the earliest. I have other business to attend to first." His words were a clear dismissal.

To his credit, Mr. Danvers didn't argue. Instead, he exited the room, bowing again more respectfully, knowing his future rested on Carrington's favorable opinion.

"Insolent pig," Carrington muttered.

"That is rather snobbish of you." The steadiness in her voice surprised her after the ordeal with Mr. Danvers.

His concerned gaze met hers. "I will not have him speak of my future wife like that."

She shook her head at his assumption but let it slide for now. "What will happen when he finds out Gilbert isn't Foxglove?"

"That won't be a problem. I've arranged for us to visit Gilbert today. You can be sure he won't be doing any talking by the time Mr. Danvers sees him."

She stared at him with a mixture of shock and awe. "Us? You're allowing me to come with you?"

He took her hand between both of his. His gaze locked on hers in solemn thought. "This has been your fight from the beginning." He spoke quietly, taking care with each of his words. "You would never allow yourself to heal if I took over your work."

He watched his thumb trail over her wrist. "Nor would you ever forgive me for shutting you out. This can't be a wedge between us." He raised her hand, kissing it gently before returning his gaze to hers. "It has to be you."

She tried to smile but settled on a small twist of the corner of her lip. She studied their hands, not sure what to say. She had judged him unfairly. He was every bit as honorable as she could hope.

Not only had he looked the other way when he had discovered her identity, but he would also help her conclude Foxglove's business. Why had she ever doubted him?

She cleared her throat uncomfortably and filled the silence with her questions. "Have you been planning to name Gilbert all along?"

"I've only known about his location since the other night, but it had crossed my mind since then. How convenient it was that Mr. Danvers paid us a visit. I'd say it solved our problem nicely."

"Then you meant to blame someone else for my crimes?" She frowned to herself. "I suppose you knew he placed the foxglove as well?"

"I'm clever, but I'm not that clever. I thought Felix might have been behind that, though he denied it. It no longer matters who takes the blame for Foxglove.

"Gilbert is guilty by his own hand, and the punishment for treason would be the same in any case. You can only hang a person once." He paused, letting his words sink in. "You don't have to see him. I can turn him over to Mr. Danvers without any trouble."

"No, I need to speak to him. It's the only way."

"Very well." He squeezed her hand and released it. "You will need your boys' clothes again and have Hope hide away. We can tell your mother we're going shopping, but you'll have to sneak out the back."

She let out a breath and lowered her feet to stand. "When do we leave?"

"As soon as you can be ready." He stood and raised her chin, kissing her lightly. "Be prepared, but know this: no harm will come to you while I'm still breathing." He watched her eyes to make sure she absorbed his promise before nodding and releasing her chin.

"Carrington?" Her voice fell, quiet, shy.

"Yes?" He frowned at her refusal to use his given name.

"If we are supposed to be going shopping, it won't be very believable if we don't return with anything." She nibbled at her bottom lip as she anticipated his answer.

He gave her a knowing grin. "Leave that to me."

A frown creased her forehead. "Doesn't that take the fun out of it?"

"Sweet, we can go shopping after this business is through, for as long as you like. Though, there is more shopping in London than here."

She lowered her lashes. "You know, I haven't actually agreed to marry you."

He sighed dramatically. "Yes, but I enjoy getting you used to the idea. I plan to do some more convincing later."

Her heart hiccuped at his words. "Indeed? Well, Lord Carrington, I will leave you to your plots."

Chapter Twenty-Six

AN HOUR LATER, Delia found herself on Crown Street in front of a tall brownstone building surrounded by a wooden fence that blocked her view of the yard beyond. She counted six stories of windows, none of them giving away their secrets from inside the building.

Guards stood watching over the entrance, and others made a tour of the grounds. They observed Delia and Carrington with matching stares that may as well have been part of the uniform.

She shivered inwardly, wanting to clutch Carrington. Instead, she grasped the medicine bag she carried, her knuckles showing white.

She wore the outfit from the night she had followed Carrington into the streets. He hadn't remarked on her choice but eyed her body approvingly. She scoffed at his appraisal. After all, she was supposed to be a boy.

He had donned a respectable but worn outfit she had never seen. The brown of his coat and trousers did not suit him, and he must have borrowed the ill-fitting costume. She had barely recognized him when he had climbed into the carriage in a lopsided wig. She wanted to burn that wig. It was sacrilege to cover such hair.

He took a deep breath beside her, watching the prison before them. "Stay close. Let me do most of the talking."

She tilted her head at him, under her cocked hat. That had been her intention, but she recognized the nervousness in his voice and chose to stay quiet.

He met her gaze with unwavering seriousness. "Above all things, you must remember our purpose. We can't help the poor souls in here."

They stood in place, studying each other's expressions. A challenge she didn't want to back down from. In the end, she was the one to drop her gaze and nod in agreement.

This prison was an evil she would have to endure. Already she had been sidetracked from finding answers and justice for Arthur. She could not let this become another one. She took one last longing glance at the clouded sunlight and trailed behind him past the towering front door.

They became encased in a frozen darkness.

She blinked at the sudden loss of light until she made out the feeble glow of an oil lamp. It was as if they had moved into night, or perhaps the sunlight refused to enter here.

She glanced up to the deep-set windows, but the clouds must have blocked what little light they had provided. The silhouettes of a foreign world surrounded her.

Carrington strode up to a long table that looked to be serving as a desk. Papers were stacked in piles across the surface. The man behind the stacks tapped a quill absentmindedly before him, listening to Carrington's explanation.

"There have been new reports of smallpox in the prison. I was sent to confirm the cases for further treatment," Carrington said as she approached. He offered a paper to the guard.

The man grunted and gazed over the page. "Dr. Carlton? And his assistant, George?" Carrington nodded patiently. "Well, Doctor, I can't say I envy you. Are you sure you want to go in there?"

Carrington frowned at the question.

The guard sighed, motioning to his side. Delia jumped when a man materialized from the shadows. Either these men were used to the darkness or she was losing her vision. The other man bent to light another lamp, illuminating the door behind him.

He beckoned them to follow, opening the door with a key dangling from his belt. She kept close to Carrington as they crept into the darkness beyond.

Horror stories had leaked out of the prison since it had been established years ago to house the rebel prisoners. The occupants were starved on old meat and moldy tack. They were confined to the oppressive air of their companions' filth. Those that didn't die of starvation were taken by disease or exposure. She had thought the stories exaggerated.

When the smell met her, a wave of nausea struck. An ammonia-like tang invaded her eyes, mouth, and nostrils in a burning rush. She fell back, covering her mouth and nose with a cupped hand. She fought the bile down. Carrington set a steadying hand on her shoulder, lending her strength to continue.

They followed the guard into the cavern of a room. She noted with satisfaction that both men had also covered their faces. Then another scent crept past her defenses. She groaned and closed her eyes, holding on to Carrington's coat for guidance.

Dread always accompanied this smell. Nothing good ever came out of it. She had only witnessed it once when she had found a forgotten beggar on the walk to her house, stiff with death. It had stayed with her after that.

Now the smell was everywhere, crawling along her skin and swimming over her eyes. A sharp bite of rotting meat, feces, and old fruit. The sweet, acrid air stung her vision as they continued forward.

The guard handed Carrington another lamp and abandoned them to their work. Delia took the opportunity to empty the contents of her stomach. Carrington rubbed her back as she tried to rid herself of the smell. A groan croaked nearby, followed by laughter of another.

She straightened from her crouch, noticing the prisoners for the first time. There must have been dozens of them etched out by the lamplight. Most of them ignored the newcomers, clinging to their wretched states.

Lumps scattered on the floor that may or may not have been men. The light brought out deep shadows in sunken cheeks and hooded eyes. Too-large pupils stared at them with hatred. She was reminded of fish from the docks, and the same vacant looks haunted many of their faces.

She tried not to breathe in the air as she steadied her nerves only to slip along a patch of floor. She cursed as she righted herself again. Carrington lifted his lamp above her feet to reveal the discolored ice along the messed ground.

They both peered up to see the roof was partially exposed to let in the elements. One glance at the floor was enough. The surface was covered in every manner of foul material from excrement, to vomit, to blood.

"I'm looking for Mr. Bryant Gilbert." Carrington's voice vanished into the darkness around them. A few grunts answered him. One of the men began weeping. "Mr. Gilbert, we need to speak with you."

"It's no use," someone grumbled lowly to their right.

They turned toward a skeleton of a man on the floor, leaning over his knees. Carrington studied him curiously. "Why is that?"

The man blinked up at Carrington without much regard. "He's senseless. Mad."

Carrington prompted him with more questions, but the man remained silent, wanting no part of their business. At last Carrington took his bag from Delia and brought out a chunk of bread to show the prisoner. The man's eyes grew, him not believing the sight before him. Carrington stashed it in the bag before the other prisoners noticed it.

"Where is Bryant Gilbert?"

The man held out his hand for the bread, but hunger brought out his answer. "Chained to the far wall behind me. Kept attacking us. I think he's mad with fever. Should've been taken to the hospital."

Carrington tossed him part of the bread. He motioned for Delia to follow him as he sidestepped and dodged around the bodies of prisoners. She tried to keep her eyes on the light and the path of his boots. When he stopped, she collided with his back, and he turned to bring her up beside him.

The sight of the man hung chained against the wall halted her breath. Her stomach churned as she grasped the image before her. She recognized the now cloudy hazel eyes of Arthur's old companion, but the similarities to her memory stopped there.

The man hung like a rotting corpse but was very much alive. His long blonde hair no longer covered his scalp but was replaced by large patches of baldness with wisps of his remaining hair. His face had been eaten away by disease and, likely, vermin. Part of his teeth and gums were completely exposed. The remaining skin on his body appeared pale with red patches threatening to worsen.

She looked away and focused on Carrington's dark coat. If only they were back in her room, taking comfort in each other's arms.

Carrington lowered his head to her. "Is this him?"

She swallowed and nodded in response. "What's wrong with him? This isn't smallpox."

"No, it's not. I'm not surprised you don't recognize it."

She looked up at his face, raising her brow in question.

"I believe he has syphilis. It appears to be in the last stages. It's no wonder he's mad."

Her gaze wandered back to Gilbert. He cocked his head at her and smiled, lifting his disfigured lip further to expose more of his rotten teeth. It took every ounce of her pride to not bolt from the prison, screaming.

Carrington stood calmly, frowning at the man. "Mr. Gilbert, do you remember Mr. Arthur Wolcott?"

"Foul worm. Foul worm," Gilbert said in a singsong, surprisingly steady tenor voice. What could he possibly mean? That Arthur was dead?

"Did you help kill Wolcott?"

"Caught worm."

Carrington glanced over at Delia and shrugged, leaving her to ask questions. She hesitated and stepped forward.

"Bryant, do you remember me? It's Delia, Arthur's sister. We have some bread for you if you tell us what you know." She reached back to the bag but stopped when Gilbert spat at her, narrowly missing her face.

She sighed, shifting tactics. "You admit you had something to do with his death?"

Gilbert laughed at this. A hideous sight of bones lifting and falling against the wall. She took a step back into Carrington. His solid frame gave her the courage she needed.

"Worm's dead." Gilbert coughed out his words through his laughs. "Pricked up, dancing in blood." He coughed louder, his chest giving a great heave. "Worms for the worm." He laughed again at his joke.

Carrington shook his head. "The man isn't all there, but that's as good as a confession for me. What do you want to do?"

"Too good for you, Tory scum." Gilbert spat, pulling at his chains.

"There's nothing left of him. Death would be a mercy. If we leave him like this, he will die soon anyway." She considered the man before them.

"More fight in me than you, traitor whore." His voice had turned coarse as if he dragged his words through broken glass.

She gasped, her gaze flashing toward Carrington. "Did you hear what he called me?"

"Whore?"

"No, traitor." Her face contorted in distaste. "The nerve of him."

Carrington chuckled at her response. "It isn't much. Do you want to borrow my knife? Make a quick end to him?"

She lowered her gaze. "No, that won't be necessary. Can we go?" She wanted to be out of this suffocating air and the guilt that went with it. She couldn't save these men. A few bread crumbs tossed their way would do little to ease their suffering.

This was what she had fought so hard against as Foxglove, and she had failed them. Soldiers and civilians alike huddled in this sore excuse for a prison. In the end, the Crown had won.

Carrington pulled more bread out of his bag. He handed her a loaf, and they both distributed it around the room, side by side. They did so silently to the murmurs of the prisoners. The small gesture gave Delia and Carrington something to agree on in this war. Mercy.

Her first breath of air outside was so delicious her eyes watered. She scarcely noticed Carrington talking to the guards and promising a visit from the hospital. She pulled herself into the carriage and dropped the empty bag to the floor. He climbed in after her and yelled to the hired driver.

She leaned against the side of the carriage. "Won't they wonder when nobody comes from the hospital?"

"No, they will come. I have friends who run the hospital, and I can spot smallpox well enough."

"How do you have friends at a hospital? When were you there?" She sat bolt upright and scanned his features for some hidden injury.

His brown gaze flickered with amusement. "I told you I was in battle."

"What happened?" Her tone went soft, an attempt to avoid causing him more pain.

He waved her away. "It was nothing, a bump on the head. It got me out of battle long enough to find a position away from the fighting. A coward's way out, but I didn't see another option to avoid slaughtering civilians."

"You are no coward, Lord Carrington."

He smiled at her fondly, taking her hand. "It gladdens me to hear you say that. You're the bravest person I know."

"Will you..." She swallowed back her hesitation. "...do something for me?"

He narrowed his eyes at her. "Will it likely get me killed?"

"Oh, I doubt it."

He let out a long breath. "Well, that's disappointing. You always give me the most interesting tasks."

She barked out a laugh. "You're alive, aren't you?"

"Indeed. What is it I can do for you?"

She studied her shoes, not wanting to meet his eyes. "Would you ask your friends at the hospital to take in Gilbert? Make him comfortable?" She blurted out her words in a rush of breath.

Gilbert had murdered Arthur, and as much as she wanted her revenge, nobody deserved the horror she had witnessed. The debt was paid; let it die with Gilbert.

She sensed Carrington grow still in front of her, and after a long moment of silence, he reached forward and placed a hand on her shoulder.

"Of course." His quiet voice soothed like warm honey. "Anything for the woman I love."

Her gaze flashed up to meet his searching brown eyes, her lips quaking. "You love me?"

"Didn't I show you last night? Yes, I love you. I want to spend the rest of my life with you if you will have me." He gave her a small, hopeless smile.

She blinked at him in surprise. "After everything, you still want to marry me? You would let me ruin myself if I chose to?"

"Delia, whatever your choice is, I'll respect it. I can't say I'll be happy if you refuse me, and I'll fight for you until Jeffrey has to put me in the ground. You've been through a lot today. Rest, take your time. I'll go back to convincing you to come back to England with me."

She attempted to smile at him, but her lips shook until she released them into a frown. Did she love him? She thought love was certain, that it would come in a blinding rush. What they had shared last night had been amazing—beautiful, even—but was it love?

He leaned back in his seat and watched her as she considered her feelings, giving her no relief from the anxiety.

"By the way, your shopping gifts will be in your room when they arrive." His manner was offhand as he gazed out the carriage window.

"You plan to go in my room?" The idea didn't offend her the way she expected.

"Hope agreed to take them up when they're brought around. Don't think that means I won't though." The threat sent a rush through her veins.

The carriage came to a halt, cutting off her response. They were a block from behind her house. He helped her out and bowed over her hand. "I must be off."

A hollowness grew in her chest as he turned away. "Where are you going?"

He gave her one last small smile. "I still have some things to take care of." Of course, he meant to finish his business with Mr. Danvers. She needed to relieve Hope out of hiding anyway. She let out a long, disappointed sigh, and he turned to her once more.

"I'll see you at dinner?"

She opened her mouth to respond, but he didn't wait for her answer and disappeared down the street.

CHAPTER TWENTY-SEVEN

C ARRINGTON NEVER CAME to dinner, nor did she see him later that night. Her brother was also strangely absent. Nobody knew where they had gone. The upside to his absence was it gave her time to take a long, heavily perfumed bath to wash away the smell of the prison.

Afterward, she idled away at her needlework, not caring about the quality or her progress. In her sullen moments, she considered stitching foxgloves and sending it to Mr. Danvers for the horrible trick he had played on everyone. She didn't realize what she was stitching until Lynette came to join her and commented on the design.

"That's lovely, Dee. Is it a gift?"

Delia looked down at the monograph she had been mindlessly creating. An intricate W. Oh my. Hopefully Lynette thought it stood for Wolcott. As it happened, Lynette was as perceptive as always.

"I suppose I did mean it as a gift." Her explanation sounded feeble to her ears.

Lynette's eyes crinkled as she smiled at Delia's progress. "He will love it."

How was it that when she woolgathered, she could do such beautiful work, but when she concentrated, her designs were a mess? And how was it Lynette even knew who it was for? Delia asked her, cautiously framing her question to avoid showing too much interest.

"Don't be daft. Father has had him shut in his study more than once, and Jeffrey seems to be sniffing him out, as he does. Mother is practically planning your wedding now. What I wonder is, Why are you hesitating?"

She opened her mouth to respond but found no words to answer her. Why was she hesitating? Surely it didn't take most women this much time to make such an obvious decision? All her excuses, her reasons for refusing him, were superficial at best and negligible at worst.

She wanted to marry Carrington, and she had only been waiting to tell him. She would have to make sacrifices, but maybe he would agree to lighten her loss.

This line of thought only increased her desire to see him. Lynette, seeing her inclination to think, stayed silent as she worked with her needle. After a time, Lynette set down her work and caught her gaze.

"There is one thing." Lynette's words were hesitant.

"What is it?" She leaned forward, intrigued by her sister's serious tone.

"If you decide to marry him, I'd like you to take me with you to England."

She squinted. "What? You can't be serious."

"It makes perfect sense. I'm afraid if I stay, I'll die here. It's far safer there than it is in New York, or anywhere in the colonies for that matter. I have a bad feeling about this war, and I don't want to be in New York if the Crown loses."

"How can you be so convinced England will lose?"

Lynette shrugged. "I just have a feeling. It's enough to make me cautious about being in the crossfire."

"I suppose that makes sense, but it isn't up to me."

Her sister's eyes brightened. "Then you will have me if everyone agrees? I promise I will stay out of your way with your honeymoon or whatever it is married people do."

"Of course, Netty. Yet I wonder, maybe you're right, and it would be best to get out while we can. No matter what side we're on, we'll lose something in this war. I'd rather it not be our lives. I wish we could take everyone, but I know the rest of our family won't agree. There's too much profit in war."

They fell into quiet contemplation, content in their companionship as they worked on their respective tasks.

That night, she dozed off waiting for Carrington, though he never appeared. He didn't show at breakfast, and once again, she didn't see him or Jeffrey throughout the day.

Restlessness consumed her, and her nerves ached with the doubt of his intentions. He had said he would see her at dinner last night. Again, they were absent at dinner. It wasn't until the next night that they dined with the rest of the Wolcotts. By then, Delia's frantic murmurings had turned to curses at their names. To add to her misery, she couldn't get Carrington alone, since he had brought along his brother as well.

The men talked amicably among themselves, forcing Delia's mother to take up a seat near her and Lynette. She stole glances at Carrington, but he appeared to be ignoring her. She did, however, get Mr. Travers's attention. He grinned sheepishly and shrugged. She fought the desire to throw a well-aimed roll at his head.

This continued when the men finally joined them in the drawing room, with the exception of Mr. Travers sitting next to her rather than the rest of his sex. He yawned and stretched out into a chair. She scowled at him, and he gave her a sluggish grin.

"Whatever is the matter?"

"If you don't know, I'm not going to be the one to tell you." She cast her gaze away.

"Suit yourself," he said in a lazy voice.

She studied him out of the corner of her eye. "Where has everyone been?" She spoke against her refusal.

"Here and there." He tilted his head from side to side as he watched the group of men.

"That isn't an answer." She flung her words at him like a dagger.

"Well, last night we went to this delightful bar where the barmaids had the most delicious, er, beer. I don't remember much after that, but Jeffrey and my brother dragged me to my bed."

He paused, remembering. "Let's see, the day before, we went gambling with the officers." His mouth tugged down to the side. "I lost my monthly pay to Jeffrey. I'm afraid I'll have to borrow from my brother again."

"So that's all? Drinking and gambling?" She had been stuck anxiously waiting over Carrington's safety and intentions, and he had been out carousing about town? At least he could have left her a note or sent word to her through Hope. Did he not understand her worries?

"Mostly, though, Jeffrey and I did a few things while my brother was at the gaming table. Things unfit for your pretty ears."

She snickered at his words. As Foxglove, being considered a delicate woman bordered on ridiculous, though she doubted that would ever change. "Together?"

"What? No, separate pursuits."

"Right. I didn't need to know that." She coughed, choking on her words.

He shrugged again. "You asked. We had a grand time."

"Why even come back?"

He studied her narrowed gaze. "For one, I'm broke and refused to go. Plus, my brother wanted a rest, or so he said. I imagine you can ask him yourself. Jeffrey was starting to show signs of boredom too, though I don't know how with his gambling luck.

"All in all, it was a great success. Jeffrey only tried to kill William twice, with moderate success."

Delia took up her needlework, but realizing what she held, she stashed it away. He noticed her action with a crooked smile and gestured for her to look up. Carrington had left the room. The scoundrel hadn't said one word to her since she had last seen him. She moved to follow, but Mr. Travers barred her with his arm.

"Not yet. It's too obvious."

"Does it matter now?" She stared at the door, willing Carrington to reappear. She had waited long enough.

"Of course it matters. Besides, he expects you to follow him, and I say you should make him wait."

She considered him, mulling over his reasoning. "Agreed." She relaxed back down with the first real smile she'd had in days.

Around two in the morning, she returned to her room. She had played cards with Mr. Travers and then Lynette until her eyes had streamed with happy tears. As soon as she shut her door, the unmistakable sound of Carrington rushed into the hall. He tapped lightly but with deliberate restraint in the rhythm.

She opened the door a crack, revealing his pained expression, which sent her into fits of giggles. The poor man was a mess. He had been neat and composed at dinner, but now he appeared to be holding back tears. Laughing at him didn't help either. He assumed a dejected stance just in the hall.

She took pity on him and pulled him by the shirt into her room. She nudged the door shut with a faint click. "Your brother is a terrible influence on me." She left him to stare after her as she took down her hair.

"I will have to kick some sense into him." He appeared sincere.

"Goodness, no." Her smile crept up to her eyes as she remembered her night. "I love him that way."

The statement had the desired effect, and he slumped against the door, the wind taken out of him.

"We'll have such a wonderful family, don't you agree?"

Not catching on to her joke, he clenched his teeth and turned to leave. She watched him in the mirror as she continued to loosen the strands. He struggled with the door, and his mind seemed elsewhere.

"Leaving so soon? I've been waiting for days to talk to you. Not to mention I've been positively mad with worry."

He frowned back at her in puzzlement. His gaze scanned her features. He seemed lost, as if he had taken a wrong turn into rebel territory.

Her chest grew heavy as she watched his reactions. "Have you nothing to say to me?"

"You're an exhausting woman." He let out a long breath and rubbed a hand over his disheveled hair.

"So I'm told." She smiled prettily at his reflection.

He groaned and gazed at her in the mirror. "Do you have any idea how much work it takes to befriend Jeffrey? My pocket is noticeably lighter from my efforts."

"Your brother said he had remarkable luck gambling."

"No, Hugh is a mediocre card player and a horrible liar. You can see right through his bluffs. Jeffrey is more than skilled, but I had to keep his good mood, meaning I had to lose."

"He would have noticed that." She had to defend her brother even if it was from Carrington.

"Maybe if he had won every match, but he didn't. Then he tried to test me by pushing women at me. It was a damned nuisance. I like Jeffrey well enough, but he's as stubborn as you, maybe worse."

"Did you come to my bedroom to discuss our brothers?" She ran a brush through her long hair. He watched her movement, mesmerized.

"Of course not. I have something for you, though I suppose if you prefer Hugh, then it is yours all the same. Your gifts arrived, and by the look of them, I assume you haven't yet opened them."

Startled, she looked to the bed, where a parcel and a small, plain wooden box sat. She reached for the larger one, wrapped in paper, and glanced at him as if asking for permission. He nodded.

She untied the string and carefully unwrapped it to reveal a leather-bound book. She studied the decorative gold etchings along the cover before opening it to the title page.

"*Flora and Their Medicinal Properties of Our Majesty's Kingdom,*" she read aloud. "My, you do like to push your point. First, you're calling me by the king's name, and now you're promoting a visit to his kingdom."

He grinned broadly, showing his teeth. "I wondered if you noticed back at the prison."

She paged through the book, but he motioned her to the other package. She picked up the box, and a pine scent met her as she lifted the lid. Inside, set off by red velvet fabric, lay the most stunning emerald ring set in gold. She stared at the stone, watching it catch the light from the fireplace.

"Wherever did you get this? There couldn't possibly be a jeweler left in the city." Her fingers flexed, wanting to test the ring on her skin.

"It was my grandmother's. I brought it over with me just in case. Reminds me of the color of your eyes, like the countryside in England. I had it resized to fit you."

She was stunned into silence. He'd brought this over for her and altered it without even knowing if she would marry him? How did he even know what size she was? She should be angry that he presumed too much, but she couldn't bring herself to care. The trouble he had gone to more than made up for it.

"Do you like it, then?"

"I adore it. It's the most thoughtful gift anyone has ever given me. Thank you." Surrendering to her impulse, she plucked the ring out of the box and, under Carrington's wide smile, placed the ring on her left ring finger.

His chuckled as he scooped her up into his arms and kissed her face over and over again. Her lips, cheeks, eyes, chin, and forehead could not escape his overjoyed attentions. She laughed as he spun her around once before setting her back on her feet.

"I have some conditions." She held out her hand to still him.

His smile didn't falter as he leaned into her, unconcerned. "Such as?"

She kept him at arm's length. "I don't want to live in England."

He gave a stern shake of his head. "That can't be helped."

Her eyes turned down. "You should know more than anyone else I won't do well in society. It will make me miserable."

"Aw, well, we don't have to stay in London. England is more than just London, you know. I have an estate in Surrey, or maybe you would prefer the more isolated one in Cornwall. It's of no consequence to me." He dropped to his knees, since he had failed to get past her arms blocking him.

"Cornwall sounds nice." Away from the noise and the judgmental crowds. "I've read some books that take place in Cornwall. It sounds beautiful."

"It is that." He rustled through her skirts.

"Would you stop that? I'm being serious here." She held back her laughter.

"I am too." He stroked his hands up her legs, building the anticipation inside her.

She wiggled her legs around, trying to evade his grasp. "You're making it hard to think."

"Good."

She slapped at his head but with minimal impact. "Also, I want to bring people with me." Sheer determination allowed her to get a word in.

"Bring a caravan of people." His voice muffled under her skirts. His fingers peeled away her stockings.

"I'd like to bring Hope and maybe Felix. This city is corrupting him." She tried to ignore his attentions. "Lynette has asked to come as well."

His tongue brushed against her thigh, and she suppressed a shiver.

"I wouldn't mind having Abigail around for a visit."

Exasperated, Carrington stopped his efforts to look firmly up at her. "My dear, you may invite who you want, whenever you want. If it pleases you to invite the Pope or the ghost of Genghis

Khan, you are within your rights to do so."

"That is oddly specific."

"You are oddly resisting my attraction."

She huffed. "Not used to being refused? Well, I'm not done. I want to be able to see my family."

"I've already thought of that. Jeffrey agreed to help me purchase a house here for when we visit. He will maintain it while we are away. A sort of bachelor residence for him. That will have to keep until we can more freely travel. It all depends on this war. We could always lose the house in the outcome."

Her jaw dropped open. "He agreed to all that before knowing I would marry you?"

"I've grown fond of New York, as dirty and chaotic as it is. I'm sorry though. I have too many responsibilities at home to move here for any length of time. Are you done?" Not waiting for her answer, he tossed up her skirts and ran his hands along her skin.

She inhaled as he deftly pulled off her undergarments and pushed her legs apart. Her gaze wandered the room as she tried to find her bearings. He kissed the inside of her thigh, his hot breath tickling her. She squirmed, and he held her still.

"Really, Carrington." A nervous laugh trickled from her.

"Stop talking." His voice was barely audible under the layers of fabric.

"I hardly think…" She shivered as he ran his fingers along the sensitive skin between her legs. He grunted in approval at her silence and kneaded the skin just below her bottom. A rush of warmth pooled deep in her belly.

His fingers skimmed along to the already tingling area before her entrance.

She gasped and spread her arms to steady her shaking knees. "Please."

He answered her by reaching around her leg to stroke the aching area from behind. When his finger penetrated her, she lost her balance and tipped forward.

Carrington laughed, delighted as she toppled into him and onto the floor. He knelt over her from the side and unfastened the front of her dress.

"This has to go." His hands yanked at the stubborn garment.

She reached out to rub the bulge in his trousers. He moaned and moved to remove his clothes. His deft hands made quick work of them, captivating her attention. If only her clothes were as simple. His focus turned back to her.

"A little help." He gestured to her dress.

She leisurely pulled down the unfastened garment, watching his mounting frustration. He ground his teeth and tore off the offending dress. She giggled as the fabric ripped and snapped under his grasp.

"You know, this gown was more expensive than five of your shirts."

He only grunted as he removed the remaining material between them. Then, taking her hand, he lay back onto the floor. She gave him a wide-eyed look when he reached for her hips and pulled her forward to straddle him.

She moved tentatively to place herself above him. Then, with a wicked grin, she teased the tip of him with the wet folds of her skin. He jerked up, but she shied away.

Leaning forward, he stilled her hips as he entered her, moaning with his victory. Her vision blurred with the all-consuming pleasure.

He guided her with his hands, and soon they found a rhythm. They rocked slowly. She leaned back, allowing him to guide her while he cupped her breasts. He ran his palms over her nipples and kneaded them in tune with the movement of their hips.

The pressure built between them, and she quickened the pace, taking over their movements. His hands fell back to his sides as she pleasured herself.

She escaped into the sensation of his body beneath hers, thrilling in the hard muscles below her thighs.

He gazed up at her, eyes half-closed and expression content.

Her fingers ran along his chest only to have him catch them in his hands.

He pulled her into a hungry kiss before allowing her to continue her movements. He grasped her legs, moving her in a rapid, blinding whirlwind.

"Oh, don't stop."

"Don't stop what?" he asked through his teeth.

"Don't stop, please."

He grunted at her avoidance of his name and refused to increase his pace. His hips jerked up hard to meet her.

A cry burst from her lips, begging for release. His hand came between them to circle the sensitive skin above their sex. With a gasping moan, she lost all sense as her body exploded in ecstasy, shivering around him.

"Oh God, William."

Her words caused him to lose control as he thrust with frenzied motions. With a deep moan, he erupted inside her.

"Oh, William." She convulsed again around him, her body melting into his. "I love you."

He stilled at her words but relaxed after her sated face sank to his shoulder. He gave her a lopsided grin. "I love you too."

For a time, they lay there in silence in each other's arms, joined by something more than just their bodies. He stroked her back, recalling her to the world. "We'll have to make it a quick wedding."

She nodded into his chest. "To avoid scandal."

He kissed the top of her head. "There will already be scandal. I'm more concerned with being able to keep you in bed for as long as I like."

She gazed up at him with raised brows. "Aren't you tired?"

"I am, but my body isn't aware of that." He looked down at himself.

She trailed her fingers in circles along his stomach. "You know, we have some hours left."

He snorted and grasped the traveling hand. "That isn't nearly enough, but it will have to do."

She laughed. "To a prolonged honeymoon and the stopping of time."

He tilted up her chin and met her gaze. His encompassing stare jumped between her eyes and lips as though he meant to memorize them. "To you in my bed with a smile on your face."

She gave him a deep frown, pouting.

He sighed, shaking his head in mock frustration. "My work is never done."

His kiss muffled her answering laughter, his lips showing her the love and devotion that awaited her.

About the Author

Mae Thorn enjoys being romanced and terrified – a combination not normally found in books so she writes them. Her favorite stories include kickass women and the men they fall for. She writes historical romance and fantasy.

When she isn't writing she battles for equal access for those with hearing loss, discovers hidden records as a volunteer archivist, geeks out about Legos, torments her feline minions, and watches bad movies.

Mae holds a Bachelor's degree in English from the University of Utah and a Master's degree in Library and Information Science from San Jose State University.

She lives near Salt Lake City, Utah with her cats; Church, Shadow Moon, and Sabrina.

Website:
Maethorn.com

Twitter:
Twitter.com/maethornwrites

Facebook:
Facebook.com/maethornwrites

Instagram:
Instagram.com/maethornwrites

Pinterest:
https://pin.it/15qQIQ6

www.ingramcontent.com/pod-product-compliance
Lightning Source LLC
Chambersburg PA
CBHW071750190726
48292CB00003B/930